'Please
Eduard

'We are s_____. 'The Exhibition is a superb venture, and _____ to be congratulated on his foresight and planning, no?'

'You are acquainted with royalty, I suppose?' Serena said sarcastically, finding his familiarity more insufferable by the second.

'The Prince and I have met several times,' he said, nonchalantly enough for Serena to believe him. 'But seeing the progress of the building was only one reason for my visit to England. You are the other.'

Serena felt her heart begin to beat faster. 'You said this before, and I would be glad if you would explain yourself, Don Eduardo.'

'My mission is to invite you to the Casa de Montalban. Your grandmother is ill and wishes to see you to make her peace.'

Sally Blake was born in London, but now lives in Weston-super-Mare. She started writing when her three children went to school and has written many contemporary and historical novels using various pen-names. She loves the research involved in writing historical novels, finding it both exciting and addictive. Conscious of the way that circumstances can change people, she applies this maxim to her fictional characters, providing them with an emotive background in which to grow and develop.

Previous Title

OUTBACK WOMAN

LADY
OF SPAIN

Sally Blake

*First published in Great Britain 1990
by Mills & Boon Limited*

© Sally Blake 1990

*Australian copyright 1990
Philippine copyright 1990
This edition 1990*

ISBN 0 263 76912 7

*Masquerade is a trademark published by
Mills & Boon Limited, Eton House,
18–24 Paradise Road, Richmond, Surrey, TW9 1SR.*

*Set in Times Roman 10 on 11½ pt.
04-9008-75497 C*

Made and printed in Great Britain

CHAPTER ONE

IT HAD always seemed such an un-*English* painting to hang in her aunts' conventionally correct household, which only made its presence there all the more surprising. As a child, Serena had begged Cook to tell her something about it, since she rarely dared to question her austere aunts.

But Cook, to whom everything beyond the Thames was unspeakably foreign anyway, always sniffed hard and said that Miss Serena should just thank her stars she had a good home here in London and never mind what went on in the outside world. Eventually, it became obvious that she was never going to hear anything exciting or intriguing about the painting, and Serena's childish curiosity had waned.

But she had always been attracted by the likeness of the huge sprawling house with its round rooms at either end of the building and its hotchpotch of curving archways and different roof-levels. Somehow she was convinced that it was a real house that existed somewhere in the world, a home of splendid proportions, as unlike her own surroundings as anything she could imagine.

Because she herself loved to draw and sketch, she was awed as much by the rich blues and greens and magentas of the oils on the canvas as by the splendour of the house itself, the dazzling sunlight struck from its window-panes by an expert artist's brush. More than just a painting, it seemed to Serena to have been executed with love.

Apparently, no one else ever saw in it what she saw. It was merely something to adorn the staircase of the London residence where Serena lived with her two elderly aunts. Inevitably, she invented her own secret dreams about the inhabitants of the house in the painting, imagining that she was its mistress, sharing its secrets with a wonderful and even more shadowy companion...

'Your head is forever in the clouds, Serena,' her aunts Hope and Dorcas scolded. 'You'd do far better to attend to your lessons than to sit gazing into space. It's what we pay your tutor for.'

But apart from the tutor's own royalist leanings which she shared with Serena, the woman with her tight grey bun and sweeping black skirt was hardly a stimulating companion for an eager young pupil who suspected there must be more to life than the rigours of an all-female establishment.

The only saving grace for the tutor was the sparkle she put into relating to Serena the story of the young queen's marriage to the German Prince Albert, and the subsequent arrival of all the little princes and princesses, which was fairy-tale enough to stir the romantic soul of any red-blooded young lady...

She knew better than to say so, of course. Neither the tutor nor her aunts would understand...any more than she had ever understood why their name was Laker and hers was de Montalban. It was one more mystery that was tersely explained by the obvious fact that it had been her father's name, in a tone that invited no further enquiry. And she was brought up to accept that a young lady did not question her elders' decisions.

Anyway, to Serena it was such a beautiful name that she simply wove her own dreams about her origins. Perhaps she was in reality a princess that they had taken in. Or a love-child...she always felt a small shiver at the thought, because it was deliciously wicked, and she was thankful enough to have a good home with two people who loved her.

One day she meant to learn the truth of it...but the chance to pursue it with her aunts never came because they both died from the fatal bout of influenza that had ravaged their district of London all that winter.

It was a very subdued and sorrowing Serena de Montalban who was summoned to the chambers of Messrs Phillips and Price on a grey and chilly Monday at the beginning of January.

It was the start of the new and splendid year of 1851 that was to see Prince Albert's wonderful Exhibition in Hyde Park, but for Serena the year had a sad beginning. The elderly Mr Price cleared his throat and offered her his condolences with the usual platitudes.

'Thank you, sir,' Serena murmured, looking down at her kid gloves and willing her thoughts well away from this sombre afternoon.

She had always been able to use that little trick, projecting her senses away from the present to more palatable surroundings, while still taking in all that was going on around her. It had stood her in good stead during the sadness of recent days.

She didn't even want to acknowledge that she now owned the small town house and all the effects of the Misses Laker who had cared for her diligently but without much outward show, simply because it wasn't their way—a fact that had often frustrated a headstrong girl with a hasty temper that needed to be checked, and an extrovert, loving nature that was also to be kept firmly under control.

She was so unlike them in every way, Serena thought, still caught up in her other world while Mr Price shuffled the pages of the joint will and droned on. Her aunts had been thin-faced and pale-haired and generally colourless, while she had flashing eyes the colour of night, and hair so dark it was almost black. She did not have the English rose's pert, tip-tilted nose, but one that was defiant and just missed being called prominent, and her cheekbones were high and covered with a smooth, tawny complexion.

Even now, in the midst of her grief, she knew she looked as if she had spent long days in the sun, instead of being cooped up for a suitable mourning period in an English winter...

'...and in particular, the painting of which you were always so fond,' the solicitor's dry voice went on, and now Serena's full attention was captured.

'The painting?'

Mr Price smiled faintly. 'So we are paying attention, are we?'

'Of course. I heard everything,' she said, impatient at his patronising tone. 'But what about the painting? Isn't it merely part of the effects of the house?'

'They do emphasise that the painting is their very special legacy to you, Miss de Montalban, and there are also two letters for you to read. They must be opened in their correct order, and if you have any queries on the contents you are to consult me. I shall leave you alone for a while to open them.'

Serena stared as he went stiffly out of the chambers. She picked up the letter-opener on the desk and quickly slit the first envelope open. She was sharply aware that her heart was pounding in a strange sick way. Did the painting hold a secret after all? Was it worth a fortune, perhaps? Or was she to discover that she was a long-lost heiress?

Sudden tears stung her eyes at the flippant thought, because her aunts' illness had struck so quickly that she had never had the chance to tell them how much she loved them, nor to thank them for all their care during all these years, and now it was too late...

She opened the crackling pages of the first letter and stared at the unfamiliar writing. She didn't recognise the signature, even though her heart had jolted as soon as she saw that the name was the same as her own. Was the writer a woman or a man? Adriana de Montalban. Serena scanned the letter, curious that it was addressed, not to her, but to her aunts, and it was dated over five years ago.

'My dear ladies,' Serena read, and immediately sensed that this was written in the style of someone who knew the English language but was not familiar with it as their own.

'Now that the child is growing up, and time moves on for us all, perhaps it is time to make amends for what is past. As you know, her father finally came back to us for a short while after his wanderings, but he has now gone to a better world, and therefore your sister's memory is no longer painful to our family.'

Serena felt a shock run through her. Her brain was quick enough to grasp the implications of the letter at once. This Adriana de Montalban must be related to her... Serena knew that her mother had died in childbirth, and she had always believed that her father too was long since dead. Had he been alive all these years and she hadn't even known it? The shock of it was tempered with a sudden impotent rage and a sharp feeling of loss. She read on quickly.

'My son confessed his regret that he never knew the child, but could never face her, knowing he would be reminded too much of her mother. The *familia* now accept that theirs was a love-match, even though it was totally unacceptable at the time to the Casa de Montalban. However, time heals, as your people say, and, since there are legal matters to consider in this respect, perhaps one day I might see the girl. I do not beg, but eventually all concerned should make contact with one another.'

It was a cold, unemotional letter, full of stilted phrases from a woman who undoubtedly never begged a favour from anyone. Serena felt nothing for the person who had written it. But the knowledge that somewhere in the world there must be a family of whose existence she had been totally unaware until now had set her heart racing painfully.

Clearly her aunts had refused to do as the person wished, and she had never been told anything... She tore open the second letter without bothering to use the letter-opener.

'Dearest girl,' it began in Aunt Dorcas's handwriting, bringing the salty tears to her eyes, because it showed much more open affection than the aunts had ever been able to show in life.

'We write with sorrow, knowing that you will only read this after we are gone. But it is your right to know the truth, and to know that your rightful home is the house in the painting of which you were always so fond.'

Serena felt her mouth drop open. That lovely place...? Her throat felt tight and raw as she swallowed and read on.

'Your parents were besotted with one another. They married against bitter opposition from his family and were outcasts from them. He could not forsake his Spanish roots, however, and took her to Spain where they lived a quite bohemian life until you were born.

'After your mother died, you were brought to us in the care of a wet-nurse with a trust for your upbringing. Mr Price has seen to everything and will advise you now. If it all sounds bizarre, dear Serena, much of it is undoubtedly due to your father's flamboyant nature and desires, which we always feared you may have inherited. Hence our wish to bring you up correctly as a proper young English lady. Forgive us for keeping the truth from you until now, dear girl. We thought it best.'

For some minutes, Serena struggled to control too many emotions. There was still anger; there was regret for the father she had never known; a new, sweet poignancy for the doomed love-affair that had been her parents'; there was such a mixture of feelings tumbling about inside her...

There was a fierce need to see and touch the house that had been a part of her all this time, and to put it in its proper perspective in her life. And there was an insidious bitter resentment towards this Doña Adriana de Montalban who could not unbend far enough to welcome a grand-child into her home.

For of course, she was not, and could never be, quite the 'proper young English lady', as her aunts so quaintly put it. There was a part of her that was foreign, that belonged in the Casa de Montalban, the more dramatic and flamboyant Serena that her aunts had always strived to suppress, and succeeded so well. The part of her that was Spanish...

She heard the solicitor clear his throat without even being aware that he'd entered the room again. She looked up with wild dark eyes, her cheeks flushed crimson.

'I presume you know something about these letters, sir,' she said. 'Do you know the address of this person?'

She indicated the letter in the larger envelope.

'Doña Adriana de Montalban is your grandmother, young lady,' he said, his face stony at this seeming disrespect. 'And of course I can show you exactly where the Casa de Montalban is situated.'

He drew out a large map of Spain from a desk drawer. Serena was familiar with its shape and size from her geography lessons, and the solicitor stabbed a finger at an area west of Seville.

'Much of the land in this area belongs to the Montalban family,' he said.

'Are they rich, then?' she asked, not really caring.

He gave a slight smile.

'My dear young lady, the Montalbans are one of the oldest families in this part of Spain. Have you never heard of Montalban wine?'

'I have not. My aunts did not drink wine, and we never had it in the house,' Serena said inconsequentially, while her thoughts whirled with all the implications of what the man was saying.

'And the house in the painting.' Her thoughts kept going off at a tangent and coming back to the one thing she wanted to know. 'The big house I always thought so magnificent——'

'The Casa de Montalban,' Mr Price said reverently. 'The house that will one day be yours.'

Serena felt the tension in her face give way as she gave a disbelieving laugh that was tinged with fury.

'*Mine?* I think you tease me, sir. How can it ever be mine?'

'I never tease, young lady.' The solicitor rolled up the map at once, his brief good humour gone. 'The Doña Adriana owns the entire property, and your father was her only son. When she dies, it will go to you. It is indisputable, however much she may wish it otherwise.'

A little chill ran through Serena. For of course the unknown grandmother would wish it otherwise. Why should she want a girl she had never met, a foreigner from England, whose mother had enticed her only son away from his rightful heritage, to walk into a way of life that had probably gone on for generations? Presumably, these were the legal matters that needed to be discussed . . . and suddenly she felt defensive. It was her rightful heritage too, and she had been denied knowledge of it all these years.

'I shall go there at once,' she declared, without serious thought.

'I urge you to write to the lady first. Naturally I have informed her of your aunts' sad demise, but she is very old and any visit from you will be a shock to her, just as all this has been to you. She assumed that since there was no response from your aunts you wished to have no communication with the family until—the proper time. Tread carefully, Miss de Montalban.'

Serena walked out of the chambers into the January afternoon, where thin patches of sunlight struggled to get through the clouds, casting a silvery sheen on the cobbled streets. She held up her skirts and stepped into the road without thinking, then leapt aside as a conveyance hurtled around a corner, its narrow wooden wheels clattering and jarring, sending a protesting flurry of birds into the sky from a narrow London rooftop.

A sudden image of what it might be like in Spain right now flashed through Serena's mind. She had never been there, yet the pictures in her mind were as clear as if painted by an artist's brush. She saw sunlit vineyards of lush, verdant green waving in soft, warm breezes, fields of green and purple stretching endlessly to the horizon, beneath a brilliant sky of a blue so dazzling it hurt the eyes to look at it ... and in the midst of all that paradise was the house Serena had loved for so long, drawn to it like a moth to a flame even when she was too young to know the meaning of empathy...

'I *will* go there,' she said slowly to herself. 'I was always meant to go, and nothing's going to stop me.'

All the same, it needed a bit of thinking about first, and Mr Price had been right in one respect. She couldn't just arrive on the unknown grandmother's doorstep like an unwanted parcel, even if it was the way she herself had been abandoned to her aunts' care.

At least *they* had wanted *her* ... but now they were gone, and, even though she had loved them, she recognised what a restricted life she had led all these years. It was as though the two well-meaning women had wanted to stifle the girl's true nature for fear that she would turn out as reckless as her mother.

And her father too...the dark and shadowy Montalban, who was suddenly assuming charismatic proportions in Serena's mind ... She pictured the two of them now, defying all for love... She hadn't thought of her parents in years, but now the very thought of their married bliss enchanted her.

One of the first things she did that night was to move the painting of the Casa de Montalban from its dark place on the stairs to a place of prominence above the mantel in the parlour. One part of her wanted to go to Spain at once and declare herself, but, despite what her aunts had always considered her headstrong ways, she was learning to be more circumspect and to think before she acted.

And in the end, the dream was too new and too important for her to act on a mad impulse. The cautious Englishness of her upbringing in her aunts' household tempered the rush to follow her instincts. And there was something else. She was almost afraid the magnificence might fade if she saw the Spanish house too soon. There had to be a right time. Perhaps later in the year, when she was able to control her still-painful emotions a little better...

In the first week of a blustery April a visitor arrived to see her. Serena still thought of it as her aunts' home. Even without Cook's incessant weeping and pressing her apron to her eyes whenever she thought of 'them poor dear ladies', Serena couldn't think of this place as her own. Cook was irritating her beyond words, but she could hardly blame the woman, who had been in service here for years and was inclined to rule it as her own.

It was Cook who answered the door that gusty, rain-swept evening, and who came back to the parlour round-eyed, holding a gilt-edged calling-card in her hand.

'There's a gent to see you, Miss Serena, though I'm not sure that I shouldn't call the constables just to make sure he ain't up to no good——'

'What are you blathering about, Cook?' Serena said impatiently. 'Let me see the card, for pity's sake.'

Cook was still reluctant to hand it over.

'Some dark foreign gent he is, miss. Oh, he's well-spoken enough, I grant you that, but with his hair all plastered down around his face and his collar turned up, he looks like a black heathen devil——'

Serena almost snatched the card out of the woman's hand. Cook couldn't read, so she wouldn't have any idea if the man was prince or pauper. And Serena didn't know any foreign gentlemen, but her sixth sense told her there could only be one explanation for the visitor, if foreign gentleman he really was...

She spoke the name aloud.

'Don Eduardo García.'

There was no formal business status, nor any address. There was just the arrogant starkness of the name, as if it needed no more elaboration. Somehow she felt it should have offended her, but instead it had the power to make her heartbeats quicken.

'Show the gentleman in at once, Cook, and bring us some hot tea. It's a miserable evening. And stop looking so disapproving. He's a...' She sought for a word that wouldn't scandalise the older woman. 'He's a kinsman.'

The term came into her head without too much conscious thought, at once familiar and remote, and seeming to cover everything.

Cook turned abruptly, muttering that this would never have happened when her mistresses were alive, letting in foreigners off the streets...

Serena realised how nervous she felt. She had never been lacking in confidence, but somehow these last few months had taken much of her confidence away. She missed her strait-laced aunts, and her first burst of anger at the deception that had controlled her life had diminished into an embarrassed hesitancy about confronting the family in a strange country.

And now a stranger with a Spanish name had sought her out, and all her instincts told her he must have some significance in her future. The fact that she was so inwardly disturbed made her tilt her chin even higher than usual as she awaited the visitor.

She smoothed her black mourning dress tidily over her slim hips, and wished she hadn't taken the pins out of her hair so that it cascaded now in dark curls over her shoulders. If her aunts had been there, they would have insisted that she go upstairs and prepare herself properly to greet a visitor, not invite him in in this uncivilised way. As it was, she suddenly felt very young and gauche and vulnerable as Cook stood aside to allow the man to enter.

Her first impression was indeed of someone very dark and very tall. He wore a long travelling coat and gleaming, close-fitting boots of a kind more usually worn for riding. Sleek black gloves covered his hands, and Serena had the feeling that everything about the man was of the best quality, which only increased her feeling of nervousness. And then she remembered her manners and held out her hand.

'Good evening, sir. I am Serena de Montalban——'

'I know who you are,' he said abruptly, the richness of his voice with its slight accent stopping her in mid-sentence. Without asking permission, he discarded his travelling coat in one easy movement and handed it to Cook, who was still gaping in the doorway.

Serena waved her hand at the woman, furious that the initiative had been taken from her so effortlessly. Whoever this man was, it was obvious he was used to being in command. And she was not used to being spoken to so curtly, especially in her own house. She felt a tingling in her blood at his arrogance.

'Won't you take off your coat, sir, and sit by the fire while you tell me your business?'

She spoke with some sarcasm, and almost believed she saw the flicker of a smile cross his angular features. One second it was there and then it was gone.

'*You* are my business,' he said.

He moved into the room, with none of the awkwardness or stooping that some men of his height affected. He chose an armchair that might have enveloped a lesser man, but which simply complemented his size. He peeled off the tight-fitting gloves and tossed them on to a side-table. He seemed to take in everything in the room at a glance, his gaze pausing briefly on the painting above the mantel.

Serena looked at him. If his words were meant to unnerve her, she wouldn't let them. She gave a short laugh.

'Please spare me any riddles, Señor García.' She gave him his full title now. 'I do not know you, and can only presume you have had some knowledge of my aunts' deaths through my solicitor, and have come to inspect me on behalf of my Spanish family.'

She spoke with complete daring, the words spilling out before she could even think logically. Her 'Spanish family' indeed! Until a few months ago she hadn't known of their existence, and the sudden urgency to see the Casa de Montalban had faded with the knowledge that she would have to see this Doña Adriana as well. The *familia* had wanted nothing to do with her all these years, and she wasn't rushing to give them the satisfaction of meeting her now.

'Then you are aware that we exist,' Señor García said calmly.

'*We?*' Serena said.

He smiled faintly, but she was too caught by the implication of his words to register its charm or otherwise.

'I am a distant cousin to the Montalbans. My father is overseer to the *viñas*—the vineyards—and I am controller of the wine-production. You and I are very distantly related.'

'Really! And does this fact mean that I am supposed to welcome you with open arms?'

He laughed aloud now, and Serena acknowledged that he was a very handsome man indeed. His naturally olive skin was sunburnt to a deep tan, his eyes flashed as dark as her own; his hair was longer than the conventional English length, black and sleek, and all his clothes were dark, worn with the air of a man very much in control of his own destiny.

'I do not insist on it, even though it would be a very agreeable situation, Señorita Serena,' he said. He paused, and then, 'You find it amusing?'

She ignored the doubtful compliment, but the title had made her lips quirk, despite herself. 'I'm sorry, but Señorita Serena sounds quite preposterous!'

'Then, since we are related, perhaps we may drop the formality altogether. My name is Eduardo.'

He took her completely by surprise as he rose to his feet again and held out his hand. Without thinking, she took it, and it was large and firm and warm. He touched his lips to the back of her hand, and she snatched it away quickly, not wanting to register the sensations the action evoked, or to acknowledge them.

'I'm sure that my aunts would not approve of such familiarity.'

'It is not your aunts' decision. And Serena is a beautiful name for a beautiful woman. It would be a pity not to use it.'

Her male acquaintances were few, and this man was unlike anyone she had ever met before. He seemed to sweep anything of no consequence aside and concentrate on things of the moment.

Even while it was irritating, and unlikely that her feelings should matter at all to him, she admitted that she liked directness in a person. It was a quality not many people had. Most of her aunts' circle had been over-polite, masking their true feelings. It was unusual and surprisingly refreshing to meet someone who spoke as he felt. Not that she had any intention of letting him know it.

'Eduardo is presumably the Spanish equivalent of Edward?' she said, momentarily nonplussed at how to deal with this strange man.

'In my country we prefer to say that Edward is the English equivalent of Eduardo,' he said coolly.

Oh, yes, there was definitely an arrogance about him. Despite his elegant appearance, Serena could almost feel a raw, untamed vitality about the man. She had the feeling that no one ever got the better of Don Eduardo García.

The door opened and Cook brought in a tray of tea and banged it down on a table next to Serena. Her disapproval was tangible. Serena gave the woman a smile, deciding that she might as well enjoy this unexpected situation that had enlivened a dull day. She liked intrigue, and this man was certainly intriguing.

'Thank you, Cook. Don Eduardo is my guest and may be staying for supper, since we have many things to discuss.'

She spoke without thinking, impulsive in a way that had rarely been allowed when her aunts were alive, relishing this rare kind of freedom in her thinking and her doing. She was the lady of the house now, and Cook had better remember it, regardless of her sniffs and swishing exits.

Her hand was not quite steady as she poured out the tea for herself and her visitor, and handed him a delicate china cup.

'I apologise for my thoughtless remark. You will have better things to do than to share a meal with me, and we can have very little to discuss——'

'On the contrary. It would be my pleasure to share a meal with a charming *señorita*,' he said in a formal manner that could never be called English in a thousand years. 'And you were right, we do have much to discuss.'

'Do we?' Serena said, conscious of the heat in her cheeks at this frank appraisal of herself. She took a sip of the strong, dark brew that Cook called tea. 'Perhaps you had better tell me exactly why you're here, Don Eduardo.'

'Only if you agree to drop my title and call me by my given name alone. Otherwise our days are going to be taken up by unnecessary irritations.'

'I'm sure our days are not going to coincide at all!' she countered smartly. 'Please tell me the purpose of your visit. You obviously don't reside in England.'

'Certainly not. I would be frozen to the marrow in your cold little country——'

Serena gasped with anger. As with most people of her acquaintance, it was considered perfectly acceptable to criticise the weather or the price of food or the state of the streets and the lack of lighting in the narrow mews— but not for a foreigner to come to England and insult them all by doing so.

'Why did you bother to come here, then?' she replied indignantly.

'For several reasons.' Don Eduardo drained his cup in one swallow in a very masculine manner.

Serena began to wonder why she had thought him attractive, even for one moment. She realised she was tapping her fingers on the side of her chair, and stopped herself quickly, because Aunt Dorcas had always said that it indicated a display of impatience in a woman. She bit her lip, remembering Aunt Dorcas...

'For one thing, I wanted to see how the great *edificio*— the building—in your Hyde Park was progressing.'

'The Crystal Palace?' His words took her by surprise. 'You know something about the Exhibition, then?'

'Of course. And it is such an elaborate and colourful name for your dour countrymen to adopt, but no doubt it was the Prince's idea to name it so.'

'And why would you be interested in seeing it?' Serena said, outraged now. She struggled not to let her temper rise any higher, determined to send this impossibly rude man on his way as soon as possible.

'We are showing Montalban wines,' he said. 'The Exhibition is a superb venture, and Albert is to be congratulated on his foresight and planning, no?'

'You are acquainted with royalty, I suppose?' she said sarcastically, finding his familiarity more insufferable by the second.

'The Prince and I have met several times,' he said, nonchalantly enough for Serena to believe him. 'His Exhibition will be a great showcase for the world, and it would be a foolish businessman who did not see its usefulness. But seeing the progress of the building was only one reason for my visit to England. You are the other.'

Serena felt her heart begin to beat faster. 'You said this before, and I would be glad if you would explain yourself, Don Eduardo.'

He looked at her without answering, and their glances clashed. It was Serena who finally looked away, expelling her breath impatiently.

'Very well. Please explain yourself—Eduardo.'

'That's better. We should not fight, you and I. My mission is to invite you to the Casa de Montalban. Your grandmother is ill and wishes to see you to make her peace.'

'Doña Adriana is not dying?' Serena asked quickly. She was already in mourning and had no tears to spare for a woman she had never known. But Eduardo shook his head.

'She has the strength of a bull,' he said, which Serena thought a very odd simile to apply to an elderly lady of class. 'But the years catch up with her, and you are her direct descendant. Is it so strange that she wishes to know you—as we all do?'

As he spoke, Serena had the strangest feeling that she was standing back and dispassionately reviewing this man and all that he was saying.

She was the direct descendant of Doña Adriana de Montalban who was growing old. Don Eduardo García was distantly related to them both, and clearly very much a part of the Montalban wine business.

He had made no secret of the fact that he found Señorita Serena de Montalban attractive. Beautiful was the word he had used... and Serena knew that she was not beautiful in the strict English sense of the word. She had never fitted the conventional requirement of the English peaches-and-cream complexion. Her features were too strong, her skin too golden-hued, like Eduardo himself...

Her thoughts were swift and certain, guessing instinctively that here was a man who wanted power. It oozed out of every part of him. And what would be more natural and devious, for a man who wanted power, to see the potential in sweeping a young woman off her feet, when that young woman was destined to be the owner of all that he might desire most in the world?

CHAPTER TWO

'Do you have a wife?' Serena said, deciding to be as direct as Don Eduardo. His eyes narrowed slightly, and she sensed that he was not altogether pleased by the question, but not for any reason she might have expected.

'I do not. A man in my family does not as a rule marry until after a certain time.'

'Really? And what time would that be?' she asked, daring to steer the conversation away from herself.

She was surprised at his bitter laugh.

'When he has proved himself in the *corrida*. When he has conquered *el toro*, then he can call himself a man and do as he wishes. It is a tradition.'

Serena looked at him blankly. In an instant he seemed to have changed from the proud Don Eduardo García to someone who knew the meaning of vulnerability. Even so, he had lost nothing of his charisma. Serena was puzzled and intrigued by his words.

'You must explain what you mean. I don't know your Spanish words,' she said, adding 'Would you like more tea?'

His mouth twisted again. 'Ah, you English! Always the tea as the complete panacea for all ills, even for when the conversation becomes a little intimate! No, *querida*, I wish for no more tea, and neither will I stay for a meal tonight. I have more people to see, but I will call on you again tomorrow, and we will discuss your visit to Spain.'

She hardly noticed then that he gave her no real explanation of the marriage requirements for the men in his family.

'I haven't decided whether I'm going to Spain yet!'

'Oh, but you will,' Don Eduardo said confidently. 'Your curiosity would not let you do otherwise. And I see one of your father's paintings in evidence. Do you not wish to see the house in reality?'

Serena felt a new shock as they both stared at the painting of the Spanish house.

'My *father* painted it?' She ignored everything else he had said.

'Of course. There is his signature in the corner. The fact that he lived such a wild bohemian life in the days before he found success was the first thing to arouse his family's anger. But did you not know that before he died he was an acclaimed artist?'

Serena was suddenly aware that her throat was full.

'How could I know that? I didn't know of his existence until a few months ago. And why should his family be angered at such talent?'

'Because he did not fulfil his obligations in the *corrida*. Instead, he chose to pursue an artistic career and to wander the world. He married an Englishwoman and refused to go back to his family home unless they acknowledged her, which obviously they could not do.'

'It's not at all obvious to me!' Serena said tautly, wondering just what kind of people these Spanish relatives were after all. Where was the passion, the love of daring? All she saw was a cold, matriarchal society.

Eduardo looked at her thoughtfully. 'This is because you've been brought up to think in the English way.'

'Of course I have. I *am* English——'

'No, you are not. Half of you is Spanish. Half of your personality has been smothered all these years.'

She was furious by all that he was implying, aghast at the revelations about her parents, yet knowing the truth in what he said. Hadn't she already acknowledged

it for herself? Hadn't she always felt that there was
something more inside her waiting to burst out like a
flower blossoming in the sun?

'What were my father's obligations in the—what was
it you said?' she said huskily.

'The *corrida*—the bullfight.'

Serena felt the room spin.

'But I've heard tell of this bullfighting, and it's barbaric——'

'No more so than your English sport of cock-fighting
or fox-hunting. We all have our own ideas of what's cruel
and what is sport, *señorita*.' He spoke drily, yet Serena
had a sudden feeling about the man.

'Is this something that the young men in your family
have to endure? And perhaps why you yourself haven't
married yet—because you fear the bull?' she taunted
him, and as she had expected she saw the anger flash in
his eyes.

'I do not fear *el toro*,' he said with arrogant pride.
'But I've no wish to draw blood unnecessarily.'

'Then perhaps even a Spaniard can have a touch of
English sensitivity in him,' she retorted.

She expected a sharp denial, but he said nothing for
a moment, and then he spoke slowly.

'That is hardly the case, although since I have spent
some time in your English university it may have temporarily coloured my outlook on life. No, I do not fear
el toro, but I think I may have met my match in you,
Señorita de Montalban. Until tomorrow.'

He bowed low and turned to walk swiftly from the
room without giving her the chance to say anything else.
Serena stood quite still for a moment, and then Cook
came storming in.

'I swear the man's a rogue and a charlatan! If he comes
here again I'll refuse to let him in, and that's that. Pushed

past me, he did, and just snatched up his coat on the way out. He didn't upset you, did he?'

Serena snapped at her unnecessarily, her head still churning with all she had learned.

'No, he did not. What's more, he'll be coming back some time tomorrow, and of course you'll let him in! You're to be civil to him, Cook. Do you understand?'

'If you say so, I suppose I must, but it goes against the grain.' The woman glared. 'I don't know what your poor dear aunts would have said to it all. Sometimes I despair of you, I really do.'

She stomped out again, and Serena slowly picked up the gloves that Don Eduardo García had left behind. There was the sharp, pungent smell of best leather about them that was almost sensual. Absently, Serena slipped her fingers inside one of the gloves, her hand small inside it, flexing the shiny black skin and touching it to her face almost as if it were a lover's caress. Just as quickly, she seemed to hear Eduardo's voice, rich and seductive...

'...we will discuss your visit to Spain...'

As if there were never any doubt. As, of course, there was not. It was as inevitable as breathing. She knew it, even while she fought with herself about everything that could go wrong. She had to go, to see for herself the house that she had always known was important in her life. The house where her father had been born. The house where her aged grandmother, Doña Adriana de Montalban, reigned supreme, and would be as full of seething resentment towards Serena as she was towards the old woman.

Even more so, perhaps, if Serena was indeed the direct descendant, and the English upstart was destined to inherit the Casa de Montalban. The very thought of such grandeur, mixed with such hate, made Serena shudder.

She removed Eduardo's glove and dropped it with its mate on to the armchair, and went to the mantel to study the painting again. She had seen the signature often enough, scrawled flamboyantly across the lower left-hand corner of the canvas. Ramón. Just that and nothing more. She had had no idea that her father's hand had written it.

She touched each letter of his name, wishing she had had the chance to know him as well as she knew this painting. And bitterness overcame all other feelings towards Doña Adriana de Montalban, who had never been forgiving enough to welcome her son back to his rightful home until long after his wife had died.

No wonder the aunts had kept the past a shadowy secret from herself. She might well have demanded that they take her out to Spain a long time ago to see her father. Serena understood their motives, but they hurt all the same.

And it was irksome to agree with Eduardo García's words. Half of her personality had been smothered. She knew without question that it was the more stormy, dramatic part, the undeniably Spanish part...

By mid-afternoon the next day Serena's fingers were drumming with impatience. Eduardo hadn't arrived, and she had spent a restless night, knowing she wanted to make plans as soon as possible. Once she had made up her mind, there was no reason to delay. She knew that she might hate Doña Adriana. She might find the heat of the country unacceptable, and the people less than welcoming. But she had to know. She had to find out for herself. There *was* another world after all, and she was part of it.

She had already told Cook what she meant to do, and received the expected tears and tongue-lashing.

'You can't mean it, Miss Serena! Your aunts'd turn in their graves, so they would. All these years they've tried to save you from knowing about your bad roots——'

'Oh, Cook, don't be so silly. Why should I have bad roots, just because my father came from another country?'

'Tain't right. People should marry their own, and not go mixing the breeds.'

Serena had had a hard job not to laugh out loud.

'Good heavens, I'm not going off with an Eskimo, am I? Don Eduardo *is* a relative, and I'm half Spanish myself, don't forget, so you could say I'm going to my other home.'

'And what about this one?' Cook's face suddenly crumpled. 'What's going to happen here while you're off gallivanting?'

Seeing her genuine distress, Serena gave her a hug.

'Nothing. You'll take care of it, the same as you always have. This is your home as much as mine, and when I come back I'll have you to come home to. I'm not going away forever, am I?'

'So you say,' Cook said darkly, without much conviction.

It was early evening before Don Eduardo arrived, bringing as a gift a bottle of ruby-coloured wine. It wasn't the kind of gift a young lady usually expected, and it was a rare sight in this house. Serena looked at it and frowned, and the man spoke coolly.

'I thought we would sample it with our meal tonight, no? That is, if you are inviting me to eat with you again.'

'Of course. A relative is always made welcome in an English home.' It was the kind of thing she had been taught to say, and she thrust the bottle into Cook's hands, who held it as if it were red hot.

'Please don't drop it,' Eduardo said quickly. 'It's one of our finest vintages.'

'It's a Montalban wine?' Serena asked.

'Naturally. Why would we drink anything else?'

She felt immediately put in her place. His was a world, after all, of which she was as yet unaware, and wine-drinking was clearly an important part of it. She felt obliged to tell him she was not used to it and might well dislike the taste.

'You will not be a true Montalban if that's the case. But don't worry. If you find this one too sweet, I shall bring another one the next time we meet.'

The fact of their meeting again would seem to be inevitable. For a moment she didn't know what to say. There was no point in flippant remarks, since if she went to Spain it was obvious that they would be in frequent contact.

'You look troubled, *querida*,' he stated.

She lifted her shoulders and let them fall. 'Wouldn't you be disturbed if you suddenly discovered you were not who you thought you were?'

He put out his hand, and without thinking she put her own inside his palm. Swiftly, he brought her hand to his mouth and brushed his lips to her fingers again in that strangely touching foreign gesture.

'You are the Montalban heir. You have your own special place in the world. When you reach that place, you will have many offers of marriage that may stun you. I pray you to think carefully before you make your choice.'

She pulled her hand away, his words unsettling. She had not considered marriage yet, except in distant, dreamlike terms. She was unworldly in every sense when it came to men. Her unmarried aunts had seen to that.

'Are you a fortune-teller, to know such things?' she said, to hide her embarrassment. Eduardo laughed.

'No. I'm someone who knows what will happen when my countrymen see a beautiful and desirable woman coming to live among them. I am no fortune-teller—I leave that to the gypsies and their dukkerin.'

'The gypsies and their *what*?' Serena said, as much to cover the stab of pleasure his compliments gave her as anything else.

'It's the Romany word for fortune-telling. Have you never heard it before?'

'Well, why on earth would I? A young English lady is hardly likely to be acquainted with gypsies!' she said, affronted with him for thinking such a thing.

'You will be when you come to Spain.'

In the hearth, the wood-fire crackled from a sudden gust of wind down the chimney, blowing a cloud of grey smoke into the room, dank and earthy from the sparking logs. Serena gave a small shiver. There was so much she didn't know about this alien country she was proposing to visit. So much she didn't know about its people...

'I think you had better explain that remark. I thought the Casa de Montalban was a splendid vine-growing establishment where you made your own wines. Have I understood correctly so far?'

'You have. But the estate is vast and there are great tracts of wasteland on the fringes where the Montalbans have allowed the gypsies to roam for generations. The Spanish gypsy is a colourful part of our culture, and your father had a great empathy with them. Don't judge until you have seen the wild flamenco danced beneath the stars to the music of the tambourine and guitar. When you see the flounced dresses of the gypsy girls glittering against the leaping flames of a camp-fire, you will feel your heart soar with a passion that is unlike any other.'

Serena listened, open-mouthed, to all of this. It was as far removed from life in London as it was possible to be. It was heathen, as Cook had described the man himself. Yet the picture Eduardo conjured up in her mind was almost heartbreakingly, barbarically beautiful, and it touched her soul . . . and his voice was so mesmeric, so seductive . . .

'Well, *querida mía*, do I intrigue you enough to come to my land?'

She shook herself, forcing her voice to be brisk and sensible and not to be swayed by these enticing images of a world she didn't know, but which had evidently held her mother in its spell.

'I've already decided that I'll come, for a short visit. But this is my home, and this is where I belong——'

She saw him shake his head decisively.

'Not from the colour in your cheeks and the ebony of your eyes. You belong where your heart is, and I think that yours is a heart that has never yet been stirred to the limits.'

'I do not care for these frank discussions, Eduardo, and if I had any idea what you're talking about——' She tried desperately to hold on to her English dignity.

'I mean you have never been in love.'

Serena felt her skin prickle. This certainly wasn't something she wanted to discuss with anyone, least of all a man she had only met for the first time yesterday. A man who looked at her with those unfathomably dark eyes that seemed to look into the deepest corners of her mind and know the essence of her, even more than she knew it herself. She swallowed, feeling the dryness in her throat.

'I'm eighteen years old. There's time enough for falling in love.'

'And I am twenty-eight. There's a good enough margin between us for me to act as your so-called Dutch uncle and adviser, no?'

Without warning, Serena's senses rebelled. He spoke lightly but she took his words at face-value. And no, she did not want him as her uncle at all. She turned away from him, knowing her wayward thoughts were spinning away in far different directions from the one he had outlined. Dutch uncle indeed. Such a person should be dull and elderly and characterless. While Don Eduardo García was vital and exciting and everything that a foolish young girl might dream about...

'I don't need an adviser. I'm quite capable of managing my own life. And I shall see my solicitor about arranging a passage to Spain when it suits me to go.'

'It is not advisable for a young lady to travel alone, and Doña Adriana would be most upset if I did not escort you myself. I shall be in London for one month. I have business here at the moment, and I shall also be supervising the arrival and display of our wines for the Exhibition. I particularly want to be present at the opening ceremony, of course. Perhaps you would care to be my guest. Have you been presented to your Queen and the Prince?'

He simply took her breath away. She no longer bothered to deny it.

'Of course I have not! What ordinary English girl ever has such an opportunity?' she snapped.

He gave a small impatient sigh. 'My dear Serena, you are not an ordinary English girl. You are the Señorita de Montalban. You will be my guest and you will be presented to Their Highnesses.'

If the prospect was simply dazzling, it was all going too fast for her. She escaped from the room, saying she wanted to inform Cook that Eduardo would be staying for supper. And once in the steamy kitchen, she leaned against the door, her hand on her chest to stop her heart from pounding.

'What's he been saying to you? He ain't touched you, has he? I told you never to trust them foreigners!' Cook looked ready to do murder for her young lady if necessary.

'No—*no*! He's going to take me to the Exhibition when it opens, and present me to the Queen and Prince Albert!' she babbled.

'Gawd Almighty, he's having you on, gel! The likes of you and me don't get presented to royalty.'

For the first time in her life, Serena recognised who she really was. It was a moment as sweet as Montalban wine.

'The likes of the granddaughter of the Casa de Montalban does! How about that thought for you to go to bed with, Cookie?' Suddenly she had to tease, to bring it down to some kind of normality, because just as quickly the enormity of it all just about scared her to death.

'A little more wine?' Eduardo García asked, leaning towards Serena to pour more of the clear red liquid into her glass. Too late, she shook her head, and immediately wished she hadn't done so, because the movement disorientated her for a moment.

'It's very palatable indeed, but I'm unused to it, and I really think I've had enough.'

'You'll become quite accustomed to it in Spain, Serena, and because of the hot climate the effect on you will not be so potent. But perhaps it is time that I left, anyway.

My thanks for an excellent meal, and I will call on you in the near future when I have visited your Mr Price to discuss the matter of your departure to Spain.'

She felt a sudden alarm. 'You do realise I am only going for a visit, don't you? This will not be a permanent arrangement, Eduardo.'

He gave a smile that seemed to see beyond her. His hand reached across the table and covered her own for an instant.

'I think the decision will be made for you as soon as you see the Casa de Montalban, *querida*. You will fit it as smoothly as a hand fits a glove.'

Her head was dizzy with wine, but she was still able to think it odd that he should have made such a simile, when her hand had not fitted into his glove at all. Not at all...

'No, you don't understand. It will be a visit only,' she insisted, annoyed to find that her words were slightly thicker than usual.

He came around to her side of the table and helped her to her feet. Before she could stop him, his arm was around her waist and she was pulled into him.

'It's a foolish woman indeed who flies in the face of destiny, Serena de Montalban,' he said, his voice flowing through her mind as warm as honey.

And then his mouth was touching hers, tantalising her in a kiss that barely brushed her lips but had the power to fire her senses in a way that was new and heady.

'Goodnight, cousin,' he said softly. *'Buenas noches, prima mía.'*

'Goodnight,' Serena whispered, knowing she should be angry at the familiarity, and by the unknown words whose flavour could somehow enchant her. Instead, she was unable to be anything but caught up in a beautiful, hazy dream inspired by the wine and the heat of the fire, and the hours spent with Eduardo García.

Serena awoke the next morning with a headache of minor earthquake proportions and was obliged to spend the morning in bed in a shaded room, while Cook spoke darkly of the wickedness of men who plied women with drink and then had their evil way with them.

'Eduardo did not have his evil way with me,' Serena said crossly, 'and if you would please stop crashing about the room, my head might have a chance to recover.'

'He plied you with drink though, didn't he, gel? And what would the good ladies of the house have had to say about that?'

'It was Montalban wine, for pity's sake, and if I went to Spain without even knowing how it tasted I'd look pretty foolish and innocent, wouldn't I?'

She caught the look on the woman's face. 'Before you say one more word, Cookie, I *am* innocent in *that* way, and I mean to remain so! And all this talking is getting on my nerves. It's a lovely day, so I'm going to get up and take a ride to the park, and I'm sure it will clear my head quicker than your old powders and censures!'

She threw back the bedcovers, wincing a little as she sat upright and put her feet to the floor. But fresh air was what she needed, and in less than an hour she was dressed and on her way in a hire carriage towards Hyde Park, to join the throngs of folk enjoying the spectacle of watching the final touches to building Prince Albert's Crystal Palace.

Serena had watched some of the early progress, although in recent months the remnants of winter and the gloom of her aunts' house had made her forget all about such frivolities as outings to the park.

But by now it was spring, and even if the nights were still cold enough to have fires the daytimes were warm. Flowers were blooming in window-boxes, and pushing their way naturally through the sweet young grass in the park. There were one or two couples in rowing-boats on the lake, young men straining on oars, their ladies trailing their fingers in the cool water and holding parasols above their heads in the sudden burst of warm sunshine.

It was a day for couples, Serena thought suddenly. Her headache was clearing rapidly, and she looked about her at the throngs of people watching the glittering building dominating the entire area. Young couples walked hand in hand. Other couples had families of children scurrying about their feet, shouting for penny ices and toffee-apples, or to pay the hurdy-gurdy man with a monkey on a stick. Other couples strolled more sedately, arm in arm... Everyone seemed to have somebody, everyone but Serena de Montalban...

It seemed as if all of London had decided to take a stroll around the park today, she thought, and all of them having someone to talk to, to share the day... She missed her aunts acutely at that moment, because, reserved as they were, they would have loved to see all the spectacle.

She forced herself to stop being maudlin, and walked purposefully towards the great glass building, where teams of workmen were still scurrying about, putting the finishing touches to its magnificence. Serena's aunts had studied the reports in the newspapers and periodicals about the building with all the eagerness of two elderly spinsters for whom vicarious excitement was considered the safest kind.

Being nature-lovers, they had applauded the fact that no trees were to be cut down in Hyde Park for the building, but that the great glass undertaking would in-

corporate three tall elm trees within the transept, a feat
to make Londoners gasp with awe that such a thing could
ever be constructed. And Serena still recalled her surprise at seeing Aunt Dorcas's misty eyes, on reading out
the emotive phrase in *Punch*, one November morning...

'They've christened it the Crystal Palace! Did you ever
hear anything so charming? It's like something out of
fairyland.'

'Oh, Aunt Dorcas, how frivolous of you!' Serena had
teased. 'I thought I was the one who had these bursts
of imaginative thinking! Did I inherit some of it from
you, after all?'

'I hardly think so,' Miss Laker had replied stiffly.
'More likely from the other side. Anyway, be quiet,
Serena, and let me finish reading the article aloud to
you.'

At the time, the remark about 'the other side' had
gone unnoticed, and Serena couldn't think why on earth
she should be remembering it with such clarity now. But
she remembered so many little incidents now that had
gone unnoticed before.

Sudden remarks from one or other of her aunts that
had the other one shushing, or quickly changing the
conversation. The desire to keep Serena under control,
bringing to the house an old-fashioned tutor who had
no thoughts about any flamboyant world that a young
and headstrong girl might aspire to know. Why should
she...? Except that this young girl had every right to
know it...

Serena sighed, stumbling slightly over a small stump
in the ground. Wishing that these thoughts wouldn't
come to haunt her at the most unexpected moments...disturbing her peace of mind, just as Eduardo
García had already done.

Besides, she had not come here to think over days that were past, nor even to ponder on the future, but to wonder and admire at the awesome building designed by Joseph Paxton. She smiled slightly. She might be unworldly, compared to many young women of her age, but she was not ill-informed. Her aunts had seen to that.

She had been wandering about for a long time and was beginning to be conscious of the ground beneath her soft-soled shoes, and, despite her determination, thoughts of Eduardo García kept returning to annoy her.

Did he *really* know the Queen and Prince Albert? she wondered sceptically. Or was it all a ploy to tempt her to put her trust in him? What did she really know about him after all, except for what he had told her? She was all kinds of a fool to believe him so implicitly, and the more she thought about it, the more she knew it.

And tomorrow she must call on the solicitor, to see if he would verify all that the Spaniard had said. She turned away from the shining glass building and began to make her way towards the road where she could call a waiting hire carriage, feeling immensely reassured at her decision, and wondering why she hadn't thought of it before.

'So you could not resist the allure of the Crystal Palace either, Señorita de Montalban.'

As she reached the road, looking to left and right, a male voice spoke right behind her. She whirled around, knowing at once who the owner of the voice would be. Besides, who else in the world would address her so?

Don Eduardo García stood a little distance away from her, one of a small party of people who had just alighted from a private carriage. Beside him was a very elegant woman, resting her hand lightly on his arm. Serena steadfastly refused to be intimidated by the beautiful bronze silk gown and matching cape and bonnet the lady wore, nor to allow herself to feel gauche and young and hot, when in fact she was all of those things.

'Oh, this is far from being my first visit,' she heard herself say in a slightly defensive voice. Did he think that a Londoner would not have knowledge of such a feat of engineering precision and beauty being built in her own city?

'I should think not,' he said with a slight smile. 'A young lady of your personality would be eager to see and share in all the excitement.'

Was he mocking her? Serena could not be sure, but before she could decide whether to rebuff him or not, or whether she should make her escape quickly, the woman with Eduardo spoke to him.

'Is this the young lady of whom you have spoken, Eduardo? Won't you introduce me?'

'Forgive me,' he said at once. 'I forget my manners. Lady Darbyshire, may I present my cousin, the Señorita Serena de Montalban?'

Serena felt the tip of the lady's fingers touch her own as she automatically responded to the introduction. The title Eduardo accorded her sounded so splendid, so *ridiculously* splendid, and she felt a sudden recklessness at hearing it said in that richly rolling accent of Eduardo's.

'I'm delighted to meet you, Lady Darbyshire,' she said, as coolly as if she were presented to ladies of quality every day.

'Eduardo tells me you're going to return to Spain with him to visit your grandmother.'

Serena murmured a reply. The fact that the lady knew so much about her was not altogether pleasing, but she was obviously in Eduardo's confidence. Serena wondered just how intimate their relationship was, and immediately decided she didn't want to know. It was of no interest to her. After a few more small exchanges, she realised that Lady Darbyshire was handing her a card.

'I'm having a musical soirée next week. Eduardo will be there, of course, and if you would like to be my guest, do come, Miss de Montalban.'

'Thank you. I'm—honoured...' and flustered, and humiliated that the party was moving away, and leaving her on the edge of the park feeling like the complete *ingénue*. She saw Eduardo turn back from his companion, after a second or two of discussion, and walk across the grass to where she was still standing, still bemused by the address on Lady Darbyshire's card.

'I'll call for you in a carriage at eight-thirty next Saturday evening, Serena, just in case you had thoughts of changing your mind about attending the soirée. It would not do to offend her ladyship, *querida*. Until then. *Hasta luego*.'

He gave a slight bow and rejoined his friends, and Serena felt her face flame. He had guessed rightly that she'd had no intention of attending this musical soirée— she didn't even know what it entailed—and he had made sure that she had no choice. Short of inventing a sudden illness, which pride would never let her do, she was committed to a social evening in a part of London that was rich and fashionable, among people with whom she would have nothing in common.

If ever she had needed every bit of self-confidence she possessed, she needed it now. But even as the thought sped through her mind, she knew that this was only the beginning. The hollow feeling in her stomach became more pronounced, for how much more nerve-racking would be the ordeal of meeting strangers at the Casa de Montalban...

CHAPTER THREE

SERENA'S first priority was to decide on something suitable to wear. Nothing in her wardrobe was remotely grand enough for the house of a real lady, and she threw aside gown after gown in mounting frustration. As her voice rose in despair, Cook stood with arms folded impatiently.

'Anybody would think it was the Queen you were going to see from all this fuss. If there's a crowd of toffs there, do you suppose anybody's going to notice you?'

'That's just the point!' Serena raged. 'I don't want to be thought of as some little nonentity merging into the background! It's—humiliating.'

She knew that the older woman was studying her shrewdly, and not to her advantage.

'Well, I never,' Cook said finally. 'So your true nature's coming out at last, is it? Your mother had too much independence too, so I suppose it was too much to hope that the good ladies would quench it forever.'

'You can talk about her now, can you?' Serena's thoughts were diverted for a moment. 'Nobody thought to tell me anything about my parents when I was a child, did they?'

Cook put her arms around the girl's shoulders, her voice more sympathetic.

'Lord love you, gel, my ladies only did what they thought was best, and would you have wanted me to tell you things behind their backs?'

Serena was shame-faced at the woman's indignation.

'Of course not. Oh, don't let's talk about it any more. I still haven't decided what to wear to Lady Darbyshire's, and you're not helping me!'

'This sudden desire to look beautiful wouldn't have anything to do with a certain foreign person, would it?' Cook said suspiciously. 'You know my feelings on that——'

'No, it wouldn't,' Serena said irritably, because it was more than half true. 'And if you haven't got anything more intelligent to say than that, then you may as well go and do whatever it is you were doing in the kitchen.'

'You're putting me in my place now, are you?'

Serena regretted her quick temper at once.

'You know I don't mean to upset you! Why do you goad me into saying such things, when you know it's only because I'm in such a state about meeting new people?'

'Maybe you'd better change your mind about going to Spain, then, if one evening's turning you so topsy-turvy.'

'That's different. That's family.'

And that was probably the most thoughtless thing she'd said yet, because the Spanish family were going to be very different in nature and temperament from anyone she would meet at Lady Darbyshire's home. They wouldn't even speak in a language she could understand...

'And you think you need something special for next Saturday night?'

Serena's smile was on the brink of tears.

'If you're going to tell me you know a seamstress who can perform a miracle and produce a special gown before then—even if I had money to pay her—I'd say you were slightly wild in the head. Or do you have some priceless garment hidden away in the attic?'

'Well, it might be something like that.'

At that moment, Serena almost wished she were the type of inane female who stamped her foot with frustration, because she could have done it right then. It was too bad of Cook to make fun of her, when all this was of such vital importance, but then it dawned on her that there was no hint of laughter or teasing in the woman's eyes, only a rather guarded look, as if she had already said too much.

'Come on now, Cook, I can see there's some secret you're hiding, and I demand to know what it is.'

Cook smiled briefly. 'I only met your mother a few times, Miss Serena, but you've got the same high-handed manner when you want something. Perhaps that's why she appealed to your father—and why that other foreign fellow is attracted to you. You be careful, that's all.'

'Is that all you have to say? I thought we were discussing my apparel for Saturday night! Do you have something tucked away or not?'

She didn't really believe it was likely. Cook was homely and round, and not given to high fashion. Neither had her aunts been, which had always made their choice of clothing for Serena serviceable rather than decorative.

'You've got your best cream silk dress that you persuaded your aunts to have made up for your last birthday. It's good enough to go anywhere——'

'But it's so plain!' Serena wailed. 'It's high to the neck and it has no ribbons or bows, and I shall just feel like the plain Jane at the Ball. Oh, you don't understand——'

'Put it on and we'll see what can be done. I'll be back in a minute,' Cook said.

Whatever she had in mind, it was going to do nothing for her, Serena thought miserably. But doing as she was told had been ingrained in her for too long, so dutifully she slipped the cream silk gown over her head. It was undeniably the loveliest gown she had ever owned. There was an almost sensual feel to it that she hardly recognised as such. She only knew it made her feel different inside when she wore it. The pity of it was that there had been so few occasions when she could do so.

And it was true what she said. Despite the glorious folds of the fabric that shimmered every time she moved, the neckline was high and the sleeves full. It was still a young girl's dress, when she wanted so much to be thought of as a woman. She wanted Eduardo García to see her as a woman.

The thought slipped into her head without warning, bringing a painful heat to her cheeks as she preened in front of the dressing-table mirror, lifting her long dark hair from her neck. Her eyes were dark and her face as flushed as the colour of the wine he had brought. Even to Serena's own eyes, she looked like a woman wanting approval from a man.

She turned away from her own image, knowing that the sight of it betrayed deep feelings that she hadn't even acknowledged to herself. She was not ready to know a man intimately, but that did not stop her body responding in a way that was new and almost frightening.

She turned thankfully when Cook came into the room, carrying something in paper so old that it crackled. She handed it to Serena.

'I've kept this in my own trunk ever since it arrived years ago. Your aunts said they couldn't bear to look at it,' she said sadly. 'It was the second gift your parents sent them. The other one was the painting, and they felt obliged to keep that. It would have brought bad luck to the house if they'd destroyed the painting of it.'

Thank God for superstition, Serena thought swiftly. But by now, her heart was pounding. There was so much about her parents she hadn't known, and yet so much of it was here, in this house, and had been within her grasp all these years. She took the package out of Cook's hands and untied the string with unsteady hands.

And then she gasped as the soft, cascading silk of the Spanish shawl slid into her hands, rich in colours of scarlet and gold and tempered by muted shades of blue. The fringed edges were a mixture of threads of all the colours. She suddenly caught sight of herself in the mirror again, and the effect of the silken shawl held against the cream silk gown was stunning.

Quickly, she threw it around her shoulders, knotting it low over her breasts, and instantly it seemed as if she took on the persona of a different person, someone she hardly knew, dark and mysterious, and as beautiful as Eduardo García might want her to be. She turned to Cook.

'Will I do?' she said, her voice husky.

'You'll do,' Cook replied, the understatement saying more than words ever could.

The Misses Laker had been much older than their sister Claudia, who was born to their parents late in life. They had treated her more as a plaything than a younger sister, and she had grown up with far more freedom than either of them had enjoyed or wanted.

The older sisters had preferred the security of a regimented household, while the pretty young Claudia had been more adventurous, even begging to accompany old friends of the family on a Grand Tour of Europe. A tour which for the Laker family had had disastrous consequences, because Claudia had met and fallen in love with the son of a vine-growing empire in southern Spain, Ramón de Montalban.

She had married him after a whirlwind romance that left both families gasping and incensed, even though communication between them had been sparse. Claudia had never seen her aged parents again and only returned to England once more.

Heavily pregnant by then, she had brought the flamboyant Ramón with her, bestowing gifts on her sisters and begging their forgiveness. And because she was the only thing that had ever brought colour into their lives, as usual they had forgiven her everything.

Long before Serena was ready to go to the musical soirée on the following Saturday evening, Cook finally told her the whole story as far as she knew it, and the girl could only feel a deep empathy with the mother she had never known, and the romantic love-story that was her parents'.

'Romance!' Cook sniffed. 'What good is that if it leads nowhere? They were ill-fated from the start, and the shock of it all did for her parents.'

'They had two years to be together, didn't they? Some folk never have two minutes of pure happiness in their whole lives. I'd gladly settle for two years——'

'That's nonsense, Miss Serena, and I don't want to hear any more of such talk. Now, are you going to let me help you get ready for this fancy outing or not? I'm not at all sure that I approve of sending you off with that——'

'If you call him that foreign fellow once more, I shall be really angry,' Serena said. 'His name is Eduardo García, and he's a distant cousin of the Montalbans.'

'And it hasn't taken you long, miss, to be putting on airs and graces. You might be some young *señorita*, or whatever they call it, but you're still my Miss Serena that I spanked on more than one occasion for sneaking a slice of fruit pie when my back was turned, and don't you forget it.'

Serena laughed.

'I never will, Cookie, even if I do end up as mistress of my lovely house in the painting! Wouldn't that be the funniest lark? It's never going to happen, though. I'll go and see my grandmother, and be very proper and dignified, and then I'll come home and it will all seem like a dream. Because that's what it's always been to me.'

But she didn't quite meet Cook's eyes when she said it, because the excitement running through her veins had nothing to do with the house or the prospect of being Somebody in the world after all... It had more to do with knowing that tonight she looked more beautiful than she had ever looked in her life, and that there was someone who was undoubtedly going to tell her so.

Eduardo García arrived on time and was shown into the parlour. It was a week since they had met, and Serena was suddenly apprehensive about seeing him again. He had occupied her thoughts far too much, and she was perfectly aware that she was unused to the attentions of young men, particularly hot-blooded young men, and was determined not to let her head be swayed by them.

He appraised Serena without speaking for long moments, his eyes taking in every detail of her appearance, until she began to feel like a fly on the wall about to receive the rough end of Cook's swatter.

'Well?' she said, in a mixture of nervousness and annoyance. 'Am I good enough for you to act as my escort?'

He spread his hands in a gesture that seemed to embrace her, even though they were still some distance apart.

'*Querida*, you are simply the most beautiful woman in the world. But you already know that, don't you?'

She lowered her eyes from his unblinking gaze, hot with embarrassment, and wishing she had never challenged him. His answers were too smooth, too foreign, too charged with meaning.

'I hardly think that a lady would admit to thinking any such thing,' she said crisply. 'Especially when she knows very well it's not true!'

He moved forward to pick up her warm cloak, and adjusted it around her. His hands rested lightly on her shoulders and she knew his presence was beginning to affect her in a way that was too disturbing to be welcome. Besides, she was still not ready to trust him implicitly.

'Tonight you have paid me the greatest compliment by wearing a Spanish shawl, and if I say it makes you more beautiful and desirable to me, then you must believe it. It's the greatest insult to throw a compliment back in someone's face, but I think that this is the English in you, so I will readily forgive it.'

She twisted away from him, more amused than outraged by his arrogance.

'Thank you, sir! Then I accept the compliment.'

She had a great temptation to giggle, and tried desperately to remember her aunts' stern admonition that a young lady never giggled. Giggling revealed either immaturity or bad taste, but it was an urge that almost overcame Serena at that moment.

She suddenly saw the preposterousness of the whole situation. Here she was, about to enter high society with a complete stranger, who might be about to whisk her off into white slavery for all she knew... and through it all, she felt more alive than she had ever done in her life before.

She was on the brink of a great adventure that might
even include her introduction to the Queen of England,
and unquestionably a visit to Spain, when she had never
travelled more than a few miles from home before. And
these forays into the unknown all began tonight with a
musical soirée in the home of a titled lady...

A couple of hours later, she wondered how she could
ever have thought of tonight as the beginning of anything. The evening was so dull she could have screamed
with the boredom of it.

The house was in a fashionable part of Paddington,
the furniture inside it heavy and ornate and dark, with
a plethora of plants in every kind of container im-
aginable, making every room resemble a hot-house. The
guests were for the most part elderly matrons accom-
panied by their husbands, who looked at Serena
cautiously and seemed to assume that she was as foreign
as Don Eduardo García.

Lady Darbyshire flitted about, looking, though it was
probably an ungallant thought, older than Serena had
at first supposed, handing out little programmes for the
evening. Maids served warm punch and nuts to nibble,
and Serena was pleased to see that there was also a Lord
Darbyshire, since it meant that Eduardo was clearly not
the object of the lady's affections after all. She refused
to analyse why this should concern her in the least.

When it was announced that the evening was about
to begin, an elderly woman with pince-nez perched on
the end of her nose started proceedings by thundering
her way through the Mozart, the first piece on the
agenda.

After half the items had been gone through—more
ponderous pieces by the same lady, lighter ditties sung
by a well-bolstered soprano, and then rousing duets by
two bearded male tenors—Serena tried not to fidget.

Eduardo had positioned himself beside the pianoforte, having offered to turn the pages of the music when required, and remained standing the entire time.

He was in direct line with Serena, and she had the uncomfortable feeling that he was judging her reaction. Perhaps he didn't think she was capable of enjoying a civilised evening such as this. He was absolutely right in that, but she had no intention of letting him guess it. She sat upright, her shoulders squared, apparently listening intently, while letting her thoughts roam quite indiscriminately, and wishing herself anywhere but here.

What would the warm evenings in the Casa de Montalban be like? she wondered. Just as dull as this, or would there be different entertainments? And would there be outings, away from the house? She had no idea at all, but vivid snatches of Eduardo's conversation began to swim in and out of her mind...

'...the wild flamenco danced beneath the stars to the music of tambourine and guitar...the flounced dresses of the gypsy girls glittering against the leaping flames of a camp-fire...you will feel your heart soar with a passion that is unlike any other...'

It was beating quickly now. Not because any of this evening's music was inspiring her, but because her gaze was suddenly caught and held by that of Eduardo García. From the other side of the room, she could feel the magnetic pull of his personality. She could almost imagine that he read her thoughts, and knew that for her this sedate English evening was not enough. That there was another part of her that needed to explore the world that he knew, that her parents had known and loved...

She wrenched her gaze away, not wanting her thoughts to be probed as effortlessly as he seemed to be doing. Unless it was all her imagination, of course. A feeling evoked by the warm room and hot punch, and the sense of claustrophobia that both the house and these heavily pampered and overdressed people so unwittingly produced.

She felt trapped among these corseted matrons and their spouses. It was as if a little chill wind ran over her, whispering that this too was meant to be her destiny. This orderliness, this *dullness*...and she saw instantly what she should always have seen. That, though it would probably be in far less sophisticated surroundings than these, this was the kind of controlled life her aunts had prepared her for, in their coldly caring way, to prevent her from making the same mistake her mother had made.

The small sense of panic Serena felt at that moment was almost akin to fear, as if she saw the years stretching ahead, knowing they were not of her choosing. The fear was so real...and in a strange moment of word association, Eduardo's words echoed again in her head...

'I do not fear *el toro*, but I think I may have met my match in you, Señorita de Montalban...'

Was he her destiny after all? Not him personally, she thought hastily, but was he the catalyst to take her to the place where she was always meant to be?

Another voice, trilling with rounded English vowels and beautifully correct diction, sounded in her ears then, a voice that was real, not imagined...

'Did you enjoy the evening, Miss de Montalban? You certainly seemed to be giving it rapt attention. It's so refreshing to see that in a young woman. So many of them sit with glazed eyes these days, not even attempting to understand what the music is saying to them.'

People were starting to move around, chatting and congratulating, and Serena turned to the powdered and scented lady who had spoken, forcing a smile.

'Oh, yes—I found it all—most stimulating,' she said, fervently glad that as she was sitting alongside her the woman couldn't possibly have seen Serena's eyes during the performances.

Thankfully, she watched Eduardo's progress across the room towards her. She was out of her depth here and she knew it. He had obviously heard the lady's remark and she saw the glint of amusement in his eyes at her reply.

'My cousin appreciates all kinds of music, Lady Faulkner,' he said smoothly, just as if they had known one another all their lives.

'You play an instrument yourself, of course, my dear?' Lady Faulkner asked Serena.

'I'm afraid not.'

'Ah.' She paused now. 'What a pity. It's such a necessary accomplishment for a young gel. Do excuse me for a moment. I must pay my compliments to Lady Darbyshire and thank her for a splendid evening.'

Eduardo dropped into the seat the lady vacated, and Serena almost hissed at him. They were temporarily alone, the way people sometimes were in the midst of a crowded gathering, the buzz of conversation going on all around them yet somehow isolating them.

'Did I detect the atmosphere going a few degrees colder because I do not have the "necessary" musical "accomplishment", or am I being oversensitive?'

He gave a small laugh. 'Both, I suspect. Don't let it concern you, *querida*.'

'I shan't,' she said smartly. 'But I'm interested to know how you can bear to spend your evenings like this? It's surely very different from what you're used to at home?'

'Very,' he agreed. 'But I hope you do not imply that we are all barbarians. We have our music, our culture, and our different levels of society. In many ways our worlds are not so very different.'

'I think that they are! Indeed, I hope so, otherwise why would I want to see yours at all? I might just as well stay here,' she said quickly, conscious that he was being critical of her.

'So. I have intrigued you, have I? And you want to know what it is that makes us all different. I have no argument with that. Just as long as you come to see Doña Adriana de Montalban, my mission will be fulfilled.'

She looked at him curiously, detecting an almost reverential note in his voice.

'She means something to you, doesn't she?'

'Of course. She is the matriarch of *la familia*. We do not cast out our old, nor expect our young to desert the nest the minute they have wings to fly. *La familia* is at its strongest when every member remembers that he is part of a whole.'

Serena recognised an unspoken rebuke towards her own father, and an extraordinary sense of defensiveness stirred inside her. She had never known him, but she had always known and felt the love he put into his painting. It seemed to Serena that this man was accusing her father now of not playing his part in this family unity which he seemed to find so all-important. She challenged him at once.

'Do you think it a betrayal that my father did not feel the same way? Do you not think it shows more strength of character and a certain pride in one's own ability to break away from filial dependence and think for oneself?'

'I think that for such a beautiful woman you talk too much like a man,' he said drily. 'It is not done in my country.'

'But we are not in your country, and if I have my own opinions and feelings why should I not express them?

And does it follow that because a woman is beautiful, she is also empty-headed?'

She was beginning to sparkle at his arrogance. If she spoke with more daring than usual, it was because she was realising that she had never had the opportunity nor the need to speak so controversially before, and she was unexpectedly enjoying it.

But just as quickly, she knew that this was not the time or place, and that one or two people were glancing their way. Eduardo had evidently noticed it too, because he stood up and held out his hand.

'It will be my pleasure to continue this discussion some other time. Meanwhile, allow me to escort you into supper, Serena.'

Afterwards, when she was able to dissect the events of the evening clinically, she knew she had not enjoyed the rest of it at all. The people were too false, and she suspected that not all of them had meant the effusive compliments showered on Lady Darbyshire. When she suggested as much as they jolted homewards in the carriage, Eduardo agreed, commenting that he had only accepted the invitation out of courtesy to old acquaintances of his father.

'Thank heavens,' Serena said frankly. 'Then I don't have to accompany you to any more of them, do I?'

'I doubt if we shall see much more of each other in the next weeks. The wines for the Exhibition will be arriving by sea in a day or so, and I shall be extremely busy seeing to their storage and display. The opening is drawing very near, and I thought you may like a catalogue.'

He drew out the bulky Exhibition catalogue from an inside pocket and handed it to her. Until she had known of Eduardo's involvement with it, she had only had a superficial interest in the proceedings, but now it was an intimate concern. Montalban wines were to be on display, and she felt a surge of pride in her own name.

It was probably just as Cook had implied, she thought ruefully. She was putting on airs and graces, however unconsciously...

'But I shall see you on the opening day, shan't I?' she said. 'You did say you would present me——'

She stopped, because suddenly it all sounded so unlikely. Ordinary folk were not normally presented to royalty, and she felt embarrassed at her eagerness.

'If the opportunity arises on that day, I will certainly do so,' he said. 'Otherwise, it may be possible to arrange a small private audience at the palace.'

'You don't mean it! Oh, I hope not. Oh, Eduardo, no! I would be too terrified to say a single word!'

'That would be a surprise to me! I thought you had enough spirit to face tigers! Anyway, I cannot promise anything, but I have said I will try, and I never go back on my word. You will learn that, Serena.'

'And did you give your word to take me to the Casa de Montalban?' she said.

'Naturally.'

There seemed little else to say as the carriage rattled through the cobbled streets. He had given his word to Doña Adriana de Montalban, and he never went back on his word. The outcome seemed as much a *fait accompli* as if she were already on the boat to Spain.

Serena was acutely aware of events controlling her, instead of herself controlling them. And even while she rebelled against it, there was also a strange sense of acceptance, knowing that her one great desire had always been to see the house in the painting.

She realised Eduardo was still thinking about her meeting with the Queen and Prince Albert.

'Look, I know that the royal party will be visiting the Crystal Palace informally on the day before the opening, as they have done many times in previous weeks,' he said thoughtfully. 'If you've no objection to complete informality, it might be simpler for us merely to be in the vicinity, and I'm certain I shall be able to introduce you.'

'I would prefer that to anything!' Serena said fervently. The very thought of being presented at Buckingham Palace was enough to set her nerves tingling, and she was beginning to realise that her Spanish family were of a very different class from that of the reserved Laker ladies.

Not that they were any the less dear to her because of it, she thought loyally. It was just that her life could be very different from now on.

Immediately, she thought that it must not. This was her home and she had no intention of staying in Spain indefinitely. It would be a visit, no more.

As if he read her mind, Eduardo spoke lazily. 'Have you given any thought to our departure for Cadiz?'

Since he presumed she knew what and where Cadiz was, she spoke just as casually. 'Not really——'

'Then may I suggest you return with me one week after the opening of the Exhibition? My work here will be done, and I do not wish to delay your visit to Doña Adriana any longer than necessary.'

'Oh, but there will be so much to arrange——' she said, in sudden fright. His hand closed over hers.

'All you have to arrange is your own baggage and any arrangements with your house. Everything else you can leave to me. I have no doubt you have verified my credentials with your solicitor, and if you wish to bring money with you he will see to it. But it is not really necessary. Everything you need will be provided at the Casa de Montalban.'

She felt a small shiver at his words. Everything was being taken care of, and she was being carried along by it all. And, after all, she had not been sophisticated enough to check on Eduardo García's credentials with Mr Price! She would check staight away.

She had fully intended to do so, and had simply forgotten all about it, since seeing that Lady Darbyshire was a close acquaintance of the man had seemed security enough. How naïve she was! She was very conscious of being a mere eighteen years of age, compared with the years of experience of this man.

The pressure of Eduardo's hand was still on hers as the carriage stopped outside her aunt's house. It was warm and reassuring, and she supposed she was beginning to trust him after all. She had to, because in this new world where he was taking her he would be the only one she actually knew. She needed to believe in him.

'Until the last day of April, Serena,' he said steadily. 'I will call for you at ten o'clock in the morning.'

'Very well.' She hesitated, and then said a little awkwardly, 'Eduardo—what were the words you used once before—*hasta luego*, or something like that?'

He laughed in delighted surprise.

'You learn quickly, *querida*! Yes, *hasta luego*—until then.'

Before she knew what he intended, he had caught both her hands in his and raised them to his lips. She could feel the warmth of his breath on her fingers as he kissed them, and the texture of his skin on hers. It was as foreign a farewell as she could imagine, neither too familiar nor too intrusive, and yet in the confines of the carriage she felt that it was as intimate as an embrace.

*   *   *

She was ready long before Eduardo arrived on the morning of April the thirtieth. She was all fingers and thumbs as she struggled to fit her hands into her gloves, and Cook scolded her time and again, but it had little effect on Serena.

'Don't pretend that you wouldn't be just as excited if it were you going to meet the Queen!'

Cook snorted. 'You don't know yet if it will even happen. I don't want you to be disappointed, that's all.'

'It *will* happen,' Serena said. 'Eduardo will make it happen.'

She avoided Cook's eyes as she said it. But by now, there was nothing the woman could say about Don Eduardo García. Serena had finally been to the solicitor's chambers and learned that everything the man said was true, and that she had no reason to mistrust him. Only in a more personal way, perhaps, and she wouldn't even think of that.

And, after all, the day had a kind of dreamlike quality. They drove to Hyde Park, two people among a vast crowd of spectators all eager to get a glimpse of royalty in a way that was refreshingly informal, because tomorrow would be all pomp and ceremony; to see the last touches to the enormous glass building that people were already calling an architectural masterpiece, adorned with the flags of many nations now, the stage almost set for the great moment of tomorrow's opening by Her Majesty.

And in the midst of the final day's bustle and excitement there was a moment unlike any other for one of Her Majesty's loyal subjects. Long into that night, Serena kept remembering it, relating it to Cook time and again, wanting to imprint it on her memory forever.

'The Queen was so tiny, Cookie, and so pretty. And the Prince is one of the most handsome men I've ever seen, and clearly adores her. The elder children were there as well, and so were the Prince and Princess of Prussia with their children.'

She paused for breath, and Cook spoke caustically.

'My, how glib we are, talking about royalty as if they were the folk next door——'

'Oh, don't spoil it! I thought you'd want to know everything that happened——'

'So I do, if you can slow down for a minute——'

'I'll try! Well, then. We watched for the royal carriages to arrive, and Eduardo gave his card to a footman to offer to the Prince. Then he was invited to approach the carriage after they all alighted, and I could see at once that they were old friends. Then Eduardo called me forward, and oh, Cookie, my heart was pounding so much I thought it was going to burst. To have the Queen saying that it was a pleasure to meet me—oh, I think I shall never know another day like it in my life. And I owe it all to Eduardo.'

Her eyes glowed like rich jewels as she clasped her hands together, still caught up in the day and the memory. And thinking that it was surely going to be impossible to ever find a way to repay Eduardo for giving her the experience of a lifetime . . .

CHAPTER FOUR

IF THE day when Serena was presented to the Queen was magical indeed, she could never say that the opening day of the Exhibition was any less memorable.

The spectacle was too grand, the precision of the day too well regimented in a way that only the British could enact. She and Eduardo had taken their places early, and Serena felt a special burst of national and personal pride as Victoria and Albert entered the arena, hardly able to believe that only yesterday those majesterial eyes had smiled kindly on her alone...

But, after all, it was something of a relief when the long-drawn-out formal ceremonies were over, and all the fanfares and singing and the speeches done. The royal party left, and the public was free to roam and gasp and explore every part of the great displays that had come from all parts of the globe.

'I never dreamed of seeing such beautiful silks as those from the Orient,' she said in an awed voice to Eduardo, imagining for a moment that sensuous fabric draped around her body. 'Their brilliance is dazzling, and they shimmer so wonderfully in the sunlight streaming through the glass roof.'

'So what do you say to the Koh-i-noor diamond?' he challenged some time later when they had paraded around the vast exhibits for what seemed like hours. Serena stood in front of the stunning jewel without speaking, never having expected to see such a thing in her lifetime.

She shook her head slightly, her senses beginning to reel with all the magnificence of the natural resources that existed in the world, to say nothing of the ingenuity of the human mind and the skill of human hands in producing such marvels of invention.

'It's beyond words,' she said simply. 'And, although I never thought I would say so, I do believe I have seen enough for one day, Eduardo. After this, I don't want to go on any more,' she said, hoping he would understand.

And, in truth, the great glass building was becoming something of a hot-house, with its thousands of exhibits and the crowds milling about in ever more perspiring excitement as they tried to see everything at once.

'Then perhaps we should retire to a tea-room for refreshment,' Eduardo said, agreeing at once. 'I, too, am beginning to feel somewhat crushed by so many people. The exhibits will be on show for about six months, so the sensible ones will spread out their visits.'

'Will you come back to England during that time?' Serena asked, as they began to push their way towards the doors, and found that it was of necessity slow progress.

'Would it please you if I did?' He answered one question with another, a habit she was starting to associate with him.

He held her arm protectively, and the crowds were pushing them together. She could feel the strength of his body, trying to shield her from the seething waves of humanity. Gentry or peasants, everyone was intent on seeing as much as they could on this initial day, to relate it all in glowing terms to those less fortunate than themselves who had not been able to be here. And not a few of them would be crowing at their good luck in being almost close enough to touch the royal personages...

Serena looked up quickly into Eduardo's face as he smothered an oath as someone stepped on his toes. Would it please her if he came back? She wasn't ready to answer that, even to herself. These last weeks had been unreal in many ways, yet they were making some kind of order in her mind.

The undisputed fact of her removal to Spain, on a temporary basis at least, had begun to fill her with exhilaration as well as a tingling apprehension. For some of the time, she managed to forget about Doña Adriana and her dictatorial ways, and look upon the visit instead as a great adventure... one that just a few short weeks ago she would never have dreamed could happen to her.

But it seemed that Eduardo did not expect an immediate answer to his question. All his concentration was on getting them both out of the Crystal Palace and into the refreshing air outside. Once there, they breathed a huge sigh of relief as they walked across the grass towards the road where waiting hire carriages lined up for people like themselves, who had had enough. They climbed into a carriage, and Serena leaned against the back-rest, closing her eyes for a moment.

'As a matter of fact, it's unlikely that I shall return to England until the end of the Exhibition,' Eduardo said lazily, picking up the threads of the conversation begun earlier. She was discovering that this was another habit he had, covering time and distance between them easily. Serena opened her eyes at once.

'Oh?'

'There will be no need. My agents will be here to see that all is going well, and to take new orders for our wines. I will certainly want to be here when the Exhibition ends in October though, to ensure that the bottles are crated properly and transported back safely—unless I decide to donate them to any organisation as an act of faith in our produce.'

'Will you call on me when you return?' Serena heard herself say. 'As a cousinly gesture, of course!'

She heard his low chuckle, and his hand covered hers for a moment in the somewhat cloying atmosphere inside the carriage. His tight-fitting skin gloves and her own silk ones that matched her bonnet and dress made hardly any difference to the warmth of his fingers closing over hers.

'As a cousin, my answer is yes, of course! But you are far too beautiful for me to think of you in such cool English terms, Serena *mía*.'

'I thought that "distant cousins" was exactly what we were to one another,' she said quickly. 'And you have not answered my question yet.'

He removed his hand from hers as the carriage driver slowed his animal to a stop outside the tea-room Eduardo had requested.

'If you are in England at that time, then I will call on you,' he said solemnly, and jumped down before she could reply, extending his hand to help her down and tossing the coins to the driver at the same time.

When they were seated at a corner table inside the establishment, with its thick velvet curtains at the windows and its plants in great jardinières in every available space, Serena looked at Eduardo in exasperation, picking up the conversation in a similar manner to his own.

'Why should I not be in England? I've already told you that I will only go to Spain on a courtesy visit. This is my home.'

He looked at her thoughtfully, his dark eyes made even darker by the rather gloomy interior of the room, which was evidently intended to give it a certain ambience. He ordered tea and pastries with the ease of a gentleman who was at home anywhere, and Serena began to find his very self-confidence irritating. She saw his mouth twitch a little, and realised that she was playing her fingers on the edge of the table.

'I see that my words annoy you,' he commented. 'Your fingers give you away, *querida*. You should learn to play the pianoforte. You would have no trouble mastering it.'

Her eyes flashed at him. 'I'm afraid my aunts did not have the wherewithal to give me lessons, and it was not considered so important in our limited social sphere. I led a rather sheltered life, but I have no complaints,' she added in swift defence of her aunts.

'You may learn what you wish in *España*. If it is your desire to learn an instrument, then Doña Adriana will be only too pleased to arrange it.'

'Please understand that it is of no interest to me!' Serena said, taking his comment to imply that he found her lacking in social skills. He was beginning to annoy her intensely, but her words were true. She had no wish now to learn to play an instrument, and never had.

The waitress brought their tea and pastries and Eduardo leaned back in his chair while Serena poured the refreshment with slightly shaking hands. Why did he seem to have the knack of disturbing her so? She prided herself on normally being well in control of her emotions, but this man seemed to bring out some reserve of passion inside her that she didn't even know she possessed. The *Spanish* side, a little voice whispered in her head...

'I have a suggestion to make to you, Serena,' he said calmly, cutting through a delicious concoction of flaky pastry filled with cream and nuts.

'What is it?' Her voice was filled with suspicion, and he shrugged his shoulders in mock despair.

'Hear me out before you anticipate the worst! I am not about to suggest we elope into the night together—although the thought has much charm for me——'

'Please lower your voice, sir! I have no wish to be thought of as a—a...'

She could not bring herself to say the word. Light-skirts were practically ten a penny when there were such crowds flocking into the capital, and a handsome Spanish gentleman leaning towards a lady in an intimate manner might well have his meaning misconstrued. Serena felt herself blush at her own oversensitive thoughts, because, glancing around, she saw that no one else was taking the slightest interest in her and her companion.

'No one could ever think of you as anything but a lady,' Eduardo said gravely. 'You have your father's proud bearing, and the Montalban hauteur.'

Serena felt a stab of pleasure at these unexpected words... and she felt something else too. She recognised it as an extraordinary feeling of loss for the father she had never known, with whom this man had apparently been on familiar terms.

'What was he like?' she asked a little huskily, and he didn't need to ask whom she meant.

'A man of strength and honour, who had to fight with his conscience several times in his life. The first was because of his refusal to perform his role in the *corrida*, choosing instead to follow his dream of becoming an artist. Then he had to fight again when he decided to marry a woman not of his race and culture, knowing it would bring disgrace on his name.'

'Are they so dogmatic, your family?' Serena said in some apprehension, yet not missing the fact that Eduardo spoke of her father with an undeniable pride and admiration.

He gave a short exclamation that she could not catch. 'The old ones were always so, but times are changing, and perhaps—who knows?—you may be the one to make them see that we are all brothers beneath the skin. You will bring a refreshing breath of life into what sometimes seems like a sterile environment.'

'You put a great responsibility on me, Eduardo!' she said in alarm. Her tea was almost untouched, and she drank quickly now, as if to reassure herself in a traditional English pastime. She bit into a cream pastry, forgetting to cut it through first in her agitation, and running the tip of her tongue around the escaping froth around her mouth.

Eduardo seemed not to notice any lack of manners. Instead he continued his earlier conversation.

'This is why I want to put the suggestion to you, Serena. You have had time to get used to the idea of coming to Spain now. You have a *familia* there, and are not alone in the world.'

He paused, seeing how her eyes widened a little, because it was something she had hardly thought about until he put it into words, but she had to agree that it was true.

'I beg you to stay longer than a few weeks,' he went on urgently. 'Your Spanish ancestry goes back for generations, and a brief visit as a *turista* will be only sufficient to skim the surface of your past. Doña Adriana wishes to know you, and to acquaint you with all that is rightfully yours. I suggest that you stay at Casa de Montalban until I come back to England for the closing of the Exhibition in October. We will return here together, and, if it is your wish to remain in England, I will not try to deter you.'

'My decision on that is already made!' Serena said at once. 'There is really no question of it, Eduardo, and I cannot think how you can expect otherwise! My Spanish ancestry, as you so flamboyantly call it, cared nothing about me all these years. Why should you think that a few weeks or months will make me want to give up everything I know and love, to stay in a country that rejected my mother, and to stay with a family that rejected my father too?'

She finished speaking with some anger, and several people at another table glanced their way.

'Perhaps you will let the country speak for itself. And I assure you we do not reject *you*, and I suspect that Doña Adriana has many regrets for what happened in the past. I pray you to allow her this time of salving her own conscience by opening her home and her heart to you.'

Serena bit her lip. He spoke with such eloquence, such charm. It was not the bland, earnest, well-intentioned charm of an English gentleman. It was more heart-stirring and emotional, and it evoked a response in her that she was still vainly trying to resist.

'Then if I give you this time—this six months—do I have your promise not to try to persuade me to stay in Spain for good? Do you assure me that this is not some kind of trick?'

Eduardo laughed, and the tension of the last few minutes visibly lessened.

'My dear Serena, what an odd idea. You speak as though I were about to abduct you. I assure you we are a very civilised race, even if we do appear more volatile than our cold English cousins——'

'Why do I always have the impression that you're patronising me when you say such things?' she said, nettled. 'We are what we are, Eduardo.'

'We are indeed,' he agreed. 'And I do not patronise you. How could I, when I am filled with admiration and pride at the thought of escorting my beautiful *prima*— my cousin—to my home? It will be my pleasure to show you everything, if you will allow me.'

She gave a sudden teasing smile. 'Can you really show me everything in six months? From the way you speak, I would have thought it would take a lifetime.'

'I hope you will remember those words, *señorita*!' He raised his cup in a small salute, and she gave a small shiver, knowing without the telling that she was being drawn into something inevitable.

Cook was all tears and red eyes on the morning she bade goodbye to her beloved mistress. Serena hugged her tightly, willing her throat to stop convulsing at the step she was about to take, or they would both end up wallowing, and that would do nobody any good.

'Now you just take care of everything and treat the house as your own, Cookie,' she said with a waver in her voice. 'Whatever you need, you're to refer to Mr Price. I've told him all the circumstances and he'll get in touch with me if there are any problems. But what problems can there be? You've run this house for years already, so just carry on in the same way.'

'It won't be the same, though, will it?' Cook sniffed dramatically. 'First of all I lost my ladies and now I'm losing you, and you're going to the Lord knows where——'

'I'm going to visit my grandmother,' Serena said, because the more she said it, the more real it became.

'A fat lot of interest she's taken in you all these years,' the woman muttered.

'It's too late now to change my mind, and we've been over it a hundred times already,' Serena said wearily, knowing that Cook was too genuinely upset at the circumstances to care how she spoke now. 'Look, why don't you ask your sister to come and stay for a while?' Serena had a sudden inspiration. 'You're always saying she hates her present position in service and wishes she could have a lovely place like.yours. Invite her to stay as long as you like and treat the house as your own. Please do it, Cookie. I would feel so much better if I didn't think of you moping all the time I was gone.'

'I might,' Cook said reluctantly. 'It would take my mind off you a bit, and I suppose that's the next best thing to going with you. Mind you, wild horses wouldn't get me to go to no foreign place, so don't go asking me at this late stage.'

'I wasn't going to.' Serena grinned. She didn't know yet how she herself was going to fit into her new surroundings, but she could never imagine Cook setting foot out of London, let alone England. Cook was essentially a home body, while Serena was... She didn't know what she was yet, but she meant to find out.

The doorbell rang while they were still standing in some embarrassment in the final moments before departure, and Cook turned quickly to let Eduardo in.

It was a dismal day for early May, the rain drizzling continuously, and he looked as dark and forbidding as he had on the first day they met. Serena quickly subdued a small moment of panic. He looked down at the pieces of baggage she had got ready for the trip.

'*Bueno*. I see you've packed enough for a long stay, but I hope you haven't included too many warm clothes. The summer will be hot in Spain,' he commented.

'If I need something more, I've no doubt I can arrange it,' she said coolly. 'You do have seamstresses in Spain, I presume?'

'Of course.'

There was an odd restraint between them that Serena couldn't fathom. She was glad when he called to the groom outside to pile the baggage in the carriage, and she gave one last hug to Cook, who let the tears flow freely now.

'I'll go and see my sister right away,' she mumbled. 'There's no point in letting the grass grow under my feet, is there? If you're sure it's all right with you——'

'I've said so, haven't I? And don't forget—Mr Price will see to everything for you—money and everything. I've arranged it all.'

She couldn't say any more, and Eduardo was urging her to get into the carriage. The boat wouldn't wait for tardy folk who were making a meal out of saying goodbye to servants. Clearly, he couldn't understand why she was making such a fuss about it all.

He was too insensitive for words, Serena raged inwardly, knowing it was easier on her emotions to be angry than to weep all over him. He would only take advantage...and this was only a visit, even if it had somehow become extended to a far longer one than she had intended...

'Have you been on a sea voyage before?' he asked her politely as the carriage took them towards Tilbury.

'No, I have not. I haven't been anywhere before,' she muttered. Did he think she was in the habit of taking the Grand Tours, the way the aristocracy did?

'There's really no need to be scratchy with me, Serena. I know you must be apprehensive about leaving England, but you will not be disappointed in your new home. Did you not tell me how intrigued you always were by the picture in your father's painting?'

'Yes,' she said in a small voice. She had made the decision to come, and she could hardly understand why she was being so prickly.

'Contrary' was the word Aunt Dorcas had always used. 'Serena's in one of her contrary moods again,' she would say briskly, 'and there's no reasoning with her until she comes out of it!'

What would her aunts think of all this? she wondered now. Would they think she was betraying their memory by going off to the Spanish house that had rejected their darling young sister? She didn't even want to consider such a thing, and pushed the hated thought away.

'I'm sorry,' she said now with a great effort. 'I expect it was seeing Cook so distraught that started me off. She's always been more like one of the family to me than a servant. And I'm a little nervous at being on the sea. I've been told of something called *mal de mer* that can make one feel wretched.'

'Don't anticipate it, Serena. The seasickness is only for old ladies and faint-hearteds, unless the weather is very rough, of course. At such times it can afflict anyone, but we should have a smooth passage at this time of year, especially on the cream of the fleet.'

Serena hoped he wasn't tempting fate in the other direction by his confident words, and at first it was very smooth sailing indeed. She found the tangy sea air invigorating and piquant, whipping up a rosy colour to her cheeks and putting a new sparkle in her eyes. But within half a day of boarding the ship bound for Cadiz her fears were proved right.

During the night a squall arose, lashing the decks with heavy, chilling rain that sent passengers scurrying to their cabins or into the lounge. It was interesting enough at first, watching as the squall developed into a downpour, then watching how the howling wind churned the seas into gigantic waves.

From their seats in the passenger lounge, Eduardo and Serena gazed in some fascination through the portholes until the motion of the waves began to make her nauseous, and she realised that the uneven lurching of the ship was doing all sorts of unpleasant things to her stomach.

One minute the ship appeared to hover above the waves, and the next it seemed to Serena to plunge to the depths of the ocean. Her senses became disorientated, and she gasped to Eduardo through chattering lips, 'I think I must go to my cabin before I disgrace myself. I'm sorry——'

She clapped a hand over her mouth and rushed out of the lounge on unsteady feet, staggering against tables and chairs as she went. Eduardo was right behind her, holding her arm and guiding her through the maze of passages to her cabin, adjacent to his own. She almost fell inside and threw herself face-down across her bunk, feeling the beads of perspiration on her brow.

'Please go away, Eduardo,' she pleaded.

Surely he understood that the worst humiliation for a lady was to retch in front of a gentleman, and her last meal was threatening to leave her stomach at any moment...

'Don't be stupid. Lie flat and I'll sponge your head. The feeling will go away soon——'

'No, it won't!'

She almost shrieked the words at him, but he was moving her swiftly over on to her back and pressing his hand gently to her upper chest to still the convulsions, while stars seemed to dance in front of her eyes.

If his actions were improper she was too scatter-brained at that moment to even think of it, and in any case the small pressure on her chest seemed to be slowing down the almost irresistible urge to vomit. On his instruction, she breathed more deeply and slowly, and when he left her side she closed her eyes, thankful to her toes that the terrible heaving sensations were receding.

The next moment she felt a cool, damp cloth on her forehead, remaining there for a few seconds and then wiping her hot eyes and moving delicately around her mouth and throat. Her breathing was more regular now, and, even though the ship still seemed to be pounding all around her, she felt as though she moved with it and was a part of it, instead of battling against it.

'You'll feel easier now, *querida mía*,' she heard Eduardo say gently.

'Thank you,' Serena said, her voice thready. 'I feel better already, and I'm sure I shall be able to get up in a few minutes.'

His hand pressed gently on her upper chest again, the warmth of his fingers replacing the coolness of the damp cloth. She kept her eyes still firmly closed as if to ward off the swaying motion of everything in the cabin.

'No. Just stay where you are a while, until this weather eases. It's no disgrace, and the longer you lie flat, the sooner you will return to normal. If it does not get better soon, some dry toast will help. I will arrange it.'

She had the oddest feeling that he could arrange anything. He'd probably arranged this bad weather simply to show her how clever he was at dealing with the effects of *mal de mer* ... She opened her eyes slowly, knowing she must be slightly light-headed to think such foolish things.

He was looking down at her, and with a swift return of self-respect she knew she must look a sight. Her hair had come unpinned in the ravages of the gale on deck before they had hastily resorted to the passenger lounge, and she hadn't had time to re-pin it. Her dress was all awry and he still sat on the edge of her bunk with his hand on her chest. She was suddenly struck by the impropriety of the situation, in the small, intimate confines of the ship's cabin, and she felt the heat in every part of her body.

As if Eduardo realised it too, she saw a small smile play about his arrogant mouth, and he stood up, his arms folded. His physical presence seemed to fill the tiny cabin, and she could not be unaware of his powerful personality.

'I think I had better leave you to recover in solitude, or I may forget that I am a gentleman,' he remarked.

'And a cousin,' she murmured in some confusion.

He laughed out loud now. As if it was an impulse impossible to resist, he leaned down to kiss her on the mouth. His breath was warm, and the tang of the sea was on his lips.

'And a cousin,' he said. 'Though I confess that it is not the way I am beginning to think of you, *querida*. Try to rest now, and I will call in on you later.'

He was gone from the cabin in an instant, and Serena lay flat and immobile as she was instructed. Involuntarily, she touched her lips, tracing the area he had kissed. Her fingers went lower, over the soft swell of her breasts where his hand had quelled the urgent retching, and there was a growing heat in her that had little to do with the seasickness or any other kind of sickness. It was a feeling she had never known before, primitive and intense, yet she felt no surprise at recognising it instinctively.

'I mustn't love him,' she whispered to herself. 'I don't want to love him. We can have no possible future together. The *familia* would see to that, and I won't let myself be hurt by rejection as my mother and father were hurt.'

It was a vow she fully intended to keep. She hardly noticed that she thought of the new family in Spanish terms, or that even in attempting to deny the inevitable she was giving herself choices.

'Cadiz has a long tradition of being an essential sea port,' Eduardo informed her, as they neared the end of the voyage. 'It has the usual bustle and atmosphere of sea-faring business about it, some honest and hard-working, some nefarious, and is a place to avoid where possible.'

Since Serena had little idea of the atmosphere of sea-faring business, she could only murmur acquiescence to his words. Wherever he took her, she was totally dependent on him now. The nearer they got to the Spanish coast, the more she realised it.

After the one dreadful spell of bad weather, the voyage had taken them smoothly southwards through the long stretch of water along the Portuguese coast until they rounded the Straits of Gibraltar, and now there was a hot, dry air that even the sea breezes couldn't disperse.

'Is the Casa de Montalban near to Cadiz?' she asked as they leaned on the ship's rail, watching the land come ever nearer as the vessel prepared to dock.

'I'm afraid not. We still have some hours' journeying to do, but we will travel as comfortably as possible. Since my return date was not pre-arranged, it was not possible to arrange for my own transportation to meet us, but I will hire the best carriage available to take us there.'

Again, Serena noticed the slightly stilted manner, as if Eduardo García too was aware of her great under-taking, and the uncertainty of her reception at the Casa de Montalban. She was becoming more nervous with every mile they travelled, and the unfamiliar heat was already drying her throat and making her palms damp and clammy. Though she freely admitted that nerves alone could do that!

'It's strange to think that England will be experiencing its usual unpredictable summer,' she said suddenly, 'while here in Spain I suppose there will be guaranteed good weather.'

Eduardo laughed. 'You English! Always you talk about the weather! When conversation flags, or you are nervous, the weather is always the safest topic, no?'

She knew her face must have coloured at this unworthy perception of her compatriots.

'What's so bad about that?' she defended them all. 'In a climate such as ours, the weather makes an interesting piece of chit-chat.'

She stopped at once. *Chit-chat* sounded so trivial and artificial, and Eduardo was still smiling in that infuriatingly condescending way.

'I think you answer your own question, *querida*,' he said drily. 'But we too have climatic changes. Since it is of such interest to you, then you should know that of course we need the rain to grow the vines and swell the grapes, and the sun to ripen them in time for the harvest. There have been times when torrential rains have flattened the crops and it has been a disaster for many *viñas*. Then, too, we are subject to the occasional sirocco—a hot, dry wind from the Sahara in north Africa, which can make life a little uncomfortable for a time.'

Serena had the fearful feeling that he was speaking very much in understatements, and muttered as much. He spoke more reassuringly at once.

'We are fortunate in that our land is widely scattered, and we have crops growing in many areas, so that when one is experiencing bad weather, hopefully the other is not and the harvest can be saved. It has been a successful method for generations.'

There was no denying the pride in his voice whenever he spoke of the Montalban heritage, to which he obviously closely allied himself. Serena sensed that whatever this family did, it would be successful. She thought at once of her own father... The proud Montalbans might think him a failure in their eyes, with his obsessive desire to paint, and his refusal to go into the *corrida*, but in Eduardo's own words Ramón de Montalban had been an artist of some note. And he had found true love, which to Serena was the most desirable and fulfilling state of all.

CHAPTER FIVE

THE overland journey was even more uncomfortable than the sea voyage. Serena wondered if her bones would ever knit together again, since it felt as though every one were broken in several places before the driver finally halted the plodding horses. By then, they had travelled well inland from the coast and the air had got progressively hotter, with an oppressive heat that threatened to curl and shrivel a delicate English skin.

Hazy, bare-sided mountains circled the rugged plains through which they travelled, and eventually they climbed through the foothills and the well-used mountain passes, to a more fertile area within their brooding shelter. And all the while the sun beat fiercely overhead, unlike any sunlight Serena had experienced before; bright, white and relentless.

The heat was making her light-headed, and the fact that Serena's own skin was not quite as delicate as most travelling English ladies was about the only thing that prevented her demanding to be taken straight back to the ship at once, announcing that this whole hideous journey was a terrible mistake. Her aunts would have found it simply appalling, she thought grimly, and wondered just how her own mother had managed to survive it.

She saw how parched and dry the earth was hereabouts, and how the slightest breeze swirled it about, so that it tickled the throat and made even breathing difficult. Compared with England's beautiful green and pleasant countryside, this was harsh and brown, and what foliage there was seemed to range from darkly green to almost black. Stunted trees with twisted barks looked dead or dying, except for their green-grey leaves that crackled in the smallest breath of air, and what appeared to be small dark fruits hanging from the branches.

'What are they?' she asked Eduardo, trying to moisten her lips with a tongue that felt swollen and dry. 'If they're fruits, they look hard and inedible.'

'Those are olives,' Eduardo informed her. 'They're quite edible when fully ripe, but their main purpose is to produce the oil with which much of our cooking is done.'

She was quite sure she wasn't going to like Spanish food. She had already made up her mind about that. But she knew better than to tell Eduardo so, or she suspected she'd be getting a lecture on the benefits of Spanish cuisine over her native English.

She leaned back against the hard wooden back of the carriage, which seemed to have few comforts in it, and closed her eyes. The great excitement she knew she should be feeling was dwindling rapidly with the exhausting journey, and she just prayed that they would reach journey's end quickly and unscathed.

All the colourful tales Eduardo had told her about gypsies dancing and singing beneath the stars to the accompaniment of guitars seemed less entrancing than threatening now. Her imagination leaped and soared. At every turn in the tracks she expected gypsies to leap out at her like vagabonds of the road, demanding money and jewels, of which she had precious little. She willed herself miles away from this alien land, wishing she'd had the courage to stay in London, and not allow her curiosity about the Spanish house in the painting to get the better of her.

'Open your eyes, Serena,' she heard Eduardo say quietly, and at the same moment she realised that the motion of the carriage had stopped.

As she automatically obeyed his instruction, she thought she must still be dreaming. She had been thinking of the house in the painting that had dominated her imagination for so long, the strong brush strokes lovingly executed by a man with a raw and passionate talent. And there in front of her, as real as if she had stepped right through the canvas and conjured up the life-size reality of the painting, was the Casa de Montalban.

For a few seconds she couldn't speak. She was caught up in the most extraordinary emotions. The feeling of coming home was only one of them. There was joy and exhilaration, pain and poignancy, and a sense of knowing and belonging in this place. The feelings were so powerful that they completely took away her voice, and she could only look and absorb and feel.

'Welcome home, Serena de Montalban,' Eduardo said in that same quiet voice that was more intensely charged than if he'd shouted the words from mountain-top to mountain-top.

Suddenly she wanted to break the spell, because if she didn't she had the strangest feeling that this place would absorb her too. And she wasn't ready for it yet...

'Is this the way you always greet your visitors? I admit it's a dazzling panorama, and it made me feel quite odd for a moment, as if I'd awakened from a dream especially to see the house.'

'Isn't that what you've been waiting for all your life? To awaken from a dream to discover your destiny?'

He motioned to the driver to move on towards the house, still some distance away in a wide valley.

Serena gave a small shiver at his words, despite the heat that was making her clothes stick to her in a very uncomfortable and unladylike manner.

'I hope I've got my feet more firmly on the ground than that,' she said in annoyance, because it was all too much like the way she *had* been feeling.

'That's the English in you talking again,' Eduardo said drily. 'Just for once, why won't you admit to your Spanish blood, Serena, and how you really feel?'

'You can hardly expect me to be over-effusive, when I didn't even know I had any Spanish blood until recently,' she said with a burst of anger.

Somehow she felt better at keeping this friction between them alive, especially right now, when she felt more like weeping. Ramón de Montalban was more real to her at that moment than he had ever been in her life before, and her regret that she had never known him was overwhelming.

'And why do you always deprecate the English so?' she went on. 'I didn't notice you despising them so openly when you paid court so gushingly to Lady Darbyshire!'

She bit her lip hard, furious that she had sounded critical and more than a little jealous, because he would surely seize on the fact.

'I assure you I never gush,' Eduardo said in an amused, tolerant voice, in much the same way he might speak to a petulant child. 'Nor do I deprecate the English. We all have our faults and differences, but I admire many of them tremendously. Your Queen and Albert, for instance——'

'*Albert?*' she said witheringly. 'Surely you're aware that Prince Albert is a German?'

'And do you think less of him for that?'

'Of course not. I think he's done a marvellous thing in staging the Exhibition, and it's obvious that the Queen and his family adore him—and so does half the female population of London!'

She caught his look and saw the smile softening the angular features. 'What have I said that's so amusing now?' she asked in exasperation.

'You've just admitted that people of different races can have a perfectly harmonious marriage——'

'I already know that. My parents married for love, didn't they? Nobody here is going to dispute that, I hope.'

The last few minutes had diverted her thoughts away from the fact that they were quickly approaching the imposing white façade of the Casa de Montalban now, and that the moment of coming face to face with Doña Adriana was imminent. Now, her own words had reminded her, and in an instant the nerves were back, the fervent wishing that this day were over... She felt Eduardo's hand clasp her own, and accepted fleetingly that there had been many times like this when his touch had reassured her.

'And you, too, will marry for love, *querida*. I am no gypsy, but if my Romany friends were here they would assure you of it too. It's written in your eyes for all to see. No one but a man who loves you will be able to conquer that spirit of yours—and that's because of the true Spanish in you.'

She hardly thought it something that applied only to Spaniards, but she declined to comment and become involved in another conversation that was too personal. Nor was she sure that she cared to be analysed so scrupulously. She agreed with Aunt Dorcas's old maxim that a lady should always keep her thoughts private, to preserve that little air of mystery about herself... and that was definitely the *English* in her coming out...

The carriage had stopped right outside the front door of the house now. To English eyes, everything about the place was excessive, yet without being really ostentatious, Serena thought in some awe. The great wooden door itself was of double width, studded and ornate, and as they arrived it opened at once, as if someone had been watching and waiting all this time. Several young men who were clearly servants ran to the carriage and began hauling down the baggage at once, while Eduardo spoke to them rapidly in his own language. He paid off the carriage driver, obviously to a degree that had the man thanking him profusely, and then he turned to Serena and helped her down.

Her feet were unsteady, and she felt as if she had been on the move for a very long time, as indeed she had. She felt in grave danger of swooning right away, and a fine start that would be. But she had to physically clamp her teeth together to stop them from chattering.

'Don't be afraid,' Eduardo said. 'Doña Adriana wishes to know you, and she is not the ogre you fear.'

'Am I so transparent?' Serena asked in a husky voice.

'Only to me. Outwardly, you look a perfectly poised young lady, but I think I know you now.'

She looked at him. And just how well do I know you, Eduardo García? She wrenched her gaze away as their glances locked, knowing that her heart always beat too fast when he studied her in that unblinking way, as if he could see inside her soul.

'Come. We will go inside the house. It will be cooler there, and it would not be the happiest way of arriving if you were to faint on the doorstep.'

He echoed her own thoughts in a light manner that was probably meant to dispel her anxieties, and only made the unreal sensations more evident. The whole world seemed to be swimming in front of her eyes, and she had to concentrate hard to stop herself falling in a heap at his feet. The ignominy of such a happening helped to steady her a little.

Inside the house it was just as he had said, blissfully cool and quite dark. Despite the whiteness of the walls in the spacious hall, with its wrought-iron candle-holders and floral display holders, and the elaborately tiled floor, the shaded windows compared with the glare of sunlight outside made it a little hard for her eyes to get accustomed to the interior for a few moments.

One of the young boys had appeared from nowhere, and spoke rapidly to Eduardo. She heard the name Doña Adriana, and Eduardo turned to Serena at once.

'Your grandmother is resting, as is her habit during the afternoon. You will find that most of our country-men take a *siesta* during the hottest part of the day. This does not mean that we are lazier than our English cousins, merely that we begin work again when the sun has lost some of its heat. It conserves energy.'

'It sounds a very sensible arrangement,' Serena mur-mured. So the moment of meeting Doña Adriana was not here after all, and she wasn't at all sure that she cared for this *siesta*, when it put off the evil moment . . . It was silly to think of it in those terms, but she couldn't think of it in any other way, and she just wanted to get the meeting over and done with.

'You'll be disappointed,' Eduardo went on, misinter-preting her expression for once. 'But it will give you time to get accustomed to your surroundings and change your clothes. I'm sure you would be glad of a rest yourself. Carlos will send a girl with some food and drink to your room, and I will return in an hour or so to present you to Doña Adriana.'

She looked at him dumbly. With every word he spoke, she felt as if he were throwing her to the lion's den—or to the poor wretched bulls whose own destiny was assured when they entered the ring.

'Where will you be? You're not going to leave me, are you?' she exclaimed in a rush. He gave a small smile.

'Your dependence on me is touching, Serena, but I wish to see my father, to catch up on events while I have been away and to give him news of the Exhibition. You forget that my reasons for being in London were twofold.'

Yes, she had forgotten. Just as she had never thought to ask if he would always be here in the Casa, or elsewhere... She had foolishly allowed herself to be swept along in a way most unlike her normal controlled self. But ever since meeting this man, nothing about her demeanour had seemed normal...

'Don't look so alarmed. You will merely remain in your room until you are sent for, and that won't be until my father and myself are here, and other members of the *familia* too. We all share the same heritage, Serena.'

He only made it worse. His father, and other members of the Montalban clan... She had always regretted not being part of a large family, but, now that she was about to be thrown in the midst of this one, she'd much rather be at home with Cookie, listening to her irascible tongue-wagging.

'Do you and your father live in the house?' she asked awkwardly, because it seemed she should have ascertained all this before.

'We have our own quarters here.' He nodded. 'And you have already seen the size of the place. It's far too large for one elderly lady, and besides, it's not our way. Doña Adriana likes her close ones around her, and we like to be here.'

And to take a share in the family fortunes, perhaps . . .
Serena couldn't stop the cynical little thought flitting
through her mind. Who was going to inherit the
Montalban fortunes? she wondered. Mr Price had told
her that she was the direct heir, and so had Eduardo,
but it was something she simply couldn't take in. It was
too impossible to believe, and she had effectively blocked
the idea from her mind. But if not her, then she began
to wonder for the first time just who was next in line.

Carlos appeared to speak no English, but he showed her
to a large bedroom that was as cool as every other part
of the house. There was a small room adjoining it that
had a bathtub and everything a young lady could need
for her toilet. The arrival of the carriage had clearly been
observed, for there were already pails of steaming hot
water awaiting her use.

Serena was pleasantly surprised. After all the talk of
gypsies and the wild bohemian life, she had been half
afraid that the Montalban house might be less than civilised. But she had needed no such fears. Before Carlos
left the room, a young Spanish girl appeared carrying
food on a tray, covered by a lace cloth, which she set
down on a side-table near the window.

'For the *señorita*,' the girl said haltingly, and Serena
felt enormous relief.

'You speak English?' she asked at once.

The girl shook her head. 'Only a little, but I learn.
My name is María. It is my pleasure to serve you.'

She was about Serena's own age, her hair black as jet
and swathed on top of her head. She was obviously eager
to please and proud of her limited English vocabulary.

'Will you teach me a few Spanish words while I'm
here, María?' she said impulsively.

'Of course.' The girl looked at Serena in surprise. 'But you have plenty time to learn. All your years now.'

Her vocabulary fizzled out, but not before Serena felt a great suspicion.

'All my years?' she echoed. 'I'm afraid you're very much mistaken if that's what you believe. I'm only here on a visit.'

And if there was too much discomfort, she would soon reverse the decision she had taken to remain here until October, she thought fleetingly. She wasn't obliged to stay in Spain any longer than she chose to, and no one could force her into it.

'What made you think I was staying all my years?' She repeated the girl's quaint phrase as María said nothing.

'I no understand,' the girl said, edging towards the door, and something in her manner made Serena quite sure that she understood very well indeed.

'Oh, well, it doesn't matter,' she said casually. She guessed intuitively that if she ever wanted to get anything out of this girl, it was best not to alarm her, or she would simply resort to not understanding...

'Thank you for the food, María,' she said instead. 'I'm very hungry.'

The girl brightened at once. 'If you want more, ring bell and I come.'

'All right. Tell me, what time does the *siesta* end? When will Doña Adriana be rested?'

'Doña Adriana takes tea at four o'clock,' María repeated parrot-fashion.

It wasn't so different from an English house after all, Serena thought. Tea at four o'clock sounded extremely civilised, and her grandmother evidently stuck to the same little rituals as her aunts had done. In their later years, they too had had an afternoon nap, though it had never had so grand a name as a *siesta*!

Serena liked the sound of it. She rolled it around her tongue, and realised she was finding the Spanish words easier to say than she would have imagined. There was an elegance about them that went with this house and almost certainly its inmates, if all that Eduardo had told her about Doña Adriana was correct. Eduardo too...there was definitely an elegance about him...

She realised that María was still hovering by the door until Serena dismissed her formally. Serena was reluctant to let her go for the moment. There was nothing complicated about the young girl, and, as long as she didn't make her wary, Serena could probably find out anything she wanted to know about this household.

'How many people live in this house, María?' she asked, without seeming to be unduly interested.

The girl shrugged. 'Many,' she said, with an expressive spread of her hands.

'But who are they? I know there's Doña Adriana, of course, and Don Eduardo and his father...' She stopped encouragingly.

'The two sisters of Don Eduardo, and his brother, and Doña Adriana's brother——'

'Doña Adriana has a brother?' Serena said in surprise, though, knowing little about the family, she didn't know why it should surprise her so much. She thought rapidly. Shouldn't this brother be the heir to the Montalban lands, or Don Eduardo's father, or Eduardo himself? She found the family network confusing, and wished she hadn't bothered to ask.

'He is old and *enfermo*——'

'You mean he's ill—an invalid, perhaps?' Serena guessed, and the girl nodded, only half understanding.

'He will die soon. *El médico* assures us of it.'

Serena stared at her. It was said without any feeling in the voice, merely stating a fact of nature. People were born, they lived and died. The entire spectrum seemed to be written in that girl's face for a second, but Serena didn't want to hear any morbid tales right now. She dismissed the girl quickly, and she could see that María escaped just as gladly.

It was probably an effort for her to speak and think in English, but it was still a relief to Serena to hear the halting words. She had never given a thought as to how many of the inmates of the Casa de Montalban would be able to converse with her. She wondered now if Doña Adriana would be able to do so, or if her antipathy towards her son's wife had killed any inclination towards it. If so, they were in for a silent time of it, Serena thought cynically.

She lifted the cover from the food, wondering what she would see. But there was only an innocuous cold platter of meats and cheese and a flat bread roll to accompany it. There was also a very welcome pitcher of a fruit drink which she poured into a glass and drank thirstily.

Once replete, she set about exploring her surroundings, and especially the bathroom, filling the bathtub from the pails of hot water standing ready for her. Finally, she slid into the bathtub with a sigh of pleasure.

Half an hour later, she was dressed and alert, her aching limbs miraculously restored to suppleness again. She looked at the ornate little clock on her dressing-table. It was not quite half-past three, but she was impatient now to see the inside of this house that had been part of her dreams for so long. Surely no one would object to her wandering about by herself. She always believed that people could drink in the atmosphere of a place far better on their own anyway. Without another thought she slipped out of the bedroom and closed the door quietly behind her.

She realised that many of the window-shades had been raised now, as the sun sank lower in the sky. On her arrival, the long open flight of stairs had seemed dark and gloomy, but now she saw that it was framed by a gloriously curving sweep of wrought-ironwork banister leading down to the lower floor of the house. And on the wall ... Serena caught her breath.

Most aristocratic English houses had portraits of their ancestors on the walls of the staircases. On this wall were portraits of a different kind. All those depicted in vibrant oils were men, dressed in the strangest garb Serena had ever seen. The colours were garish, the trousers tight and figure-hugging, the waistcoats short and encrusted with glittering jewels. The hats were strange, black and flat, and in most cases the hands held a swirling red cape on the ground.

Even if she didn't guess from past experience that these could only be past members of the house, there was something in all of them that said the men were unmistakably Montalbans, proud and unyielding. And Serena knew in an instant that these were the faces of men who had faced *el toro* in the *corrida* ... She was beginning to think in Spanish terms, she thought in some alarm, just as though it lessened the impact of knowing that a bullfighter fought a bull to the death, and there was only one victor...

'Do you recognise your ancestors, Serena?' Don Eduardo's voice floated up the stairs to where she stood motionless for a moment. She gave a start and looked down at him, surely as fearless as any of these, and yet unwilling to prove himself for the sake of family tradition.

These Montalbans might despise him for that, but Serena could only approve. Besides, in refusing to do battle with the bull, Eduardo followed the new tradition her own father had set. She was already suspecting that it was as brave to face these arrogant ancestors and defy them as to face any bull...

She spoke to him with slightly more warmth than usual as she went down the stairs to join him.

'I recognise the trappings of the so-called sport that fills me with horror,' she said, careful not to speak too loudly and offend anyone who might be listening. She was still a visitor, after all, and bullfighting was Spain's national sport...

'You do well not to raise your voice,' he said warningly. 'In fact, I suggest that it's a subject it would be wiser to ignore as far as possible, unless Doña Adriana herself brings it up. Have you been shown the rest of the house yet?'

'I was about to look for myself—or is that not allowed?' she asked, expecting a sort of flippant reply that, since this was her destiny, she could go where she wished.

'It is not usual,' he said gravely, 'and I do not think Doña Adriana would approve. I will show you around the grounds instead, since there is still some time before she comes downstairs for afternoon tea.'

He pointed towards long windows that opened out on to a wide patio, and Serena realised she had evidently made a small mistake. Young English women were evidently not supposed to wander freely about a Spanish home, even when they were presumably part of the *familia*.

'I keep having to pinch myself to remember that my father lived here,' she said suddenly, reminding him that she had every right to be here. And besides, if it hadn't been for Eduardo García's persuasiveness, she would probably still be in London. She hadn't really wanted to come, and he owed her something.

What would she be doing at home now, she wondered, on a lovely summer evening? Walking in the park, perhaps, or sitting in her favourite window-seat, reading to her aunts... She bit her lip, sad for times that could never come again, and with the sudden lost feeling that she belonged nowhere. London would never be the same again, and as yet she certainly didn't fit in here.

Seeing her wan face, Eduardo squeezed her hand. 'Cheer up,' he said. 'Nobody's going to eat you.'

'So you've said before, but it still feels like it to me! I feel as if I'm about to be inspected and picked over like tomorrow's breakfast.'

He laughed, and the sound reverberated around the white walls and uncarpeted floors. He threw open the long windows and they stepped outside on to the patio. The heat immediately assaulted her, almost taking her breath away.

'What an inelegant phrase, my sweet Serena. Nobody wants to harm you, I promise you that. I would introduce you to the rest of the *familia*, except that politeness demands that you meet Doña Adriana first. But they will all be here for dinner this evening.'

'You make it all sound as important as meeting royalty,' she said nervously. 'You're not going to tell me you have royal blood flowing through your veins, are you?'

'I'm afraid not——'

'Please don't apologise! I'm relieved. I've had enough shocks since meeting you. But I'm told you have sisters and a brother. How old are they all? Younger or older than yourself?'

'Elena's only fifteen years old, and Juana's twenty. You would have plenty to talk about, but I'm afraid their English is not so good. I am sure they will try to converse with you though.'

There was something in his voice that told her it was most unlikely. Something that told her these young Spanish girls didn't want her here at all, and if they did converse with her it would only be because they had been instructed to do so.

'And your brother?'

She heard him give an imperceptible sigh.

'Ricardo is twenty-four, and in a few weeks' time you will be able to see him perform in the *corrida*, if you have the stomach for it. Naturally Doña Adriana will expect you to attend. It is always one of the highlights of a visit to the Casa de Montalban, especially if Ricardo is taking part, but since you have English blood in you it will be no disgrace if you refuse.'

His tone told her now that it was to be fully expected that the English were made of lesser stuff than himself. Despite her own feelings on the matter, she tilted her chin at once.

'If Doña Adriana wishes it, then of course I must attend,' she flashed at him. 'And presumably Ricardo does not have your sensitivity when it comes to facing *el toro*.'

'Nor your father's,' he retorted, and she was immediately shame-faced for her snide little remark.

But the pattern of family life here was becoming clearer to her now. She assumed that, apart from her own father, Eduardo's father was the only one who had produced any children. Serena de Montalban was the direct descendant of this matriarchal Doña Adriana she had yet to meet, and after herself...

'Tell me something, Eduardo,' she said, as they wandered out beyond the tiled patio to an avenue of shady trees, where the air was heavy with the fragrant scent of flowers more brilliantly hued than Serena had seen before.

'What is it?' He took her arm and pointed out a little running stream, and he didn't relinquish his hold when they had passed it.

'Did you mean what you said, about my being the heir to all of this?'

'But of course. Why should you doubt it? You are not stupid. You understand the meaning of inheritance.' He spoke with frank surprise in his voice that she could ask such a thing, and she felt her face go even hotter because of what she was about to ask now.

'And after myself—who would inherit it all?'

His eyes grew narrow as she turned her unblinking blue gaze on him. She could feel the tension in his arm as he pressed her own close to his side.

'Ah, I see how your thoughts go far ahead, *querida*. And yes, you are perfectly right. It would be my father— who is growing old—and then myself. But you need have no fears. My family has always been content to take charge of the *viñas*. It has always been enough.'

'And will it always be enough? Even when a woman holds the purse-strings of the Casa de Montalban?'

'A woman holds them now,' he said shortly.

They had stopped walking, and somehow Serena had shaken her arm free of his, and they stood facing one another. The shadow of a tall tree placed them in a welcome patch of shade, and she no longer had to squint against the sunlight to look up at him.

'But not an Englishwoman who will probably marry one of her own kind and bring a new English family into the Casa de Montalban,' she said with slow deliberation. 'What then, Eduardo? How would my ancestors react to it all, do you suppose? And how will you?'

For an instant he didn't speak, and then he gave his smothered oath again and pulled her roughly into his arms. It happened so quickly she had no time to react, other than to gasp and become aware that she was being held so tightly in his arms that she could feel his heart-beats mingling with her own. They beat with a wild, fast rhythm as if they did some crazy dance. For a second she was reminded of the gypsies and the wild exhil-aration he had promised her when she first saw the flamenco beneath the stars. Something of the same was running through her veins now, just when she had least expected it.

They were in the seclusion of the twisting paths and quite hidden from the house, and it was suddenly as in-timate as if they shared a lovers' tête-à-tête.

'I would react the way of any man who has marked out a woman for his own,' he said roughly. 'The feeling has nothing to do with wealth or position, but, since I can already see the glint of possession in your eyes, *querida mía*, I hardly expect you to believe it. All the same, I will take this here and now, and to the devil with the future.'

Before she could protest, his head blotted out the day-light and his mouth was on hers in a kiss unlike any she had ever known. She had known only a few, and those had been mostly chaste...but this was a kiss of pos-session of a very different kind from the material pos-session of which he spoke.

This was passion, hard and blatant and demanding, and despite all her carefully nurtured upbringing Serena felt her spirit soar to meet him, and she was kissing him back with all the fervour of a wanton.

CHAPTER SIX

'DOÑA ADRIANA, may I present to you Señorita Serena de Montalban? Serena, this lady is Doña Adriana, your grandmother.'

It was all terribly formal, especially after the moments in the garden when he had all but swept her off her feet. Serena wondered if it had really happened, or if she had dreamed it all... Certainly, glancing now at Eduardo García's handsome face, he was the complete aristocrat, cordially introducing two members of a family to one another for the first time.

And Doña Adriana herself... All this time, since Serena had first learned of the woman's existence, she had resisted forming any preconceived idea of her appearance. And now that she saw her, she was shocked by how tiny she was, how frail, and how... how inexorably *Spanish*...

Doña Adriana wore a black water-silk gown buttoned high in the throat and fastened tight into the wrists. The skirt swept the floor with a rustling sound every time she moved, and she wore jet mourning beads around her neck. The severely piled up hair was iron-grey, neatly caught by an elaborate comb at the back of her head, and draped around her shoulders was a fringed shawl in grey and black. She presented a small, austere and lonely figure, and her bright eyes assessed Serena for a long moment before she gave a small, unsmiling nod and held out both hands in welcome.

'Yes. You are Ramón's child,' she said, and Serena was momentarily relieved that she spoke English well enough to be easily understood.

'How do you do?' she answered a little helplessly, hardly knowing how to behave in this presence. Doña Adriana might be small in stature, but the forceful personality was undeniable. Serena wondered anew how her father had ever dared to defy her, and guessed that few people did so.

'Are you going to kiss me, child?' Doña Adriana said, and Serena leaned forward quickly to kiss each wizened cheek that was offered in turn. Her thoughts turned immediately to that other kiss, the one she had run away from in something of a fright, until Eduardo had caught up with her halfway through a small copse of trees and demanded to know where she thought she was going and what was wrong with her...

What would he say if he knew her world had turned upside-down because of the surge of her feelings for him at that moment? Feelings she didn't dare let him know existed, not yet, not until she knew for sure if he wanted her for herself, or for her inheritance...

'I think we had all better sit down, Serena. You look as if the long journey has been too much for you, or do you find the heat troublesome?' Doña Adriana said keenly.

'Both, I'm afraid,' Serena said, glad to grasp at the excuses given to her for her brilliant face.

She averted her eyes from the older woman. 'Please forgive me, but I'm not sure what I should call you...' she finished in embarrassment, wondering how she was ever going to be on familiar terms with this stranger who had turned her father out of his own home.

'I'm your grandmother, my dear,' Doña Adriana said without any apparent emotion. 'What else would you

call me but Grandmother? Unless it offends you, of
course. Do you have another grandmother in England?'

'No. I have no one at all.' Why did she think Doña
Adriana had dragged the words out of her, and knew
very well that there was no maternal grandmother in
England! As if she wanted to make Serena appreciate
this new family, and fully intended her to stay forever...

She went on in a strong, defiant voice, 'I'm very happy
to be here and to get to know you. I'm not sure how
long my visit will be, but I'm sure Eduardo must have
told you that I have a home in England——'

'I know of your aunts' deaths, Serena, and all about
your little house. Naturally, Eduardo and the London
lawyers have informed me of all I needed to know.'

Serena looked at her dumbly. Of course she would
know that there was only Cook and herself in the London
mews house now. Of course she would know that Serena
had no other living relative in the world except those
who lived in this house—the house in her father's
painting. She simply didn't know what else to say to this
cold little woman, who was seemingly struggling to make
conversation as much as Serena was, and so she blun-
dered on.

'There was a painting of this house for as long as I
can remember in my aunts' home in London, but I never
knew it was a real house until I met Eduardo and he
told me it was this one. My aunts never told me anything
about it, you see, but I was always fascinated by the
painting——'

She stopped again in some horror at the way she was
rambling. It was her *father's* painting, the outcast
member of this family, and it was very unlikely that Doña
Adriana would want to be reminded of him at every turn.
But with a stab of anger, Serena told herself that she
was Ramón's daughter, and she had no intention of pre-

tending he had never existed. Besides, it had been this old woman's wish that she came to Spain...

She saw Eduardo glance at her fingers, drumming in some agitation on the side of her chair, and she stilled them at once.

'My father was a wonderful artist,' she heard herself say evenly, and to her astonishment Doña Adriana inclined her head.

'So I am led to believe. But it was not to discuss your father that I invited you here. We will have tea and then we will talk.'

The ritual was to be religiously followed, and Doña Adriana would say nothing more until it had been served and taken away. Tea-drinking was obviously a serious business at four o'clock in the afternoon. The tension began to unnerve Serena, and she wondered if Doña Adriana was doing this deliberately. If she had expected to be welcomed with open arms as a pseudo-prodigal child of the Montalbans, it was certainly not the case.

'Just why did you invite me here?' Serena finally burst out. 'It wasn't necessary. I had known nothing about you all these years, and surely you never needed to meet me at all.'

For the first time the old woman's eyes flashed, and her nostrils pinched together as firmly as her mouth. The yellow cheekbones were high and proud and seemed even more exaggerated as Doña Adriana registered the strongest disapproval without ever saying a word. And Serena knew at once just how her father and all the strong Montalban men must have quailed before such a look.

'You think I did not need to meet the person who would inherit the Montalban lands? Would you not say it was important to know that the ghosts of past generations were to be left in safe hands? If your people in

England think so little of heritage, then they would do well to learn from other races——'

Serena sprang to her feet, her eyes blazing. She didn't care who this woman was, nor that she was a guest in this house. She had no intention of being belittled when it was obvious she was only here under sufferance.

'Why do you despise us so? I'm sick of hearing what lesser mortals we English are! We're as proud a race as your own, madam, and I did not ask to come. It was you who wanted to see me! I care nothing for any inheritance, and I did not travel to Spain on account of it! I was perfectly happy in my own home, and obviously the sooner I go back there, the better.'

'Serena, please watch your tongue. I told you earlier that Doña Adriana is unwell.'

Eduardo spoke angrily at her outburst. He moved towards the old woman and spoke to her in rapid Spanish, to which Doña Adriana responded just as quickly, brushing his solicitous hands aside.

'Eduardo is concerned for me,' her grandmother told Serena. 'But I am made of sterner stuff than I look, and I am well able to deal with an ill-mannered visitor.'

Without even trying, she put Serena firmly in her place. 'I'm sorry,' she muttered after a small silence.

'So now we begin again,' Doña Adriana said quite briskly. 'You wish to know why I wanted to see you, and naturally I needed to know if you are a fit person to be my successor. Now that I have seen you—and heard you...'

Suddenly the old eyes were twinkling, and the expression on the face changed completely. It was actually softening towards Serena, and she felt a little shock at feeling the sudden lump in her throat. She didn't even know this woman...and yet she was aware of a flicker

of pleasure because Doña Adriana hadn't sent her
packing because of her rudeness.

'Thank you,' Serena murmured. 'But I assure you that
if—when—the time comes...' She was floundering again,
realising that what they were actually discussing was this
woman's death, and Doña Adriana was taking it all far
more calmly than Serena.

As if the woman knew exactly how she was feeling,
she leaned across and patted Serena's hand.

'Don't concern yourself, *Nieta*. I have lived my span
and am quite ready for the next great adventure, although I hope it won't be for some while yet. I want to
know you better first.'

'I want to know you too,' Serena said, to her own
surprise. 'And please, what was it you called me?'

'*Nieta*—it means granddaughter.'

'Oh!'

Serena was tongue-tied. All her life she had never felt
she had anyone of her own who really cared. The aunts
had done their duty and she had loved them, but they
hadn't found it easy to show affection. And here was
this tiny woman to whom she had closer ties than with
anyone else on earth, and she wasn't sure yet whether
affection would or could grow between them. But in a
sudden burst of awareness she knew how much she
wanted it to. She wanted it very badly.

'Perhaps you'd like to know the Spanish word for
grandmother,' Eduardo said, seeing her discomfiture. 'I
know how you English have a strange way of avoiding
personal relationships, and you may find it easier to
address Doña Adriana as *Abuela*, as the rest of us do.'

'Would that be all right?' She looked directly at Doña
Adriana, ignoring Eduardo's pointed remark about the
English, and putting it down to masculine anger because
she had run away from him in the garden.

'I think it would be very agreeable,' Doña Adriana said, as solemnly as any titled lady presiding over an afternoon tea-party in an English summer.

If the meeting with her grandmother was one hurdle she had overcome, dinner that evening presented Serena with several more. The introductions were less formal, the reactions more predictable, especially since she had been forewarned by Eduardo's guarded descriptions of his family.

The elderly brother of Doña Adriana never left his room, and so she was spared another ordeal by someone who would presumably despise her parents the way the older members of the Montalbans did.

'My great-uncle is very old,' Eduardo told her briefly. 'Since in Spain dinner is a social occasion—a real chance for the family to spend an evening together, and to do our meal justice—the effort would be too much for him.'

And again she had the feeling that his words were a criticism of everything that England stood for. She bristled inside, but stolidly refused to swallow the bait and enter into yet another defensive argument with him. She didn't deny that she enjoyed their little arguments, though, she thought in surprise. They spiced up the days, and warded off the thought of many a nervous encounter with her new family.

But here they all were now, grand and stiff in their evening attire, and the whole family clearly thought of this meal as the greatest ritual of the day. And yes, she admitted, it rivalled anything England had to offer, especially this beautiful dining-room with its costly paintings and Spanish artefacts on the white walls, and the inevitable tiled floor. Serena appreciated the cool floors now, realising that they helped to dispel some of the heat of the area.

She began to realise, too, the status of this family. It was still impossible for her to accept that she was its heir. She had never seen such richness in a house, and adding to the scene was the stunning silver table service that must be worth a fortune, and the many crystal glasses beside each place setting. They were evidently to go through quite a quantity of Montalban wines that evening, Serena thought uneasily, and hoped that it wouldn't all go to her head and make her disgrace herself on this first evening.

But even the plush setting was dimmed by the elegance of the company. Doña Adriana was content for the moment to stay in the background while Eduardo made the introductions, and Serena was obliged to rely on him to smooth the way for her. The group milled about in the ante-room beside the dining-room before dinner was announced, taking a light aperitif to whet their appetites.

'I'm so pleased to know that there are other young people in the house. It makes me feel much more at home,' she said as easily as she could to the two lovely young girls who were the García sisters.

Juana and Elena looked back at her without smiling, and she remembered that Eduardo had said they spoke little English. It seemed highly suspicious to her now, when even the maid managed tolerable sentences. They resented her, she thought instantly. They didn't want her here at all. They probably thought she would change everything once she was mistress of the Casa de Montalban...

Thoughts flitted in and out of her head like quicksilver. It was all so absurd, so ridiculous, and so very unlikely. What did she know about the running of a Spanish house and a huge estate and wine-producing empire? And why should they think she was in the least interested in learning any of it?

She turned quickly as Eduardo introduced his brother Ricardo, and Serena looked into the first pair of friendly eyes she had seen since arriving in Spain. It was as refreshing as a breath of mountain air to see black eyes smiling admiringly, and feel him raising her fingers to his lips as delicately as if she were made of porcelain.

'I am enchanted to call you *prima*, Señorita Serena,' he said in an accent that told her instantly that he too had had some education in England. She thought it odd that these people were perfectly willing to send their sons abroad to be educated, but closed ranks when it came to intermarriage with one of a different race.

And yet, hadn't Eduardo suggested that she would have many offers of marriage while she was here? She felt a sliver of anger. Evidently, the heiress to the Montalban estate was permitted to rise above the stigma of being half English...

'I'm so happy to meet you as well.' She smiled full into the charming Ricardo's face. Let Eduardo think she was enchanted with his brother too, she thought caustically. It would do his ego good to see that he wasn't the only attractive man in the world.

They were alike in features, dark-eyed, gaunt-faced with that typically hungry Spanish look, charismatic. But, in fact, she could see at once the difference between the two brothers. Ricardo was dashing and handsome, and typified the daredevil he presumably was, since he played his Montalban role in the *corrida*. But he was still a boy, eager to please, while Eduardo was a man...

'You will come to see me fight *el toro* in two weeks' time, Serena?' Ricardo said expansively now. 'You will be my honoured guest and it will be my pleasure to present the bull's ears to you.'

She recoiled in horror at the words. Out of the corner of her eye she saw his young sisters giggling together. Ricardo had spoken in English, but the girls had understood every word. She spoke quickly.

'I would prefer a different token of friendship, if you don't mind, Ricardo. I am new to your ways, and I'm afraid I would not have the stomach for accepting such a gift.' She turned swiftly to the girls and spoke directly to them. 'What about you two? Have either of you had such a favour given to you by a handsome young bullfighter?'

'Only once,' Juana said proudly. 'Elena is not yet of an age to receive such a favour.'

She stopped abruptly, seeing the look on Serena's face, and knew how she had been trapped into her reply.

'I'm so glad you understood me, Juana. I hope we will be able to have many conversations in the future. I will tell you something about England and you may tell me something about Spain.'

She made a great effort not to snap that she considered she and Juana understood one another very well, even in so short a time. The girl's eyes flashed.

'Perhaps. There is much to understand about tradition in my country,' the girl said with a small shrug.

'And much to understand about manners in mine,' Serena flashed back. She saw the girl smile faintly before she turned away to talk to her sister in their own tongue.

'They are like butterflies, *querida*,' Ricardo said lightly. 'Don't be offended. They will come to accept in time.'

Serena didn't have the opportunity to ask what he meant by that, but she hardly needed to. Resentment towards the English interloper simmered all around her, and it was not of her making. But she would much prefer to make friends with her girl cousins than to make enemies, and if it meant swallowing a little pride, then she would have to do it.

'Why did you tell me the girls' English wasn't so good? They understood me perfectly!' she hissed to Eduardo when they were momentarily alone in a corner of the ante-room.

'It was only a little game they played, *querida*. Girls in a family like ours are brought up in a cloistered atmosphere, and they're really quite shy. They prefer to assess people from a distance before being thrown into the company of strangers,' he said coolly.

Serena felt her mouth twitch. 'Shy? I think you underestimate your own family, sir. There's nothing shy about anyone in this room!'

'Why are you so angry with me?' he said suddenly. 'Does it disturb you that I find you a desirable woman?'

You disturb me, she found herself thinking. You disturb my days and my nights, and perhaps... in any other circumstances...

The arrival of the last member of the gathering prevented the need for her to try to find an answer to his uncomfortably direct question. The newcomer was tall and silver-haired and brought an air of authority with him. He was so like the younger García men that he could only be their father.

He greeted Doña Adriana first, and then walked immediately to Eduardo and Serena. His dark eyes had the same friendly smile as Ricardo's. He held out both hands to Serena and without a second thought she placed her own in his grasp.

'Welcome to the Casa de Montalban. I have heard much about you from my son, and now that I see you I know that it is all true.'

Such smooth and artless flattery was more acceptable from one of his years, and Serena gave an answering laugh.

'I begin to suspect that all Spanish gentlemen are gallant to ladies, sir. Or have I been exceptionally fortunate in meeting three so talented with words in the same family?'

'We only speak what is true for all to see,' he replied, quite unperturbed. 'Eduardo has not yet introduced us formally, but I am his father, Leandro García, and it would be my pleasure if you would address me as Uncle Leandro. That is the English term, I believe?'

'It is,' she said smilingly, 'and I shall be happy to do so. But will you also tell me the Spanish term for uncle? I am enjoying learning a few words in your language.'

'Me gusta!' he said. 'It pleases me! And the word for uncle is *tío.'*

The younger girl, Elena, drifted towards them, young and gauche, but still with that proud Spanish hauteur Serena recognised in all of them.

Leandro smiled at his daughter, and turned again to Serena, encompassing them both with his words.

'If you wish to learn more, perhaps you would care to join this young one in her lessons. She learns English from a tutor, as did Juana, and it would be a novelty for you to learn the equivalent in Spanish.'

'I would like that,' Serena said, noting the fiery colour that flooded into Elena's cheeks.

So much for the girls' pretence that they didn't understand her, she thought, but somehow it amused her more than angered her now. The girls might be jealous of her arrival, but the men in the family appeared to like her.

And Doña Adriana... She couldn't yet fathom whether she had her grandmother's approval or not. It was too soon to tell from those enigmatic eyes whether

Doña Adriana was pleased with the product of her son's marriage or not.

The rest of the evening passed off in something of a dream for Serena. The food was of the best quality, beginning with gazpacho, a cold soup she had never tasted before, but which was absolutely right in this hot climate. Then came succulent beef, whose origins she didn't want to consider, concentrating instead on the tender way it fell to pieces in her mouth. Vegetables were piled high in great serving dishes, to which she was helped silently and efficiently by a small army of servants.

Finally came the pudding—*el postre*, Uncle Leandro instructed her solemnly—a creamy concoction that seemed to melt to nothing as soon as it touched the tongue, and left behind a delicious tangy lemon taste to clean the palate.

And interspersed with every course was yet another glass of superb Montalban wine, so that Serena's head was spinning by the time they had finished. Everyone else seemed perfectly capable of handling this amount of wine, she noted, even the young Elena. It was evidently something one needed to get accustomed to from a young age.

'Are you enjoying your first Spanish meal, Serena?' she heard Eduardo say from across the vast table. He was seated opposite her, his face becoming somewhat hazy in the flickering candle-light. He looked absolutely splendid in this light, she thought haphazardly...

'It's wonderful,' she answered quickly. 'And not as— as...' She sought for the right words. She could hardly say it was not as foreign as she'd anticipated it might be!

'Not as unpalatable as you expected?' Eduardo suggested, a hint of arrogance in his eyes.

'I never even thought such a thing,' she protested. 'But you did tell me that olive oil is widely used here, and I am unused to that.'

'You will hardly notice it,' Uncle Leandro put in. 'It evaporates during the cooking and leaves only the tenderest effect on the food.'

'How knowledgeable you are about cooking,' Serena said, turning to him and away from the uncomfortably penetrating eyes of Eduardo. Leandro laughed.

'You think it unmanly to take an interest in domestic things?'

'Oh, no! Goodness me, I didn't mean to offend you——' And here she was, putting her foot in things again, she thought in agitation, but she saw that he was still smiling.

'Dear child, don't look so shaken. Men and women take equal interest in eating and drinking, so why should they not take equal interest in its preparation? I do not personally cook the food, but I like to know what's going into my stomach.'

'My cousin has an enquiring mind that continues in his children,' Doña Adriana observed from the head of the table. 'You will find that there is little he cannot tell you about the *viña*, Serena—do you know what that is?'

'Yes,' she said, with a small lifting of her head. 'Eduardo has already told me something about the wine-production, and I am eager to know more. In fact, I want to know everything!'

Doña Adriana gave a faint smile. 'To know everything is asking a great deal, *Nieta*. Even the old ones do not know everything.'

'But it will be our pleasure to be as informative as we can, Serena,' Eduardo put in quickly. 'I have already promised to show you much that is typically Spanish and especially pertinent to the Montalbans.'

Including the gypsy flamenco beneath the stars, she thought, and absorbing the wild dancing that will fill me with a passion unlike any other...

'I too,' Ricardo said eagerly. 'She will accompany you all to the *corrida* for my performance, *Abuela*, and I will give her my favour.'

'But not the bull's ears, I beg you,' Serena said involuntarily, and Ricardo laughed.

'Not the bull's ears,' he promised.

He was nice and uncomplicated, she decided. He didn't have the stature of Eduardo, nor the power to stir her heart. But as a friend she was drawn to him immediately. He was a small oasis of calm in a room filled with all kinds of emotions.

But she fancied that the two girls seemed to be gradually unbending. Neither addressed her during the meal, but several times she caught them glancing towards her uncertainly, and she thought there might be a chance of friendship between them after all. Serena certainly hoped so. She hadn't come here to make enemies.

She was discovering that the evening meal was an important occasion in the day, and one to be taken with all due ceremony. It was obviously not to be rushed, although Doña Adriana left the dining table to retire before everyone else, urging them to linger as long as they wished, and saying that she would see them all in the morning.

'The lady does not have the stamina of old,' Leandro commented to Serena. 'It is good that you come to see her before the inevitable.'

'I might have come before if I had known of her existence,' she found herself saying. 'It was something that everyone chose to keep secret from me, and it was a strange feeling to discover I was not quite alone in the world.'

Since he would obviously know all there was to know, she saw no reason to keep silent, and he nodded.

'You have a family now, Serena. You know the word in Spanish?'

'A *familia*,' she said a little diffidently, seeing the eyes of the girl cousins watching her.

Elena gave an imperceptible nod, so Serena assumed she had said the word correctly and was not about to be laughed at. She saw Eduardo glance at her approvingly, and was glad she had listened to him, making sure she put the right inflexion on the syllables of the words he had taught her. There was so much to know, so much to learn . . . and she wanted his approval.

By the end of the meal the different wines were beginning to have quite an alarming effect on Serena, and she began worrying that she might disgrace herself by tripping over the furniture if she dared to get up from her chair too quickly, or that she would simply fall headlong across the table and sleep off the rest of the evening among the costly silverware . . . The incongruity of such an event was so ghastly and suddenly so visual that it made her smother a hasty giggle.

'You find something amusing, Serena?' Eduardo asked smilingly from across the table. She looked at him, wondering if stars really were dancing in his eyes, or if the faintness she felt was real or imagined.

'I'm feeling a little warm,' she murmured evasively. 'As we've all quite finished, would anyone mind if I had some fresh air—always assuming that it's cooler outside by now?'

Eduardo stood up at once, moving swiftly around the table to hold the back of her carved high-backed chair.

'Come, and I will escort you on to the patio. The nights are always warm, but there will be a breeze tonight, and we will sit in comfort. The others may join us if they will, and we will take a last glass of wine together.'

'I think I've had my last glass of wine for one night,' she said as she rose carefully from the chair.

'Perhaps you would prefer a glass of a chilled chocolate drink, my dear?' Leandro suggested. 'You will find it very refreshing and will take the edge off the effects of the wine. I suspect that you are not used to it.'

'I am not,' she said. 'But a chilled chocolate drink sounds delightful, thank you.'

Juana spoke to her father and he gave a sigh and then answered just as quickly. He turned to Serena.

'My daughters wish to be excused, and I think I will go with them. Please do not think us rude on your first night, Serena, but in any case I'm sure you will wish to sit quietly and get used to your surroundings without these chattering magpies around you.'

Considering the chattering magpies had barely exchanged two sentences with her all evening, Serena gave them a small smile.

'We'll have plenty of time for talking, and of course I don't mind. Goodnight.'

'*Buenos noches,*' Elena said directly to Serena.

'*Buenos noches,*' she replied evenly.

Let them think she was going to be put off by their sudden little Spanish phrases that were obviously meant to keep her on her toes. She would learn as much as she could as quickly as she could, she vowed, without ever considering just why it should be so important to her.

'Come, Ricardo. You too have studies tomorrow,' Leandro said, and almost before she realised it Serena was left alone on the patio with Eduardo, and a maid was serving them both with the chilled chocolate drink that was delicious and refreshing, and then gliding silently away.

It might have seemed like a contrived assignation, but somehow she knew it was not. They were cousins, and she was new in the country and this house, and her association had been primarily with Eduardo. He was the one she felt most at home with, though it was an odd way to describe her feelings for this man who alternately infuriated her and filled her with such new longings...

'Was it so bad, *querida*?' he said softly, when the fragrance all around them seemed to charge the atmosphere with peace. The house and the surrounding lands were bathed now in all the glowing colours of a beautiful sunset, the shadows blue- and purple-hued, the barrenness of the hot, dry land tempered by the growing softness of the evening.

'It could have been worse,' she admitted, knowing that her senses were aroused by something she couldn't explain. It was more than the presence of the man, more than the relief after the ordeal of meeting this new family. It was to do with the land itself, with being here where her father had lived, with continuity... It was too emotional to explain, and she was too wine-filled to try...

Eduardo's hand reached out for hers and it was the most natural thing in the world to put her fingers in his, and it was as though she put all her trust in him also.

The night was so beautiful. Again, she thought that it was a night made for lovers, too beautiful to break the spell by mere speech. They sat close together, and only their fingers touched, yet the sexual tension between them was vibrant and undeniable. It was a spell indeed, Serena thought tremulously. It was as if she were bewitched...

From out of nowhere came a plaintive, haunting sound that made her catch her breath. It started slowly, caught on the smallest breeze, and then gathered momentum.

It gradually became louder until finally the sounds seemed to be whirling in her brain as the night was filled with music more barbaric than she had ever heard in her life before. Gypsy music... She knew what it was without being told, even as Eduardo turned to say the words.

They turned towards each other at the same instant, and their glances locked and held. And then it seemed as if the wildness was in Serena's soul, in her very being, because suddenly she was in his arms. And, just as before, she was returning his kisses as if she had been born for only these moments they shared.

CHAPTER SEVEN

SERENA could never say that the first few weeks in Spain were anything but difficult. It seemed that, no matter how much she had wanted or intended to make amends for the past, her grandmother simply couldn't unbend totally towards her. And neither could Serena feel completely at ease in her company. She wanted to love her... but each time she looked at the stern old woman she saw a stranger.

'It will take you a little time to get used to everything,' Eduardo told her a few days later when they had all eaten breakfast, and she said as much to him.

The others had dispersed by then, and the two of them were taking cool drinks on the patio before Eduardo began his working day. 'As the days pass, you will find it less strange. Remember that your father grew up here and would have wanted you to know his home and his land. And I have always understood that your mother was enchanted by it.'

'So people have spoken about her, then? I suspected that her very name was taboo here,' she said, trying not to sound sarcastic and hurt.

Eduardo shrugged. 'It is far better not to mention those days, *querida*. Your grandmother was sorely wounded with the upheaval, and the old ones find it hard to forgive. Be content that she has made this gesture to you now.'

She was struck by a sudden thought. 'Your own father does not seem to resent me, does he? He was perfectly charming to me my first evening.'

116

'He does not. The Garcías have never coveted power and possessions the way the Montalbans have always done. My mother was a Montalban, and perhaps things would have been different for us if she had lived. She may well have urged my father on to be more aggressive about his share in the estate than he has been.'

'Really?' She was sceptical, although his words revealed more about his own side of the family than she had previously known. And if his own attitude was the same as his father's, then it would seem to belie every notion she had been harbouring about Eduardo himself. She heard him give a dry laugh, and knew he had seen through all her suspicions.

'You think I court you for my own ends, *querida*? You do yourself a grave injustice.'

'I wasn't aware that you were courting me at all,' she said coolly, knowing that her heart was beating very fast at his words.

He was being strictly conventional this morning, so much so that she could almost think she had imagined his passionate kiss of that first night, if it weren't for the fact that the memory of the wild gypsy music still flowed through her senses each time she looked at him. There was something of the gypsy in Eduardo, she thought instantly.

Not in his breeding, of course, but in the simmering passion that was inside him... She knew instinctively that a woman who was truly loved by him would be loved and cherished forever...

'You promised to show me the gypsies' encampment. Will you take me there soon?' she said impulsively.

'I think you are not quite ready for it yet.'

'Now just what is that supposed to mean, for pity's sake?' she asked, exasperated.

He laughed, and his black eyes were full of the stars she had seen there on that other night. It was an illusion, she thought faintly, a trick of the light, a bewitching of the senses... She deliberately looked away from him, pretending a disapproval she didn't feel.

'All this is new to you, *querida*. You have many things to learn about us yet. Don't be impatient to see everything at once. Learn gradually, and when the time is right I promise you I will take you to watch the gypsy flamenco. They do not permit every gringo around their camp-fire, and will need to be sure that you are one of us.'

'You keep assuring me that I am,' she said, not bothering to ask the meaning of the strange word. 'And you know I can't stay here forever!'

'But it's said that nothing is forever. And neither can I remain here with you forever, much as it would please me. Your grandmother awaits you this morning and I will see you again at dinner this evening.'

A moment later he was gone without any formal goodbyes. She kept thinking of his phrase. 'Nothing is forever.' It was an odd remark, at once sincere and somehow significant, but for the life of her she couldn't think what she was meant to read into it. She gave up wondering, and went in search of Doña Adriana, who awaited her...

As the days passed, she realised time and again that she had been thrust into the midst of a family life that had its own traditions, one that was dogmatic and nothing at all like that of an English household. The very food they ate was different, and the hours they kept were haphazard to her ordered English mind. Especially the *siesta* during the hottest part of the day, when the whole countryside seemed to go silent and to be in the grip of somnolent lethargy.

Serena hadn't wanted to succumb to it at first, and preferred to do some exploring on her own, whether it was approved or not. She dutifully spent the first mornings with her grandmother, both trying hard to discover common points of interest between them, while skirting carefully around the most pertinent of all, Serena's father.

She was introduced to the elderly invalid, Paco de Montalban, Adriana's brother. He was permanently confined to his bed, and merely held Serena's hands and whispered a cracked greeting in Spanish that she didn't understand.

Guiltily, she was glad to escape from the sick-room to breathe air that wasn't tainted with the smell of approaching death. There was no mistaking it, and Serena acknowledged that the maid María had been right in her assumption. After what seemed to Serena to be a daily audience with her grandmother, Doña Adriana always left her to her own amusements, and Serena felt able to move about the house freely now that she was part of it. She didn't yet belong, but she was growing used to the surroundings.

The house itself was more beautiful than any she had ever seen before, and she tried to imagine her father here, growing up and longing to paint everything he saw. Outside, the home grounds were extensive and well tended. The scent of citrus fruit was everywhere, and she was enchanted to find a profusion of oranges and lemons growing on trees near to the house.

She enjoyed this breathing-space when it felt as if everything here truly belonged to her alone... She caught her breath, because if all that she was told was true, then one day that was exactly what it would be. It was still hard to take in, and it didn't make her feel comfortable, knowing that there were others who must think her an interloper. There was Eduardo's family...and for all his fine words, she still had to make friends with the two girls who had practically snubbed her on her arrival...

She had been in Spain for over a week before one of them sought her out. Eduardo's younger sister found her as she was wandering through a shady part of the garden after her morning time with her grandmother.

'The skin suffers if you stay long in the sun, and the head aches,' Elena said abruptly.

It was not so much a warning as an expression of resentment oozing out of her, as unrelenting as the girl's dark eyes.

'How do you say that in Spanish?' Serena forestalled any more discussion and took the girl by surprise. 'How do I say my head aches?'

'*Me duele la cabeza,*' Elena said, too rapidly for Serena to repeat.

'I'm sorry, but you'll have to speak more slowly——'

Elena interrupted rudely. 'Is not for me to do. I am sent to invite you to the lesson. We begin soon. Señora López arrives—has arrived,' she corrected herself.

Serena felt a stab of alarm. It was one thing to try out a few words, it was something else to be faced with a Spanish tutor and a cousin who would laugh or sneer at every stumbling word she said. Elena's English was far better than she had pretended, and Serena knew she was the one who was going to feel foolish. She saw the look in the girl's eyes and knew this was what she expected. She clenched her hands for a moment, refusing to let the girl rile her, and spoke cheerfully.

'Lead the way, then. I'm ready if you are.'

In the end, it wasn't so bad. The tutor was experienced enough to bring both of them into the lesson, and even asked Serena's advice several times on English pronunciation. She informed her that she would be a great asset in helping Elena in her lessons. The girl responded in a stream of words in her own language, and from the flush on Señora López's face, Serena was quite sure that none of it was complimentary to herself.

'Look here, I'm not exactly thrilled to go back to the school-room,' she told the girl when the tutor had gone. 'But you could at least be civil to me and not make difficulties. *Abuela* would want us to be friends.'

She used the Spanish term quite deliberately, and saw Elena throw back her head. Her glossy black hair was loose this morning, and flew aggressively around her shoulders like a horse's mane.

'I choose friends. And you no belong.'

She turned and ran away from Serena, leaving her white-faced and shocked. It was said quite viciously, and she knew now that she had many hurdles to overcome before she was fully accepted in this place.

And she wanted to be accepted. She owed it to her father. In some strange way, she wanted to make amends for the unhappiness he had caused, and it was an unexpected feeling. Ever since she had learned the truth, she had felt more resentment than anything else towards these people who had made him an outcast.

But she began to understand their feelings at having her suddenly brought among them now. In fact, some of her own resentment was beginning to turn towards her aunts, who should have told her everything when she was young enough to accept the truth and not old enough to be so hurt by it.

Knowing how curious she had always been, Serena knew she would then have been the one to make contact.

Letters could have been exchanged, and this meeting, which would seem to have been inevitable, would have been less harrowing for everybody concerned. Yes, Serena thought sorrowfully, Aunts Hope and Dorcas had done her no favours by keeping her ignorant of who and what she was.

She felt awkward and embarrassed at dinner on the evening after her first formal Spanish lesson. There seemed no point of contact between herself and Elena, and she discovered that the older girl, Juana, was spending the evening with the family of her fiancé.

'So there's to be a wedding in the family?' Serena said, when Uncle Leandro explained his daughter's absence.

'Not until the end of the year, and probably in December,' he said. 'Spanish betrothals are not hurried affairs, and Jorge has many relatives over a wide area, who all wish Juana to visit them between now and then.'

'What a pity it's not earlier,' Serena said, disappointed. 'I shall be back in England by then. It would have been lovely to see a Spanish family wedding.'

'Why can you not be here to see it?' Eduardo said. 'Besides, I am quite sure Juana will want to suggest you act as an attendant.'

'*No!*' Elena broke into an angry tirade, interrupted at once by Doña Adriana. It was not so much a request as an order, her voice sharp and decisive.

'You will have the courtesy to try to speak in English while we have a guest in our house, *Nieta*. And I will not have this rudeness at my table.'

'*Pero*—but Juana wanted two attendants only, myself and Jorge's sister.'

'So now there will be three,' Eduardo said, giving his sister a freezing look.

'I've told you—I shan't be here——' Serena began, but her words were lost in the sudden family furore and she might as well not have been there at all.

Ricardo gave a hoot of a laugh at his sister's chagrined face. 'What an excitable little chick you are, Elena. Our lovely cousin will bring a breath of *primavera* to the occasion.'

'Of what—I'm sorry——' Serena began.

'A breath of spring,' Ricardo said apologetically.

She gave up trying to tell them she wouldn't be here for the wedding. They simply didn't listen. But whatever they said would make no difference to her plans. She couldn't possibly stay here indefinitely. Cook's sister would want to return to her own employment or find another situation, and Cook would be dying to see her to hear every single blessed thing... Already it seemed a world away, Serena thought with a little shock, and she had to think hard to remember what the little London house was like.

She noted the new word Ricardo had mentioned. *Primavera*—the spring. It flowed with a rippling sound on the ear. She enjoyed hearing these odd little words. She was storing them away in her head, surprised to find how quickly she was learning them. Señora López had been agreeably surprised too, offering to bring her writing materials, so that she could write down the words she learned in the lessons and practise them in her own time, and she fully meant to do so.

There was a small lull in the chatter, and she broke in at once, speaking directly to Elena.

'I shan't be here in December, so you have nothing to worry about. There will be only two attendants at your sister's wedding,' she said, noting the fiery cheeks on the little madam's face.

Aunt Dorcas would have given Serena a short, sharp smack if she had misbehaved so in public, and Serena wondered what punishment, if any, Doña Adriana would have in store for the girl. It was significant that she never thought of Elena's own father meting out the punishment. Such was the presence of the matriarch of the family.

'There's nothing to stop you coming back again, is there?' Eduardo said. 'We'd all like you to stay forever, but it's not as if England is on the other side of the world, is it?'

'It rather felt like it when I had the *mal de mer* on that wretched ship,' Serena said, managing to divert the conversation without giving an answer to his question. She turned away from those penetrating black eyes to speak to his brother. 'You must have been on a sea voyage to England, Ricardo. Have you never suffered the way I did?'

And even while he was boasting to her that anyone who could face *el toro* could face the high seas, Serena was recalling the misery of part of that voyage, and most of all the gentle touch of the man sitting opposite her at the dinner table. She remembered the caring way he had sponged her eyes and her throat, and the way his hands had lingered on her body as he prevented the awful nausea from overcoming her. And glancing into Eduardo's eyes, she knew instantly that he was remembering it too.

'Would you like to see the *plaza de toros* before I meet *el toro* there, Serena?' Ricardo asked. 'I can take you one morning and explain the finer points to you.'

'I suppose it might be a good idea,' she said doubtfully. The very last thing she wanted to do was see a bullfight at all, but she realised that all eyes were watching her with various expressions in them, and she had no intention of letting them see she was afraid.

'I think that now she has recovered from the travelling, the most important thing to do is to show Serena around the estate.' Eduardo took the decision out of her hands, and she threw him a grateful look. 'You'll have become more accustomed to the climate by now, and perhaps early next week we will take a tour of the vineyards and the production sheds, and I will show you the cellars where the wine is stored and labelled and graded. It will take all of the day, so we will take food and wine with us. Does that agree with you, Serena?'

'It agrees with me very much,' she said. 'Can we really see it in a day?'

'Only superficially,' he answered. 'But it will give you some idea of what the Casa de Montalban stands for. You will see that we are a force to be reckoned with.'

Just as if she had ever doubted it . . . And whether he himself was García or Montalban, there was no disguising the pride in his voice as he said the words. The ambition he denied was all there, just beneath the surface. Just like herself, he was half Montalban, Serena realised, and she wondered uneasily if there was something of the same ambition in her too. Certainly she was conscious of a need to find her rightful place in this family and to have the rest of them recognise it. She had only thought of it as wanting to be part of a real family. But perhaps she and Eduardo were more alike than she supposed after all.

She struggled with the lessons for the rest of the week, although most of the struggle was with the antagonism of Elena rather than with the Spanish language itself. Serena might never have known her father, but she found a great pleasure in learning his language, and it didn't help the situation when Señora López said tartly that she would be overtaking Elena in her grasp of a foreign language soon, if the girl didn't pay attention to her grammar.

But she was glad to abandon the idea of a lesson on the day Eduardo suggested they tour the estate. She was looking forward enormously to being driven around it in the company of her cousin, whom she quickly recognised to be an authority about the vine-growing and the wine production, and every word he spoke on the subject enhanced her feeling of respect for him. It was clear too that he loved this land and its produce, and it was very evident that he was no parasite in the Montalban hierarchy.

'I had no idea the estate was so enormous!' she exclaimed eventually. But then, why would she know? It seemed as if they had been driving in the elegant little mule-drawn cart for hours, and they were still enveloped in the regimented rows and rows of flourishing vines, now heavy with fruit. The sun was high overhead, and there was little shade anywhere, and Serena knew she was beginning to wilt.

'It's time we took some food and refreshment,' Eduardo decided. 'There are *cuevas* nearby, where it will be cooler out of the glare of the sun.'

She didn't need to ask the meaning of *cuevas*, and saw that she was right as they approached the dark openings in the hillside.

'I'm not too happy to be inside small dark places,' she said at once. 'We don't have to go right inside, do we?'

'Of course not. Just in the shade of the entrance.' Eduardo gave her a quizzical glance. 'Are you afraid of the intimacy, *querida*?'

'I am not,' she replied, already anticipating the teasing remark. 'I am a little surprised, though, at the lack of chaperoning in this country. In England a young lady would not be allowed so much freedom with a man.'

'It is allowed for betrothed couples, and for relatives. And we are relatives, no?' he said with a disarming smile.

'But not close relatives—and until recently I didn't even know of your existence.'

'Do you think you know me now?' He helped her down, and she was aware of a small pulsebeat in her throat as she was momentarily held close to him before he released her.

'From what I have seen and learned, I begin to wonder if anyone really knows the members of this family,' she said.

Eduardo didn't answer as he spread a blanket on the ground and brought the basket of food and drink into the entrance of the cave. He had obviously prepared carefully.

She eyed him thoughtfully, realising the truth of her words. They all had a similar enigmatic look about them, except perhaps Ricardo, who was the frankest of them all. As for the others... They seemed to be constantly assessing her, as if to see if she came up to Montalban standards...

'What do you think of us all? You approve, I hope?' he said, too casually.

'Is it so important that I should think well of you, when *la familia* discarded my parents so callously? I hardly think they care overmuch what I think,' she commented.

'Of course they do. Your future children will inherit this land, and will carry on the traditions of its forebears. You must realise that.'

She didn't touch the fresh-baked bread and creamy cheese for the moment, even though she was extraordinarily hungry after the ride.

'Its traditions? You mean like the sons having to prove themselves in the *corrida* before they marry? Who decided on that barbaric tradition, I wonder?'

'Your grandmother,' he said shortly, startling her. She had expected the idea to go back far longer. 'But please eat now, and drink, and stop looking at me with that fearsome frown on your face. I do not make the rules here.'

'What rules?' she asked in some exasperation. 'And are you going to tell me just why my grandmother should make such a rule?'

She refused to use the Spanish term. These were alien ways, and she felt a great need to preserve her own identity at that moment.

Eduardo shrugged. 'Will you please eat, Serena? If you do not, you will probably spend a miserable evening suffering the effects of the sun.'

Her head was already beginning to throb. She ate silently and drank a little wine, thinking privately that it was more likely to add to her discomfort than aid it.

'Now tell me about Grandmother's rules.' She sat with her arms folded, leaning back against the cool rock of the cave's interior and watching Eduardo's handsome face. 'Since I'm a member of this family, I have a right to know.'

'Yes, you do,' he acknowledged. 'And, despite what you may think, bullfighting in Spain goes back to Roman times, but the family tradition came about because of an accident to Doña Adriana's own grandfather.'

Serena noticed at once that he too used only English words now instead of his occasional Spanish. 'Adriana was a small child when Luis de Montalban was gored to death by a wild bull, and even amid the sorrow there was a feverish excitement in the entire household while her uncles hunted the bull for a week before taking their revenge.'

'You mean they killed him,' Serena stated.

'Of course. Until then, the family had no special interest in the sport, but the uncles acquired the taste for its dangers, and learned all they could about the *corrida*. They practised with the *toreros* until they felt able to take part themselves. Each time they killed a bull they proclaimed it for Luis de Montalban, and by the time she grew up, your grandmother had decided that it would be a fitting thing for every male member of the de Montalban family to prove their strength against *el toro*.'

She didn't fail to note that he had reverted to the Spanish terms and that there was an odd mixture of pride and disgust in his voice. Had her father too felt like this, on learning of his family's bloodlust? Serena simply couldn't think of it as anything else. She was suddenly thankful Eduardo had insisted on her eating before he told his tale, because she had no stomach for food now.

'And all those portraits on the stairs of the Casa— they are the men in the family who have proved themselves stronger than the bulls?'

'That's right. There is also a room in the house with their mementoes—a shrine, if you like. I will show it to you when you wish. It is in my part of the house, and contains suits and weapons, and other items of interest.'

Serena shuddered. 'And the ears of the bulls?' she asked, remembering Ricardo's words.

'Serena, you must realise that our ways are as normal to us as English ways are to you.' He avoided answering directly. But there was still something else she needed to know.

'And did my grandmother also decree the absurd rule that the men in the family should not marry until they had proved themselves with the bull?'

If she insulted him she didn't care, but she saw by his set mouth that his anger was not directed at her.

'She did, but with the approval of the elders at that time. You will find that the Montalbans are accustomed to holding family councils, Serena, but the head of the house has the final word on everything. Naturally, there was a council meeting about inviting you here.'

If he heard Serena's gasp of outrage at such an imposition on her privacy, he chose to ignore it.

'When *Abuela* became head of the family, she had the power to change anything she chose and to override the suggestions of the family council, regardless of any majority vote. *Abuela* is a traditionalist, and sees nothing wrong in putting the strength of the family above all things. She has come up against a problem with Ricardo and myself in several ways though.'

'Not with you, surely? I'm not sorry that you refuse to obey the rules regarding bullfighting, and no sane woman would think less of you for it. How could *I*, when it was what my own father did? But does she really have so much power over you and Ricardo?'

Eduardo gave a short laugh. 'You mean because we are Garcías, I suppose. Since our mother was a Montalban, and there are no Montalban male heirs, *Abuela* takes a keen interest in our futures. The oldest son must marry first, but he must also prove himself with *el toro*. This also causes something of a problem between brothers, since Ricardo does not want to wait forever to take a wife.'

'But that's—that's awful! How can she arrange your lives like that? Don't you have any minds of your own?'

'Naturally we do.' And with that flashing anger and that harsh voice, how could she doubt it! 'We also respect the past and our elders. But there is another possibility of solving our dilemma which need not concern you yet, *querida*.'

'You mean you could do as my father did and leave the Casa de Montalban——'

'No, I did not mean that. Neither would I wish it, since my whole life revolves around my work and this land. But we will talk no more of it today, Serena. Perhaps when you are head of this great house, you will have your own ideas on these matters.'

'I certainly will. And those that you've mentioned will be the first to end!'

She stopped, appalled. Again, she was discussing what was to happen after Doña Adriana's death, and, while these things seemed quite natural to these people, to Serena it was in bad taste and courting bad luck to discuss the future so blatantly.

'Does Ricardo wish to marry someone?' she asked, suddenly realising that Eduardo's single status was preventing any such plan for his brother.

'Perhaps,' Eduardo said, in a voice that told her nothing.

'And what about you, Eduardo? Is there a lady somewhere, perhaps, who has taken your fancy?' She gave him a straight look, wishing she could get past this mask he seemed able to cast over his features at will.

She was aware of a new tension between them, as intangible and yet just as real as the hot, whispering breeze rustling through the sloping rows of vines that stretched away as far as the eye could see. They were both standing now, and Eduardo had gathered up the remnants of the meal into the blanket. They were still within the small intimacy of the cave, and without warning he pulled her close to him.

'There never has been until now, *querida mía.*'

His arms were around her, holding her captive. Serena felt her eyes close for one blissful moment, because it would be so easy just to lift up her face to his and feel his mouth on hers. But there was still some little devil inside her that whispered that he was merely playing games with her. She opened her eyes and wriggled free, watching him from beneath her lashes with a provocative look.

'And I think you take advantage of me, sir. You said yourself that it was quite acceptable for betrothed couples or close relatives to be alone together. I hardly think we qualify for either of those states, and your attentions are beginning to embarrass me, so can we please take another ride and forget this conversation? I'm sure there is plenty more for me to see.'

She hardly knew why she rebuffed him so deliberately. But his presence was becoming too disturbing to her peace of mind, and this continued closeness he seemed to favour was alternately filling her with elation and throwing her into confusion.

She wasn't a silly miss who took flirtations lightly. Nor did she want to fall in love with Eduardo García. For one thing, it would create far too many complications in her life. But she was beginning to learn that matters of the heart were less easy to control than those of the head.

'Forgive me.' He released her at once with a little formal bow. 'You slip into your rightful role so easily that I forget that part of you is still a little English rose. I must go more slowly.'

He turned to load up the cart while Serena stared at him suspiciously. Go more slowly? It almost sounded as if his intention was to court her, and that was surely unlikely. If he toyed with her affections at all, it would only be for his amusement, and that was no less than insulting. Besides, she had told him often enough that she didn't intend to make her home here in Spain.

She remembered him once saying that many men would make her offers of marriage. But so far, she had seen no one except the family, their servants and workers. The Casa de Montalban was like a beautiful oasis, she thought in a sudden flight of fancy. Eduardo had brought her here across miles of rough terrain, and she had no idea how to leave it.

Vast as it was, the estate was its own small empire, insular and remote. Serena had never given it much thought until this moment. When the time came for her to leave, she would be entirely dependent on someone in the family to take her to Cadiz and put her on a boat bound for England...and if they refused, then she would truly be trapped here in this unfamiliar land...

She realised she was breathing heavily, and that she had been staring unseeingly at Eduardo for some minutes as the horrendous thought struck her that she was a virtual prisoner here. It seemed that he sensed her distress immediately, and came swiftly to her side once more to take her trembling hands in his.

'Are you ill, *querida*?' he said, obviously concerned. 'Suddenly you look so pale. If I have done anything to upset you, then I apologise for it. It was not my intention.'

For a moment she didn't speak, and then she did so hesitatingly. 'Just what is your intention, Eduardo?'

He lifted her fingers to his lips. His dark eyes looked at her above her hands, and surely his expression was one of tenderness now...? She couldn't resist the hope that she wasn't mistaken. Because, despite everything, she was so drawn to this man, so filled with a sudden longing she didn't fully understand, a longing that she was trying so vainly to fight.

'I want you to be happy, my love,' he said, the English endearment taking her by surprise. 'I want to show you a world that is yours for the taking, and perhaps one day you will understand why your destiny is here. It was always meant to be, Serena. I beg you not to make hasty judgements, but accept us for what we are.'

His voice could deepen without warning, sending her pulses racing. She thought he was going to kiss her again, but, as if he sensed that enough was enough, he dropped her hands and spoke in a more practical way.

'Perhaps we should go now to the *bodegas* and I will show you our vast quantities of wine, and you will see just how impressive an empire you inherit.'

She thought it very strange that he should use the same word to describe her inheritance as she had used earlier. An empire... And, leaving personalities aside, destiny decreed that one day Serena de Montalban would be its head, and could then do anything she wished. She could change all the rules...

CHAPTER EIGHT

SERENA sat in a shady part of the patio and reread the letter she had just written. It would have to be sent to Mr Price's chambers in London, but she knew she could trust him to read its contents to Cook. Before she left for Spain, he had promised faithfully that he would do as much. Cook would be overcome by the gentleman's arrival, but at least she would have news of Serena, and that would put her mind at rest.

Serena thought guiltily that she had become so involved in her new life here that she had been tardy in remembering to write, but now the letter was ready to be taken to a ship bound for England. She scanned her words.

'I am quite well, Cookie, and everyone is being very kind. There are many people here, and they have all made me welcome.'

She gave a rueful smile, remembering Elena. The girl was one person who clearly still resented her, and had never unbent towards her. But Juana, at least, had taken pleasure in showing Serena her preparations for the wedding in December, and told her the details of the lovely gown already being stitched for her. Serena read on, skimming over the rest of her letter until she reached the end.

'Spain is very hot, and you would certainly not be comfortable in the summer heat. It seems to suit me tolerably well, for obvious reasons, I suppose. I am happy to stay for a while yet, and I hope that you and your sister are finding pleasure in being together.'

'Your affectionate Serena.'

There had seemed little more to say. The London house was so far removed from this vital place that Serena began to wonder what she ever did with her time there. Here, there were the hours spent with her grandmother, the family eating rituals and the exploring of the house and estate in which there was always something new to discover. There were the daily Spanish lessons that she doggedly continued, delighted to know how much progress she was making. So much so that Señora López said she had a natural aptitude for languages, which only annoyed Elena more.

How dull England was going to seem after this... The thought ran through her head, and she dismissed it at once with a little fright. England was *home*, she reminded herself fiercely, but even to herself the words didn't hold quite the same conviction as they once had.

Quite unbidden, she remembered something that Cook had once said, in the far-off days when references to Serena's mother had only ever been whispered in the house.

'Miss Claudia always said that home is where the heart is, and if home with her man had to be in that heathen country, then who could argue against it?'

Who indeed? And at least Serena was intelligent enough to know that Spain was no black heathen country, but one with a culture as proud and correct as any other. There was much to admire here... and much to resist.

She looked up at once as she heard footsteps on the tiles, and smiled at Ricardo's approach.

'I know. You want me to come with you to the *plaza de toros*,' she forestalled him, knowing that she couldn't put off the moment much longer. His performance was only days away now, and as yet she had resisted all his offers to show her the surroundings where he felt so at home.

'I know that you don't have a lesson today and that Elena has gone out with Papa, so shall we go this morning? Eduardo can spare me for a couple of hours and it will not take us long to get there and back.'

'All right,' she gave in with a little shiver. 'I'll fetch my bonnet and parasol first, though. I've no wish to be burnt in the sun.'

He gave her an admiring look. 'You have beautiful skin, Serena. It's not so coarse as some of the Spanish *señoritas*, but it is not so pink and white as the true English either.'

Serena laughed, assuming correctly that his words were not meant to insult her. Though it did make her sound like neither one thing or the other, she thought.

She informed the maid that if anyone asked for her, she had gone with Don Ricardo to the *plaza de toros*. María nodded approvingly.

'The young one has such bravery against *el toro*,' she sighed, and Serena saw at once that there was no disgust in her eyes. She was the only one...

A short while later she was standing inside a bullring for the very first time in her life. It was only a small one, Ricardo informed her, and to Serena it did indeed seem frighteningly small, when she considered that a maddened bull would be charging around it. Briefly, she acknowledged that anyone who faced one in this confined space was indeed brave—or mad.

'Is it as you imagined?' he asked.

'I hadn't even thought about it.'

She gazed around, absorbing the scene. The circular floor was covered with sand, and there were tiered seats all around the arena. Was it so very different from the times when Christians were thrown to the lions? Serena thought instantly. Except that the lions were always the victors . . .

'There is *la música* where the musicians play,' said Ricardo, 'and here the barriers for the matadors to run behind when *el toro* gets too ambitious.'

Serena looked at the flimsy wooden stalls around the rim of the arena, with just about enough room for a man to slide into out of danger from those lethal horns. She shuddered, looking instead at the tiers of seats, some in brilliant sunlight, some now in shade. He followed her gaze.

'The seats are more expensive in the *sombra*,' he said. 'Also, you do not have to close your eyes against the sun and miss the action.'

'I think I would prefer to do that rather than watch a bull being killed.'

'You may speak our language quite well already, Serena, but you do not yet think as a Spaniard——'

'If that means thinking of this barbaric killing as a sport, then I never will!' she said forcefully.

'*Abuela* will be disappointed in you.'

She hardly cared. The *plaza de toros* was quite silent and empty, and yet to Serena its very silence had a sinister atmosphere about it, as if it was just waiting . . .

'Can we leave now?' she said abruptly. 'I think I've seen enough.'

Ricardo had caught her arm, and his grip was surprisingly strong.

'I have upset you, and I should not have done so. I am sorry. *Abuela* would not approve——'

'For pity's sake, can't any of you ever think for yourselves? Do you have to stop and consider what she thinks every minute of the day?'

She bit her lip, aghast at her outburst. The truth was, she was totally unnerved by the way everything revolved

around that small, black-clad woman. What Doña
Adriana decreed was what took place. She knew very
well that it was no different in English families where
the head of the household was a dominant personality.
She simply found it hard to accept that she too was
expected to be subservient to her grandmother, and all
her instincts told her to rebel against it.

'We consider her because we love her,' Ricardo said.
'Some of her wishes are against our own, and certainly
some of the present ones, but we will strive to carry them
out for the good of *la familia*.'

'What present ones?' Serena demanded. 'Being nice
to the English cousin, do you mean? Your sister doesn't
seem to be trying very hard!'

'Perhaps it's because she doesn't want her nose put
out of favour.'

'Why should she worry? I'm only a cousin. I won't
be here forever.'

To her surprise, Ricardo slipped his arm around her
shoulders, pressing her close to him. It was hot and stuffy
in the arena, and Serena was already feeling slightly
claustrophobic. He bent his handsome head to look
straight into her eyes.

'But you will be if *Abuela's* wishes are carried out.'

'You mean she wants me to make my home in Spain?'

'Not just that alone. I mean that you must agree to
marry my brother or myself. For this, *Abuela* is willing
to break the rules.'

Serena gasped. Sunlight was doing all sorts of things
to her eyes, dazzling her and making her feel decidedly
faint. And she had no wish to fall senseless in this young
man's arms. She needed to fight off the nausea and the
hot surge of anger at Ricardo's words and all they implied, and to think sensibly.

'Take me home please, Ricardo. I've been in the sun too long,' she ordered tightly.

He released her at once and looked at her uneasily.

'Serena, I was not meant to tell you this——'

'You mean I was the last to know? It was decided in a family council meeting, I suppose?' she said with heavy sarcasm, and saw by his face that her wild guess was right.

What kind of people were they, she raged, to try and determine her future in this way?

'You will please forget my words——'

'Don't worry,' she told him. 'I won't give your secret away, but I assure you I won't be manoeuvred into marrying anybody.'

Whatever he might have said never had a chance, because she pushed past him and sat in the mule-cart looking straight ahead until he took up the reins and goaded the animal home. Serena seethed all the way, her fingers drumming on the side of the elaborate little cart. She was angrier than she had ever been in her life before.

And in the midst of her anger there was also a searing misery. All this time, she had allowed herself to dream that perhaps Eduardo's attentions had been honourable ones. In time he might have declared his love for her, and she would have had no hesitation then in following her heart...but how could she ever trust him now, knowing what she did? That any attentions he paid her were for the good of the *familia*, and on Doña Adriana's orders?

Even the stringent family rules could be rewritten if Serena de Montalban succumbed to the needs of the family circle and married one of their own. Presumably even marriage to the daughter of Ramón de Montalban was preferable to her bringing in more English blood to the proud house of Montalban... She was seeing every-

thing so clearly now, and, if she thought about it long
enough, it was enough to break her heart...

'Is it true?' she demanded, the moment she saw Eduardo
that evening. Why did he have to look especially
handsome in the crisp white shirt and tight-fitting black
trousers the Spanish men favoured, she raged, when all
she wanted to do was forget that she had been brought
up a lady and tell him exactly what she thought of him.

He had been strolling around the orange grove at the
far end of the garden in the comparative cool of the
evening, and was startled to see something resembling a
small tornado whirl to a standstill in front of him.

His face broke into a faint smile, aware that he was
in for something of a tirade, and as yet not knowing
what it was all about.

'Since I don't know what stories you've been hearing
now, I find it impossible to answer that, *querida*——'

'And please stop calling me by that ridiculous name.
I am not your darling, and nor am I ever likely to be.'

She saw his eyes narrow. If she had insulted him by
her reference to the Spanish term of endearment she
didn't care. The fact that she knew what it meant, and
that to him it meant nothing, simply humiliated her.

'I would question that——'

'Would you indeed? You mean you are so steeped in
your ridiculous family tradition that you would even
marry someone you did not love for the sake of Doña
Adriana's peace of mind?'

She was breathing heavily as she spoke, her breasts
rising and falling beneath the soft blue gown she wore,
and she was very aware of the rapid beating of her heart.
This time it had nothing to do with the man, she told
herself. It was the sheer indignity of being an unwilling
party to what she could only think of as a conspiracy.

This whole idea to bring her here had been no more than a ruse to ensure that the future heritage of *la familia* continued to be as Spanish as Doña Adriana could make it. And she was the one English interloper who could still confuse those plans.

'So someone has been talking to you,' Eduardo said, his voice harsh. 'It was Elena, I suppose? She is young and foolish and often speaks without thinking, and if she has begun inventing wild tales I suggest you ignore them.'

'It was not Elena.' Serena tried desperately to be icily calm, but it was simply beyond her, and she was still in the grip of a blind rage.

'Then who?'

'I am indebted to your brother for enlightening me about the family council meeting to decide that the Englishwoman should marry one of you, and that in such an eventuality the rules may be broken. Ricardo will be permitted to marry first, if he is the one who charms me the most. Or you may relinquish the dubious honour of having to face *el toro* if you succeed in persuading me into this farce of a marriage!'

For the life of her, she couldn't prevent all the hurt she felt from spilling over in her voice. Marriage to Eduardo García was something she had never seriously contemplated, but now that she knew of the family discussions and the proposed arrangement she realised it was the one thing she desired more than anything else in the world. But not on these terms! Never just for the sake of the Casa de Montalban!

Eduardo had grasped her shoulders and she could feel the warm pressure of his fingers digging into her flesh through the thin gown. His voice was hard and unyielding, and could in no way be compared to a lover's voice.

'Would it be such a farce? Do you really think I do not find you a beautiful and desirable woman? Haven't I told you often enough?'

'You've told me,' Serena said bitterly. 'But how much of it is to turn the head of a gauche English girl in a foreign land?'

'You insult me——'

'I—insult you?' she began scathingly.

'Did I not pay court to you in England? Did I not show you tenderness on the voyage to Spain? And you were surely not unaware of the effect you were having on me, *querida mía*. I do not think you are a stupid woman, even if you are an innocent one.'

No, she was not stupid. There had been times when she had read the quickening of Eduardo's breath quite correctly, and felt his body harden against hers. She was not unaware of the needs of a man for a woman, nor of a woman's for a man...

'However, I regret that my brother was reckless enough to inform you of Doña Adriana's wishes.'

He was so formal now, and yet he still hadn't released his hold on her, as if he was afraid she would turn and flee if he did so.

'But I assure you it would have made no difference to me. If my heart had already belonged elsewhere, nothing about you would have persuaded me to do as she wishes. But it was always my intention to make you mine, Serena, from the moment I saw you.'

Serena swallowed the sudden dryness in her throat. How could she believe this? Yet how could she not, when it was so very much what she wanted to hear?

She felt his fingers tip up her chin so that she was forced to meet his eyes. They were as unfathomable as ever, but before she had the slightest chance to analyse them she was in his arms, and his embrace was as passionate as that of the most ardent lover. It literally took her breath away, so that she struggled against him, gasping.

'You will always be able to overcome me by force, Eduardo, but I will never give in to blackmail. I've no intention of marrying anyone to save the pride of a house!'

He gave a short laugh. 'Blackmail? You have an odd choice of words for a suitor.'

'You're not a suitor. You're a—a——'

She couldn't find the words, and he looked down at her intently.

'I'm a man who wants you as much as your father wanted his English bride. Perhaps you will mull over that when you return to your virginal bed tonight.'

He *wanted* her . . . but although he made obscure references to the way she affected his heart, he never actually said he *loved* her, Serena thought instantly, and the two words had very different meanings. She spoke abruptly.

'I think we should go back to the house. The family will be wondering where we are.'

'No, they will not. They will assume correctly that I am escorting my lady around the garden. No one will question our absence.'

So it was all an accepted part of the plan. He made it sound too inevitable, and Serena felt a stab of alarm, remembering, as she had done once before, that she was entirely dependent on these people now. If she decided she wanted to leave at any time, she would simply have no idea how to begin.

'My stomach questions it,' she said baldly, at which Eduardo gave a more natural laugh and, although he released her from his embrace, he kept her arm firmly tucked inside his own.

'You English! Always so prosaic!' he said indulgently.

'Yes, we *English* always are,' she said, emphasising the word deliberately.

At dinner that evening Serena was seeing things in a very different light from previously. She saw the way Doña Adriana approved every time Eduardo made some little gallant remark. She noted the small nod when Ricardo informed her he had shown his cousin the *plaza de toros*.

The old lady was probably already calculating which of her young men was going to succeed, Serena thought angrily. And perhaps she'd just play them along and see what happened. It would serve them all right when she announced that she wasn't marrying anyone and that she was more than ready to go back to England.

She realised with a small shock that she was not at all ready yet, and that this country was beginning to get beneath her skin in a totally unexpected way. And then, perversely, she wished the moment of departure could be this instant, before she fell any deeper in love with a man who only wanted her for material gain. For why else would Eduardo agree to it all? He wanted eventual control of the Casa de Montalban, and he would go to any lengths to get it.

She gave him a sudden brilliant smile through the candle-light, and she saw his eyes widen a little. Because her aunts had kept her strictly under control, she was not familiar with the art of coquetry, but she would learn, she thought grimly.

'Eduardo, have you taken Serena to see the flamenco yet?' Doña Adriana said, apparently unaware of the sudden interchange of glances between the two. Or perhaps she was very aware, Serena thought ... She was starting to get confused as to what was real and what was imaginary now, and the feeling wasn't helped by the copious glasses of wine at her side that seemed to be always filled.

'Not yet. I thought she needed to get to know her surroundings better first, but perhaps now is the time,' he said agreeably.

You think the time has come when I can be swayed by music and dancing and an enchanted evening beneath the stars...?

She almost said it aloud and bit back the words, because undoubtedly she had already felt the allure of nights that were unfamiliar to her as yet. There were nights when she had heard the soft music drift across the plains of rustling vines from the distant slopes of the mountains. There were other nights when the music of the gypsies had sounded louder and was raw and sensuous and reached something inside her she hadn't known existed before. She hadn't known herself before...and perhaps Eduardo was right. Perhaps now was the time.

'I would like that very much,' she said, looking straight into his eyes.

Was she playing with fire? Her heart leapt as she saw the answering flicker in his dark eyes. She turned away abruptly and concentrated on her food, aware that her heart was beating too fast with an excitement she didn't fully understand. Was it because of what she had learned, that, whatever their feelings, one of the García men was determined to marry her...?

Or was it because she was actually going to meet the Romanies at last? She felt a shiver run through her and tried to recall what sketchy information she knew of them, barely touched on by her prim English tutor as part of English folklore. According to her, gypsies were colourful, bohemian, devil-may-care, rogues of the night, never-to-be-trusted individuals with access to dark se-

crets in their fortune-telling... They frequented English
country fairs and were experts at riding and horse-dealing
and called you dearie and looked at you in a superior
way as if they could see inside your soul...

'Are you feeling quite well, Serena?' It was Eduardo's
father who was leaning towards her now, and she realised she had been staring down at her plate for some
minutes, as she conjured up a picture in her mind as real
as if she saw it in a gypsy's crystal.

'Oh—yes—I was just feeling a little nervous, that's
all.' She decided she might as well be honest. 'I've never
come into contact with gypsies before. My aunts——'

She stopped in embarrassment. She had been about
to say that her aunts would never have allowed it, but
that implied that they thought themselves better than
these Spanish relatives. So they did, Serena remembered... and how she wished she could show them all
of this magnificence now.

'You have nothing to fear,' Uncle Leandro said kindly.
'The gypsies are our friends and have been so for generations. Eduardo would never take you to a place where
you would be harmed.'

She avoided Eduardo's gaze. There were more ways
to be harmed than the physical. There was the harm to
her peace of mind, and the growing certainty that she
must be mad to stay here and get more and more en-
meshed in this way of life. She should go, and go now,
before it was too late.

'I will take great care of my cousin,' he said gravely,
emphasising the harmless-sounding relationship between
them. 'She is the jewel in the Montalban crown, and I
never forget that.'

'Well said, Eduardo,' Doña Adriana said.

Well said indeed. To Serena it seemed to be a carefully
constructed phrase to please the matriarch. He never

forgot that . . . and it would just seem to affirm the fact that he knew his duty and would do it.

She spoke without thinking. 'Have neither you nor Ricardo thought of marrying yet?'

The minute she said it she wished she hadn't. She knew the circumstances well enough. She knew the absurd rules this small, black-clad woman had inflicted on her family. But surely they didn't have to obey them without question? They were men and could surely leave the parental stranglehold at any time. After all, her own father had done so and had come to no harm. Unconsciously, Serena put her own interpretation on Doña Adriana's code.

She felt the atmosphere in the room become slightly colder. Even the congenial Leandro García spoke too fast, covering the awkward moment Serena had created.

'My sons will marry when the time is right,' he intoned, and at that Serena lost her patience. She saw Eduardo glancing at the way her fingers drummed on the table, and continued her show of impatience with a feeling of recklessness.

'It seems to me there's a great deal of weight put on this elusive moment when the time is right,' she said. 'How does anyone know when the time is right for anything? My father chose his moments——'

Doña Adriana had risen from her chair even before Serena had got the words out. The rest of them stood up at once as a maid hurried from the room. Elena and Juana took the opportunity to follow their grandmother and Serena gaped at the three men remaining at the table with her.

'What have I said that was so terrible? Does no one in this country ever question the word of an elder?' she said angrily, but in some distress as well.

'You would do well to study the customs of our house and consider Doña Adriana's feelings before you speak, *querida*,' Eduardo said, as if the endearment could soften the anger sparking in his own eyes. She had a sudden suspicion.

'Are you referring to the fact that I dared to bring Ramón de Montalban's presence to the dining table? I would remind you that it's already here. I am Ramón's daughter and I see no reason to deny it.'

'Well said,' Ricardo murmured.

Despite his support, Serena was becoming more enraged than embarrassed now, even though it was obvious that they all considered she'd committed a social sin.

'I don't see why my father's name is taboo here. So he married an Englishwoman and refused to fight the bulls. Was that so terrible? And if it was, don't you people ever forgive? But if it's what you all want I will apologise to my grandmother later, even though for the life of me I don't really see why I should——'

'Then I will show you,' Eduardo said suddenly. He came around the table and caught hold of Serena's arm. There was no tenderness or false affection in his demeanour now.

'Eduardo, no——' his father began.

'She has the right. Doña Adriana would show her eventually. And even if she did not, the house will one day belong to her, and she will know it all then.'

They spoke in riddles that she couldn't follow. There was clearly some secret that Doña Adriana was keeping from her. Serena felt bitter at the thought, knowing now that secrets had been kept from her all her life, and there was apparently one more...

'Where are you taking me?' she gasped as Eduardo took her out of the dining-room and marched her through the house, giving no concession to her long skirts or shorter strides.

'You'll see. Then perhaps you will understand a little.'

She had expected to be taken to see the gypsies tonight. She had expected brightness and laughter, music and dancing, and yes, perhaps a little flirtation beneath the stars, whether real or pretended... She had not bargained for this ruthless stranger tugging at her arm until it felt bruised, nor knowing that it was her own thoughtless words that had caused all the furore...

The house was very large and sprawling and there were several wings. One of them was where Eduardo and his family lived. Another was what she discovered to be Doña Adriana's sanctum, and nobody went there without a prior invitation. She realised that Eduardo was taking her there now.

'No!' She pulled back, her footsteps faltering. 'It's not allowed—even I know that——'

He paused too, and there was a look that was almost triumph in his eyes.

'Ah. then I see that our ways are beginning to make some sense to our little English cousin at last.'

'I've asked you before not to patronise me, Eduardo,' she snapped, then spoke with heavy sarcasm, 'Even an Englishwoman knows enough to respect another person's privacy. I've no wish to intrude here.'

'You have already intruded,' he said.

Before she could even think what he meant by that, a door opened and she could see Doña Adriana standing inside it, evidently disturbed by voices. Eduardo spoke to her in rapid Spanish, and Serena couldn't understand a word of it. But she saw the old woman nod and reply just as quickly, and then to Serena's complete surprise her grandmother reached forward and pressed her thin hand against the girl's.

The next second she had retreated behind the heavy door of her room and Serena was staring at it with a strange lump filling her throat. It was clear that she had been given acquiescence on something she didn't even understand, and she turned to Eduardo blindly.

She had been so angry, and now, with that one brief touch of a scrawny hand on hers, she knew she wanted to say she was sorry for causing all the fuss, but the words wouldn't come.

'She understands,' Eduardo said, as if he could read her mind. 'Come, my love.'

Serena followed him mutely, still not knowing what it was all about, until they reached a room at the end of a twisting corridor, and he drew out an ornate metal key from inside his jacket. He turned it in the lock, and from the way it resisted Serena guessed that this door wasn't often opened. The instant she was inside the room, she knew why.

'This was my father's room,' she whispered.

It wasn't a bedroom but a studio. There was still a strong smell of oils and there were rags and cleaning materials beside several easels. On one of them an unfinished painting remained just as it was when Ramón de Montalban left it. There were finished paintings stacked all around the walls, and some were already hung. They were beautiful, dramatic paintings, bringing a culture to life as Serena had never seen it.

There was the bullfight, bloody and magnificent, the matador resplendent and proud in his *traje de luces*, the dazzling tight-fitting suit studded with jewels. In these violent paintings, the oils appeared to have been stabbed on to the canvas, and Serena could almost taste the heat and dust and smell the blood. The creative talent was so real she could feel the passion in the massed onlookers' faces...

The feelings evoked were so powerful that she had to turn away to gaze instead at the group of paintings depicting the gypsy flamenco, the vivid swirling skirts of the dancers a mass of movement, their black hair unkempt and wildly beautiful, just as Eduardo had described it . . .

A group of less flamboyant portraits suddenly caught Serena's attention and made her draw in her breath sharply. She had seen enough likenesses of Claudia de Montalban, her mother, to recognise her at once, but never portraits like these, and one in particular.

The eyes that looked out of the canvas were the eyes of a woman in love, created by the artist who loved her. The full mouth curved softly, as if it was about to be kissed, or had just been kissed, or was constantly being kissed throughout the sitting.

It was an intensely personal, intimate portrait. The tumbling light brown hair fell on to the woman's bare shoulders. In some of the other paintings the smooth, rounded shoulders were sheathed in soft folds of fabric as if the artist's brush caressed even the canvas on which he stroked his beloved's image.

'I think I've seen enough,' Serena said thickly. 'But I think I would like to come back to this room again when I've had time to get used to the fact that my father's still here.'

She didn't quite know why she had used those words, except that it was searingly obvious that Doña Adriana, for all her sternness, hadn't had the heart to be rid of all her son's work. The essence of Ramón de Montalban was still here, as strong and alive as he must have been when he painted these canvases. The woman wasn't all hard—and neither was Serena.

She turned away from the poignant reminders so fast that she almost tripped over her own feet. She found herself caught up in Eduardo's arms and thought he was going to kiss her, to take advantage of the moment, but instead he spoke quietly.

'You've reacted in the way I expected, and will have much to think about. It has put sadness in your eyes, but also some understanding. I think that now is the time for you to see the flamenco, to understand still more.'

She was still caught up in the glory of her father's paintings, and somehow those of the flamenco seemed to have conjured up the spirit of the music in her head. Then she realised it was not all in her head at all. It was reaching out to her from somewhere in the darkness of the Spanish night, a night filled with stars and music and magic...

CHAPTER NINE

THEY travelled in the small ornate cart again, and the nearer they got to the foothills of the mountains, the more vibrant the music became. The very air throbbed and reverberated with it, until Serena felt that she and Eduardo were no longer a separate entity but a part of its rhythmic enticement.

It only added to the importance of this strange night. She had discovered a love in her grandmother that was clearly still too great for her to destroy all memories of Ramón de Montalban, and because of it Serena was deeply affected. It put a good many things into perspective, and aroused even more questions in her mind.

But the night was so unlike any other she had ever experienced that she finally gave up wondering and worrying. She gave up suspecting Eduardo's motives in bringing her here, and just let herself be motivated by fate or destiny or whatever life had in store for her.

'I think you begin to relax at last, Serena.'

He hadn't spoken on the journey until she realised that the shooting sparks and flames from a camp-fire were more than a figment of her imagination, and took shape and form in front of her. The scent of wood-smoke was pungent and sharp, spiced with something sweet and pleasant that she couldn't identify, and she gave up worrying about that too.

'I'm not sure if that's the right word to use to describe how I feel,' she said. 'I think I'm relaxed and excited at the same time, if you can make any sense of that.'

He laughed, and she hadn't heard him laugh so naturally for a long time. There was a tension among all the inmates of her grandmother's house, she thought suddenly, and admitted that meeting Serena de Montalban for the first time must have been quite a trial to her relatives.

'I understand perfectly. And I promise you that before the night is out you'll be more intoxicated than by any wine.'

'Well, I don't know whether that pleases me or not,' she said instinctively, and felt his hand close over hers.

'Just for once, forget your English reserve and take what comes, Serena. Enjoy, and don't question the enjoyment. Feast your eyes on the spectacle of the dance, and let your senses expand to take in all the pain and pleasure of past, present and future.'

Sometimes he spoke with an emotion that went straight to her heart, and these were the times when she was most vulnerable, she thought weakly. When she could almost forget that the family instructions were for one of the García men to marry the English cousin, to ensure that the Spanish heritage would continue as pure as possible.

For a moment she tried to follow their reasoning. Presumably, with the children of such a marriage, and with their children's children, in time the English interlopers would be only a memory. That was evidently the plan.

Ever since Ricardo's careless revelation, her thoughts had been so wrapped up in the outcome of her visit here she realised she had even been in danger of accepting it, because the future of *la familia* was everything... But she was still woman enough to refuse to marry anyone except for love, and strong enough to stick to her own ideals.

She gave a small start as the group of brightly clad gypsies caught sight of the approaching cart and came running towards them, shouting a greeting to Eduardo, but he murmured to her to sit still and not to be frightened.

Eduardo began talking to these strangers, in a different patois from the usual. She couldn't follow the words at all, but she was not so much scared as curious. She was armed now with the knowledge that her father must have known and loved them, to have been allowed to sketch and paint and walk freely among them. She saw the oldest man among the group step closer, smiling and bowing low to her. To her relief, he spoke now in hesitant English.

'It honours us to receive the daughter of Don Ramón, our best-loved. Come to the fire and our women will dance for you and bring gifts.'

'Oh, but I don't expect——'

'Don't refuse,' Eduardo's voice said in her ear. 'It will be considered a grave insult to refuse any gift that's offered. Eat and drink and watch.'

A short while later, Serena began to wonder with mildly rising hysteria whether it was all a dream. Here she was, in the middle of nowhere, sitting cross-legged on the dusty ground with a man made even more handsome beside the leaping flames of a camp-fire, the two of them surrounded by a band of gypsies, as exuberant as children.

It was a world away from London life. In fact it was truly like a scene from the pages of a child's play-book. She hardly noticed how her eyes smarted from the woodsmoke, because the sounds of guitars and fiddles rang in her ears, and the glitter of the gypsy girls' dresses were far more dazzling to the senses.

In her lap there was a selection of gifts, ornaments fashioned from wood, hooped golden earrings, sachets of herbs to put beneath her pillow to ensure all kinds of good fortune and well-being. She drank from a goblet made from stone and ate titbits of meat of a kind she didn't dare question.

The night seemed to be endless, as if everything within the circle took its place in eternity, and she hardly knew how she came to be having her palm turned upwards in an old crone's hand, or how the ancient fingers were tracing the deep indentations across her palm. The scratchy voice invited no denial of her truths. The old one spoke very little English, and Eduardo translated the gypsy's words in a low voice.

'She says that you don't suffer fools gladly, nor will you be persuaded against your will. You have the strength of your ancestors, which will cause you to fight with yourself regarding your destiny.'

'How do I know if you're telling me exactly what she says?' Serena said, because the words were too near the truth either to be scoffed at, or believed so implicitly.

She knew, too, that these canny gypsies would be sure to know the truth of her situation, so it wouldn't be too difficult for them to assess her feelings.

'Because El García, he never lie!' a soft voice said on the other side of Serena.

She turned quickly to see a young gypsy girl sit down beside Eduardo with a sinuous movement, her body still glistening from the dance, her eyes glowing with fire and exertion and something else.

She adores him, Serena thought instantly, and a stab of jealousy as keen as a knife ran through her at the way Eduardo laughed at the girl's adoration. Serena didn't miss the way his eyes took in the voluptuous curves of the girl's shape in the flimsy dress. He gave her a quick hug before releasing her as quickly. There was clearly protocol to be observed, Serena thought instinctively.

'You honour me, Rosanna,' he said.

'I say only truth,' the girl said indignantly. 'No one shall say that El García lie!'

She glared at Serena, only to have the old crone still holding Serena's palm screech a stream of words at her. The girl sat sulkily and silent while the hand-reading went on. This was the dukkeripen, Serena remembered, similar to that strange word Eduardo had told her so long ago in London. She had never thought then that she would be sitting here like this beneath a great yellow moon, in a circle of enchantment...

'She says you must not be persuaded by the wishes of others,' Eduardo was saying reluctantly.

And now she knew that he was indeed translating the gypsy's words accurately. Otherwise, he would surely have said what he wanted her to hear...but perhaps he could not, with the other gypsies listening intently.

'Ask her when I will go home,' Serena said suddenly.

That would teach him to meddle in her life. There were enough people in the group who understood her words tolerably well, and so did the old crone. She traced another of the curving lines across Serena's palm with great solemnity, and this time she spoke her own halting words.

'Your time here will end before the end of summer.'

To her own amazement, Serena felt a bitter disappointment. She wanted to snatch her hand away, but it was held too firmly in those wizened little fingers. What had she wanted to hear, for pity's sake? That the gypsy would say it was written in her hand that she was to stay here forever? Hadn't she been protesting against that very thing all these months?

'But you will surely return,' the voice continued. 'You will discover what you really want and you must make a choice.'

She stopped abruptly and dropped Serena's hand.

'Is that all? I must make a choice?'

'It's not so very different from what we all have to do, all through life,' Eduardo said in an odd voice.

She glanced at him. Was he intimating that he, too, had a choice to make that was not of his choosing? Perhaps he was implying that he didn't really want to marry Miss Serena de Montalban from England, and would rather choose one of his own kind. Even the gypsy girl who was gazing up at him with a blatant invitation in her eyes...though such a match would never be sanctioned, of course. It would be as impossible as that of a Montalban heir running off to marry an English girl without performing his duty in the *corrida*.

'My daughter will now sing for you,' the old man whom Serena assumed to be the head of the gypsies said quietly, and the whole company fell silent as the girl called Rosanna moved away from Eduardo.

She sat on the ground alongside the fire so that light and shadow played on her smooth amber skin and caught the glitter of her hooped golden earrings every time she moved her head. The seductive curves of her young body were clearly revealed in the firelight, and when she threw back her head before beginning the song the long line of her throat was as delicate as a swan's.

Serena knew that the strongest feeling inside her at that moment was indeed jealousy. She was jealous of the way Eduardo watched and enjoyed all that he saw, and that very definitely included the lovely Rosanna.

And then Serena forgot all about being jealous as the haunting notes of the song filled the air. Rosanna's voice was pure and clear with a slight hint of huskiness in it, and accompanying it was the plaintive sound of a single guitar. It would never sound sophisticated enough for the London auditoriums, Serena thought incongruously, but here, it seemed to complement the very essence of the night.

The poignant music was saying everything that was necessary. Without knowing the words, she sensed that it was all about a lost love, heartache, sadness and tears... By the end of it she felt so emotional she could have wept. She joined in the applause to be polite, but she ached to be somewhere alone to contemplate...

'Did I not tell you it was beautiful?' Eduardo said.

'It's too beautiful,' she said huskily. 'I wish—I wish it ended right there. I'm not sure I'm capable of taking any more tonight,'

'Then we shall leave. It's been something of a day for you today,' he said, understanding at once.

'They won't be offended?' she queried, under cover of the general chatter starting up again.

He smiled faintly. 'They wait for us to leave, *querida*. They would sing and dance all night if we wished it, and never suggest that the night is ending until we are ready to go. This is their way of pleasuring us.'

She revised everything she had ever heard about the bad manners and bad tempers of the gypsies. These might be more civilised than most, but there was nothing she could fault in their behaviour towards her and Eduardo.

They said a formal goodbye and climbed back in the cart, and Serena felt more tired than she had ever been in her life. Her eyes stung a little, and she felt as if she wanted to sleep forever. Unconsciously, she leaned her head against Eduardo's broad shoulder.

'I wish I could keep you there always,' he said in a deeper voice than usual. 'I wish we did not have this obstacle between us that puts suspicion in your lovely eyes every time I want to hold you in my arms. I wish we had met in other circumstances, in another time and place, and then you would know that my feelings are very real.'

'Please stop,' Serena said tremblingly. 'I just can't deal with any more emotion tonight.'

And if he continued, she might be the one to throw her arms around his neck in a way that no lady ever did except in the intimacy of marriage. She could be swayed so easily, far too easily, if she didn't hold on to her self-respect now.

'You still don't trust me, do you?' His voice was tinged with anger and sorrow in equal measure. 'What must I do to prove that I want you for yourself, and not for all that you will one day inherit?'

He flicked the reins to tell the mule to stop his plodding gait, and turned to look at Serena in the silver glow of moonlight. Distantly, they could still hear the faint sounds of gypsy music. It was the only thing that disturbed the peace of the night, except for the faint rustling leaves of the vines in their tiered rows, and the beating of two hearts.

'I wish you hadn't reminded me,' Serena said with an effort at being jocular. 'Because of my grandmother's order, I think there will always be the obstacle of the Casa de Montalban between us, Eduardo.'

'I am not a man who obeys impossible orders blindly,' he answered. 'I promise you I will marry whom I choose.'

'And so will I.'

They seemed to have reached an impasse, since he clearly assumed that she was rejecting him out of hand, and she didn't choose to enlighten him. But the pleasure of the night was already dimmed. They rode back to the estate without speaking or touching, and, for all their enforced closeness in the little cart, Serena thought miserably that they might as well be half a world apart.

She could have changed all that by one word, she thought, when she had taken off her finery and lay sleepless in her own bed. She only had to say yes to the only man she had ever loved, and she would be his wife. And surely with such a status she would be cherished forever. But not yet loved...and until she heard that other special word, and stopped doubting his reasons for proposing, her own pride would let her do nothing other than refuse him.

It was only a few days later, when Serena was still unsettled as to her own feelings, when the day of the *corrida* arrived. Serena viewed the day with great misgiving. She had learned enough about the so-called sport by now to know that men were hurt and sometimes killed by the bulls, and what price their bravery then? There was nothing so wonderful in leaving behind women to weep because of masculine pride and obsession in risking their lives by facing *el toro*. A dead hero was no less dead, Serena thought cynically.

Ricardo García awoke that morning in the usual state of excitement and nervous tension he had felt in the practice arena. He was especially eager to show himself in a good light, because his lovely English cousin would be watching. He was not a professional matador, and his part of the performance was a continuing concession to the sons of Montalban, just as it was to other courageous young men. The only proviso was that they had done sufficient training to ensure a good fight with the least risk of blood-spilling to themselves and unnecessary cruelty in prolonging the death of their opponents.

'But in the end, whatever happens to the matador, the bull always loses, doesn't he?' Serena said to him on the morning of the *corrida*, unaware that his nerves were razor-sharp.

'Naturally *el toro* dies,' he said edgily. 'But you surely would not rather it was the man?'

'Of course not. But why does the bull have to die at all? Couldn't it just be a fair fight and then let the animal go free? It would still prove the man's courage.' She felt belligerent this morning, and couldn't seem to let the argument go.

'If you do not yet understand, Serena, there's no means of explaining it. Perhaps it is inbred in all men that when they fight, they fight to kill. I cannot say more.'

Elena had joined them on the patio in time to hear her brother's words.

'Perhaps Englishmen do not have the courage of the Spanish,' she said slyly, knowing very well that Serena would rise to the challenge.

'Of course they do. They simply choose to use it in other ways,' she snapped.

Ricardo snapped just as sharply. 'You think that fighting the chickens and badgers and dogs is more admirable than fighting something of such great strength as the bull? Which is the worthiest opponent and which the smallest and weakest?'

Serena felt her face flush. Put like that, it did her countrymen no service at all.

'You're the one who does not understand now. Englishmen do not fight chickens——'

'No, they set them to fight against each other and put wagers on them,' Ricardo said, airing his knowledge with a sneer. 'What courage your countrymen show. Is this your idea of heroism?'

'It is not. And anyway, I think that all killing for killing's sake is shameful. But I don't want to argue with you about it, Ricardo. I'm sure you should stay calm before the *corrida*, and, whatever my own feelings, you know that I wish you good luck.'

She stood up and went inside stiffly. She had already guessed that today was going to be an ordeal. She was about to witness the very thing her own father and Eduardo had refused to do, and she hated the idea of watching senseless slaughter.

But it would be expected. Doña Adriana herself would be present with all her family, and the English upstart must not be seen to be afraid. She owed it to herself not to flinch, whatever happened...

She found her way to the library, where she had been struggling to read a child's book in simple Spanish, and sat down heavily in one of the deep armchairs. She thought she was alone, and then she heard Eduardo's voice from the other side of the room, and, as she swivelled her chair around with a start, he did likewise.

'You won't get the better of him, you know,' he stated, and she knew he must have heard everything through the long open windows. There was no point in pretending she didn't know what he meant, nor for soft-treading her argument.

'I'm not trying to get the better of him, but I have an opinion and I don't see why I shouldn't voice it.'

'But not today of all days. You spoke the truth when you said he needed to stay calm. His nerves will be strained to the utmost and he needs love and support from his family.'

Serena stared. 'You would give him love and support when you refused to go into the *plaza de toros* yourself?'

He shrugged. 'It does not diminish my admiration for his courage.'

'Even though I might decide that such courage means he would make a worthy husband?'

She hardly knew why she had said such a foolish thing. Just lately, her tongue seemed to run away with her far too often when she was nervous. And she was nervous now. Here in the dim interior of this room with the sensuous smells of leather-bound books and furniture to match, she was highly aware of the last time she and Eduardo had been alone together. She was still remembering one beautiful night when she might have had her heart's desire and had thrown it all away... That was making her tense enough, and besides that she was scared silly about what she—and Ricardo—had to face this afternoon.

'If that is what you think, then it is your decision,' Eduardo said in a wintry voice.

'Then you would not try to prevent me from choosing him?' she demanded. If she had expected to see him squirm, or to flare with anger, she was disappointed.

'I would not fight with my brother over a woman.'

'In other words, blood is thicker than water,' she muttered, deflated. 'Is that it?'

'I think perhaps you have already made up your mind on your future, and I am not a man to beg for favours, *querida*.'

The fact that he used the endearment at that moment made her throat fill. It contrasted so tenderly with the harsh words he used. And suddenly she felt like weeping, because this conversation was so wrong. It shouldn't be like this between them. From the first, she too had been drawn to Eduardo García, and her own grandmother had created the foolish barrier between them. In trying to get her own way, Doña Adriana had effectively prevented Serena from doing the very thing they both wanted the most.

'As a matter of fact, you're quite wrong in your assumption,' Serena said abruptly. 'I have no desire to marry Ricardo, and never will. To me he's just a boy.'

And this was despite the fact that he was nearer her own age than Eduardo. But it didn't alter the way she saw Ricardo as a callow youth, while Eduardo was a man, in every sense of the word.

She got up clumsily and went quickly out of the room before she said too much. Let him think she didn't intend marrying either one of them. It was the most likely outcome anyway. She realised everything had gone quiet outside, and that it was nearly siesta time. For once she was thankful to go to her room and close the shutters against the glare of the sun, lying dry-eyed on her bed. Tears wouldn't come, but they were all there, too deep to be expressed.

It seemed no time at all when María woke her, and she knew she had slept after all. She had dreamed uneasily, and the dream was still vivid in her head. She had seen Ricardo lying broken on the blood-stained sand of the *plaza de toros* and Eduardo rushing into the arena to defend him against the charge of *el toro* on his defenceless brother.

The dream had ended too soon for it to be resolved, but to Serena it had been violent and real, and she was white-faced and shaking when she felt the maid touching her arm and telling her the siesta was to be kept short today because of the performance.

'I come to see Don Ricardo fight *el toro*,' María said proudly. 'Doña Adriana say it all right.'

Serena simply didn't know how to answer this obvious adoration, so she said nothing, merely splashed her face with cold water from her washing-table while María fussed about laying out her clothes on the bed before leaving her alone as Serena always requested.

As she dressed, her fingers fumbled with buttons and ties, and she wished desperately that the day were over. She tried hard to project her thoughts several hours ahead, when they would be back here once more, but for once the trick deserted her, and all she could think about was the immediate future. Her mouth was dry, and she hoped she wasn't going to disgrace herself.

When she was ready, she reluctantly went down the stairs, past the portraits of past generations of Montalbans in their garish bullfighting garb that made heroes out of every one of them. Yes, she admitted, there was something splendid in the suit they wore, that *traje de luces* that sparkled in the sunlight and proclaimed everyone who wore it as something of a king. But it still changed nothing...

'Serena, come and take some wine,' Eduardo called to her from the *salón*. 'It will settle you before you leave.'

She went into the room obediently, feeling ridiculously hunted. There was nowhere she could hide, no one with whom she could share her panic. The family were all there except Ricardo, all drinking Montalban wine and chattering excitedly. There was also a young man Serena hadn't seen before.

'Serena, this is Jorge,' Juana said, drawing her fiancé into the family circle. 'He's heard all about you, and we're both still hoping that you'll stay in Spain for our wedding.'

'I'm enchanted to meet you, *señorita*,' Jorge said, taking Serena's cold hand and raising it to his lips.

'And I you,' Serena murmured, regretting that there was time for these little niceties that only prolonged the important business of the day.

Eduardo placed a glass of wine into her hand. It was a beautiful deep red, the colour of blood... She wished she hadn't compared it so readily, and drank too quickly, sending the blood to her cheeks and her head spinning.

'Where is Ricardo?' Serena murmured.

'He will be here soon. Right now he is in the chapel, praying for continued health and luck,' Eduardo answered casually, and Serena drank deeply again.

When Ricardo finally appeared, they gasped in admiration, but to Serena he looked totally unlike the Ricardo she knew. His suit was as red as the wine, with gold embroidery encrusting the sides of the figure-moulding trousers and completely covering the short stiff bolero jacket, on which the epaulettes were of studded gold and silver. Around his waist was a brilliant red sash, and in his hand he carried his *montera*, the black hat of the bullfighters.

His hair was pinned flat and heavily sleeked down with oil, and a pigtail had been attached to the back of it. On his feet were soft black shoes tied with elaborate bows, presumably to assist agility around the arena. Over his arm he carried the cape with which the bull would be enticed and goaded into charging.

This was a different man from the brash young García brother that Serena knew. This was a man with a purpose, intent on proving his strength and courage, and she just hoped that his secondary purpose in today wasn't to win her hand. The fact that he had been to pray for his success in a killing ritual seemed to her to be almost blasphemy, but she put her own feelings aside and told him he looked simply splendid. At least she could be totally sincere about that.

The *corrida* began promptly at five o'clock in the afternoon. Since the whole family would be present, they went in two carriages; Serena and her grandmother, Eduardo and Elena in one; Ricardo and his father, Juana

and her fiancé Jorge in the other. Any of the servants
who wished to attend came behind in a mule-cart.

Serena soon discovered that this was an outing at-
tended by people from miles around. She began to realise that the Casa de Montalban couldn't be quite as
isolated as she had imagined, if these others could arrive
in carriages like their own and be greeted like old friends
and acquaintances. She concentrated on being introduced and speaking a few carefully chosen words in
Spanish to each group, who were obviously delighted at
her attempts.

It all helped her from recalling the horror of why they
were actually here as the spectators took their places in
the arena and *la música* played relentlessly all the while
the matadors and their attendants and assistants were
preparing.

'There are six bulls to be fought today,' Eduardo told
her. 'Ricardo will be last, as is usual for the *aficionados*.
If you feel faint at all, no one will be offended if you
close your eyes or simply lower your head. For new-
comers it is often a little harrowing.'

'You underestimate it, I think!' she muttered, already
feeling so faint she could hardly see properly. She felt
him touch her hand, and her fingers were enclosed com-
fortingly inside his palm.

'It will not last for ever, *querida*,' he said quietly.
Nothing did, she remembered...

But in the end, she was thankful for the potent red
wine she had taken before leaving the house. Her head
swam continuously, but at least the heady feelings
deadened the sensation of knowing what was happening
down there on the sandy arena.

The only acceptable part of the day to Serena was the
initial parade of the matadors and *cuadrillas*—each
man's team of assistants. She was quite stunned by the

spectacle of colour and strutting arrogance of the performers. It was nothing like anything seen in England, and Serena was almost deafened by the roars of applause for the crowd's favourites.

But once the real business began she was forced to turn away time and again as the stab of a *picador*'s lance weakened the bull in preparation for the performance of the matador himself. These were the worst moments, when *el toro*, proud and maddened, charged in a kind of bewildered frenzy, rocking the whole ring, and was inevitably brought to the ground by the final thrusts of the matador's sword.

Then the crowd really roared, stamping their feet and screaming their approval to the matador, while *la música* surged into triumphant chords to acclaim the victor. There were few accidents that day, only a gashed arm for one of the *picadors* and a jacket ripped to shreds in a goring that would have been fatal if it had been a few inches nearer the matador's heart. And then it was Ricardo's turn.

'I don't think I can bear it,' Serena mumbled to Eduardo. The stench of blood was sweet and strong in the late afternoon heat, and it was turning her stomach.

He put his arm around her, and she buried her face in his shirt. She didn't care if she was being cowardly or not. The whole scene was so bestial, and she just didn't want to be a party to it... She realised there was an announcement from the ring, and opened her eyes to listen. She was able to translate the Spanish well enough.

'As on previous occasions, the matador from the house of Montalban dedicates his bull to the memory of Luis de Montalban. And today, in addition, he dedicates it to his cousin, Señorita Serena de Montalban.'

She gasped. She didn't want this. She hated Ricardo for making her a part of this hideous ritual, especially

as he was down there now, awaiting his enemy, and lifting
his *montera* to her so that everyone knew exactly who
she was.

'Stand up and raise your hand to him, Serena,' Doña
Adriana instructed. 'Until you do, permission to begin
will not be granted.'

Serena felt beads of dampness on her forehead.

'Do as you are asked, Serena. It will all be over soon,'
Eduardo urged.

She stood up and raised her hand, and the roar of
approval from the crowd was as much for her as for
Ricardo. He threw her a kiss and smiled, and for a
moment she saw past the bravado and the elegance, and
saw only the boy that he was. And she sat down abruptly,
silently praying for him as she had never prayed before.
She realised she was holding on tightly to Eduardo's hand
without knowing quite how it came to be there.

'I'm so afraid he will be hurt,' she whispered, unable
now to take her eyes off the huge bull that came ambling
into the ring, searching and snorting and pawing the
ground.

'The *médicos* will take care of him if anything goes
amiss. There is a special room at every *corrida* for such
an eventuality,' he told her. 'But don't worry. Ricardo
has practised well. He knows all the moves to make and
is very skilful.'

'Perhaps the bull knows them too,' she said, attempting a joke.

He shook his head, taking her seriously. 'It is the first
time for *el toro* too. They face each other on equal terms.'

His reasoning was beyond her understanding. How
could they be on equal terms, when men with lances and
swords hidden beneath capes pierced an animal's hide
so relentlessly? She kept her eyes tightly shut through
almost all of Ricardo's performance, hardly daring to

look when the crowd roared, for fear of what she might see.

But then at last it was over, and Ricardo stood unscathed and triumphant, one foot on the inert body of the animal, one hand proudly waving aloft his *montera*. And then he walked across the blood-stained arena, to bow low before Doña Adriana and his family, and to throw another kiss towards his English cousin. There was a buzz of chatter in the crowd as they saw the gesture.

'They wonder if there is to be an announcement of any sort,' Uncle Leandro said, leaning towards Serena. 'It often happens to crown the day, especially when a victor has made his feeling clear.'

'What kind of announcement?' she said stupidly.

'Often it will be a betrothal,' he said. 'Is it your wish, Serena?'

Her mind might be fuddled, but she knew exactly what he meant, and she didn't need to think twice.

'No, it is not. It most definitely is not!'

Involuntarily she squeezed the hand that still held hers tightly, and immediately felt its answering pressure. It was as if Eduardo's hand was the only safe thing to hold on to in this entire unreal day, she thought sickly, and that was certainly the last thing she had expected to feel.

CHAPTER TEN

THE morning after the bullfight, Leandro García and his sons had a private audience with Doña Adriana. Serena sat with Elena on the patio after breakfast, still finding it difficult to get used to the formality of this family. In many respects they were more autocratic than princes.

'Is it usual to have such a discussion after the bull-fight? Does my grandmother discuss the finer points with Ricardo or something?'

Serena spoke half in jest to lighten the atmosphere, since there seemed an abnormal air of tension in the air that morning.

'Papa will put Ricardo's thoughts and feelings to *Abuela*,' Elena informed her solemnly, although by now she had begun to mellow towards the English cousin.

'Not regarding the so-called betrothal, I hope,' Serena said at once. 'It was too bad of your father to make me feel so beholden yesterday——'

'I wonder why you always think we are concerned with what happens to you above all things. Is it the English way to be so full of self-importance?' Elena said. There was less malice in her voice than curiosity.

Serena felt her face go hot. 'I think not, but your father's suggestion yesterday gave me a restless night. I felt as if all eyes were on me, expecting me to reward Ricardo for his bravery with my favour, and it put an undue burden on me. Especially as I understand that such an outcome wouldn't be unwelcome—at least in some quarters.'

She knew she was getting muddled, and, whether Elena could follow it all or simply chose not to comment, she gave Serena a swift explanation of the minor family council.

'Well, it will not be you that Papa and my brothers discuss with *Abuela*, but Ricardo's future. It is men's business, but Ricardo has a certain choice now. He can pursue a career in the *corrida* if he has the taste for it, or remain working with my father and Eduardo in the *viñas* and donate his *traje de luces* with the others.'

'Others? What others?'

Elena was becoming bored with the conversation and spied her older brother coming towards them, and she rose to leave them.

'The meeting must be over and I wish to talk with Papa. Eduardo will tell you what you want to know. Ask him to show you.'

'And just what will Eduardo tell you and show you?' he said, as he reached Serena on the patio.

'I'm not sure, but it has to do with Ricardo's future. She spoke about whether he continues in the *corrida* or places his suit with the others. What does she mean, Eduardo?'

'Have you forgotten what I told you about the shrine?' There was a faint tinge of bitterness in his voice. 'Perhaps now is the time for you to see it.'

She remembered at once. 'A kind of museum, you mean, where the special matador suits of past Montalbans are kept, with all kinds of mementoes?'

He nodded shortly. 'That's right. I have half an hour to spare. Shall we go now?'

Suddenly he was too polite. It was as if he was indulging a visitor because it was necessary for the manners of the house. Perhaps others wouldn't have noticed it, but Serena was too perceptive to his moods, and to her there was a subtle difference in his attitude towards her. She felt it keenly, and wondered what she had done.

She followed his elegant strides, and realised they were going into the García wing of the house. Serena had not been there before, since it was entered by invitation only, and the central part of the house was where everyone met daily. She wondered which was Eduardo's room. She wondered what it would be like.

She didn't want to imagine it, to place herself mentally beside his possessions, to feel absorbed by his ambience, but she couldn't help herself. The room would be dark and masculine like himself, she guessed, without a woman's touch to soften it, yet with that essential male charisma that surrounded the man. She acknowledged freely that for her no other man in the world could have so much, nor ever would.

She felt the heat in her cheeks again, realising where her thoughts were going.

'Did your meeting with *Abuela* go as you expected?' she said, as polite as himself.

She was unsettled by this new cool and silent manner, and she could hardly associate it with the hot-blooded man who had caught her in his arms after the gypsy flamenco, running his fingers through her hair and filling her senses with a passion as wild as the gypsies'.

'Some of it, yes,' he said. 'The rest was certainly not what we thought to hear.'

'I see. And I suppose I'm not allowed to ask what it was?' She hardly cared, except that it was unnerving her more by the minute to see the hardness in his angular face, and now she began to wonder if something momentous had occurred in her grandmother's sanctum.

'You will know it all very soon, especially as part of it concerns you. But I must ask you to curb your impatience a while longer.'

His words took her by surprise. She'd quite expected him to say it was none of her business, but whatever she was going to hear was evidently going to wait at least until she had seen the special room he referred to so mockingly as a shrine. Anyway, whatever was inside, it wouldn't be as emotive to her as that other room, she thought fleetingly, where all her father's paintings were stored.

That was a room that had really touched her heart and shown her a different side to Doña Adriana, if she could have kept everything intact all these years... And then she stepped inside the room that Eduardo unlocked, and gasped.

There were glass cases all around the room. Inside each one was a matador's regalia, the *traje de luces*, the hat, the sash, stocking and shoes, the swords and the lances. Each glass case evidently contained the belongings of a member of the family who had faced *el toro*.

In a few of them there were the ears of the bull and in one of them there was also a tail. Some of the weapons still bore traces of blood, and several of the suits were torn, the visible evidence of goring. Serena shuddered, still too close to yesterday's spectacle to dissociate her thoughts from what all this implied.

'These artifices belonged to your relatives,' Eduardo said stonily. 'Each one tells the story of months and months of practising and a few moments' glory in the *corrida*. Each one of them was glad enough to donate his possessions here and return to normal life.'

She caught her breath. 'And what of Ricardo? Will he do the same? He has the choice, I believe.'

Somehow she guessed at once, assuming that this was the reason for Eduardo's coldness. He disapproved strongly, and Serena could only ally herself with that.

'You are right, it is his choice.' He shrugged. 'If he wishes to become a matador for all time, then of course I can only wish him well.'

She realised that there was no anger in his voice, only sorrow. So perhaps it wasn't only Ricardo's future career that was riling him. Serena spoke boldly.

'Do you have regrets that your own *traje de luces* is not among these? Or my father's?'

'I do not,' he said at once. 'I feel no sense of shame or loss of family pride that neither Ramón de Montalban nor myself availed ourselves of the dubious honour of facing *el toro*.'

'Then what is it?' Serena said. She put her hand on his arm and felt it granite-hard. 'I know you well enough by now, Eduardo. You look at me as if I'm a stranger and it—it makes me unhappy——'

She said it without thinking and knew at once that the old Eduardo would surely have taken advantage of this moment of weakness. The fact that he did not made her feel cold to the ends of her toes. He looked at her intently, and she caught her breath. Why did he not smile and let the wide curve of his mouth soften his features? Why appear so cold and distant when she longed to tell him she appreciated everything he said, and it didn't matter a fig to her...

'You were a stranger when I paid court to you with less than honest intentions,' he said slowly. 'It could be that you were right all the time, and it was for the Casa de Montalban that I forgot all else——'

She felt a deep shock run through her.

'Why are you saying this?' she whispered, removing her hand from his arm as if it were red-hot.

'Perhaps to release you from any idea that I am a fortune-hunter,' he said brutally. 'Because Doña Adriana has today released my brother and myself from her own dictum that one of us should marry you. She has also rescinded the age-old tradition that the Montalban men must face *el toro* before they marry. It will be made clear in a complete family council, but she wished to inform the two of us in private that she has given us a kind of freedom we may not want but must accept.'

Serena's thoughts were whirling. 'Why would you not want it? I don't understand. You and my father were opposed to blood-spilling and were strong enough to refuse——'

'You cannot understand, can you, Englishwoman? She has taken away my strength and my pride.'

Serena lost patience with all this noble talk. She spoke tersely with English no-nonsense common sense.

'Well, don't you think I intended to do exactly the same as *Abuela* when I inherited? I would never have allowed this tradition to go on——'

'No one would have questioned your decision. You have a different culture and see things differently.'

'I certainly do. I think you're quite mad,' she said, her voice rising. 'And because you've had your own choice not to fight taken away from you, should I now think you less of a man?'

'Well, don't you?'

She could hear her own breathing, no less harsh than his own. To her, it was all a storm in a wine glass, but she could see how vitally important it was to him. It was that damnable fierce pride that seemed to be ingrained

in this family whether they were Montalbans or
Garcías... Without a second thought she put her arms
around him.

'You fool,' she said softly. 'Don't you know that no
one was ever more of a man than you are, Eduardo?'

If she was throwing her own pride to the four winds,
she didn't care. What mattered more was keeping this
man's pride intact. He gave a mirthless laugh.

'Your sensitivity does you credit, cousin. But if I were
to do as my heart dictated right now, I dare say I would
have it all thrown back at me with accusations of cashing
in on the situation. That is your English expression, I
believe? And I do not crave your pity.'

As he put her away from him she felt the sharp stab
of tears on her lashes, but her feelings were laced with
exasperation and anger. How could a man be so short-
sighted as not to see what was right beneath his nose?

'So when are the rest of us to be informed about the
new arrangements?' she said, as cold as he. 'I presume
I'm to be included in any other family council meetings?'

'Of course. This initial one was between men only,
but there will be a full meeting after the meal this
evening, and our family lawyer will draw up a new document regarding the bullfighting.'

'You mean it's all done legally?' she said, startled
anew.

'Naturally. Why should it not be?'

Why did she even need to ask? She might have known
there would be a document drawn up and witnessed
properly so that there was no loophole to the requirements of a Montalban male. And it all seemed less
frightening than sad, that a small, birdlike woman like
Doña Adriana should have had such power over future
generations of strong men, that so few had had the

strength to refute it, and that she could remove it all
with one stroke of a pen.

'You may find it hard to believe, Eduardo, but I'm
more proud of you and my father than if you had killed
a dozen bulls between you,' she said unsteadily.

And then she turned swiftly and walked with her head
held high, out of the hideous little room with its barbaric mementoes and into the sunlight. She needed to
be alone, and she needed to think. It wasn't only
Ricardo's future that deserved serious consideration.

'*Abuela*—everybody—while we're all here together, I
want to tell you that I've decided to return to England
as soon as possible.'

She spoke as steadily as she could that evening when
dinner was over and the family council meeting had taken
place amid yet more wine-drinking. 'I thank you all for
making me welcome, but lately I've felt more and more
a great longing to go home.'

She stopped abruptly, and the first startled silence in
the room was broken only at Doña Adriana's wine glass
thudding on to the table. Then everyone began talking
at once, and Doña Adriana held up her hand for quiet.

'I cannot oppose your intention to return to England
so soon, *Nieta*, but let me say that I do not wish it, and
I think I speak for us all. I had expected you to stay for
some months more, if not for the foreseeable future,
and I beg you not to make a hasty decision, Serena.'

'It's not a hasty decision,' she answered in a low voice,
not looking at anyone else but Doña Adriana. She looked
so old and so frail, and she remembered Eduardo saying
as much the first time he came to the London house.
Impulsively, Serena moved swiftly around the table to
kneel by the stiff-necked old lady.

'Please don't think it hasn't all been wonderful here. I've seen a way of life I never knew existed, and I shall remember it all my life. And especially this house, because it has been in my heart for many years, ever since I first saw the painting——'

She bit her lip hard, partly because the essence of the father she never knew was too poignant and too real in this place, and knowing too that she was reminding Doña Adriana of the son she had rejected. And then she felt the touch of her grandmother's hand on her hair.

'I have been thinking of many things these past days, and it has been a bad thing that you cannot speak freely of him. Ramón's name has been banished for too long in this house, but I see his spirit in you, and you will be a worthy successor to the Casa de Montalban. But you cannot think of leaving, child. This has been no mere holiday for you. This is your rightful place.'

For all her frailty, the words were uttered in too dictatorial a way, the gaze fixed on Serena too intense. They tried to pin her down like a butterfly, and she wasn't ready to be trapped where she didn't belong... She got to her feet clumsily, feeling a sudden panic.

'I'm sorry. I want to go home, and if you won't agree to it——'

'Of course we will agree to it, if it's what you really want,' Eduardo said harshly from the far end of the table. 'No one will try to keep you here against your will. But I had hoped you would stay until October when I shall be in London for the closing of the Exhibition, and I would have escorted you safely back to England——'

'I need no one to accompany me,' she said swiftly, as if she spoke only to him. 'There were plenty of gentlefolk on the ship coming here, and will be others I am sure who will see that I come to no harm. I'm perfectly capable of travelling and I don't wish to put people to any inconvenience. Actually, I would prefer it, if you would be kind enough to make the arrangements.'

'Naturally. It will be done whenever you wish it.'

'Serena, I do wish you'd change your mind.' Juana spoke with genuine distress. 'In fact, I hoped you were going to stay forever. But if you must go back to England, will you return for my wedding? I would so dearly like you to be one of my attendants.'

Serena looked at her numbly. Couldn't she see that a wedding was the last thing she would want to attend? But why should she, when Serena had never allowed anyone to see that to leave here would be to leave her heart behind...? She didn't dare look at Eduardo again, and as she hesitated Elena's voice broke in.

'Yes, and I want you to be an attendant as well. I know I was horrid to you about it at first, but I hate Jorge's sister, and I don't want just the two of us——'

'Oh, Elena, you don't hate her!' Serena began to laugh, but there were tears in her eyes too, because this difficult girl was offering her friendship at last, even though it was all too late...

Ricardo put in his piece, though he was less concerned with family nuptials now than with the prospect of a glorious career ahead of him, and without the need to try and woo his pretty English cousin against his inclinations.

'Just say you'll come back for the wedding, Serena, or we'll have to put up with Elena's bad temper from now until December.'

'Well, if you're sure you all want me——'

'We all want you,' Eduardo said.

But nothing was going to change her mind about going home. She felt a kind of frenzied need to get right away and consider her Spanish relatives from a distance. When the time came, she knew it was inevitable that she would inherit all this land and the wealth that went with it, and she had to consider what she was going to do about that too. And she was too close to it here, too involved with feelings and emotions that she couldn't always hide.

Everyone expected that eventually she would simply leave England and settle into the Casa de Montalban to become the rightful owner of one of the largest vineyards in all of southern Spain. It was the natural order of things. But it didn't necessarily have to happen that way. She had choices too. They had to be thought about very carefully, and it was impossible to do so here.

Eduardo arranged a passage on a ship bound for England in two weeks' time. It was mid-summer in Spain, blisteringly hot and airless, and Serena kept reminding herself that England's climate would be blissfully mild and gentle after such excessive heat. She refused to accept how easily she had grown used to it, or how she had blossomed like an exotic flower in the sun.

There were times when she peered at her face in her bedroom mirror and anticipated just how Cook would exclaim over her golden, un-English complexion and insist that she administer a concoction of oil and lemon juice to whiten it as much as possible before she met any of her old friends.

But who were they? Serena's life had been sheltered to the point of being almost stifled by her well-meaning aunts. She had no real friends, only acquaintances, and most of these were friends of her aunts. It had never really concerned her before, but it seemed as if she was seeing everything more objectively now, and, whatever the future, it still seemed uncertain and frightening.

The final few days before Serena was to leave seemed to be a constant round of fiestas. Jorge's entire family came to the house to meet her, and wine flowed like the proverbial water. She must be getting used to it, Serena thought faintly, because it no longer made her head spin, and when Ricardo told her laughingly she was a true Montalban she felt an absurd pleasure in the words.

But already Serena sensed that her leaving was only a part of the pattern of life here. There was much talk of the grape harvest in September, and the casual aside that it was a pity Serena wouldn't be here to see it all.

'You won't tempt me,' she said a little ruefully to Ricardo. 'My passage is already booked and I leave from Cadiz on Friday at six o'clock in the evening.'

She said it in precise terms, to ensure that it was really happening. Even to herself, the days seemed to be running out too quickly, and she didn't dare examine her heart to discover why she felt so saddened. It was her own decision, after all.

'Anyway,' she went on talking to her younger male cousin, 'you won't be here to see many more grape harvests, will you? I presume your new career will take you far away from home.'

'But I shall always be here for the harvest, and besides, the season for the *corrida* is short, and is over in September.'

'Oh, I see.' So there was still much that she didn't know. 'And the harvest is an important time, is it?'

It was a foolish question, and she knew it as soon as she had said it. It was the fruitful culmination of the year's growth on the vines, and Eduardo moved to join them and added his words to the conversation.

'It's a time for rejoicing, naturally. Even the air we breathe is filled with the aroma of fermentation as the carts are loaded with the grapes and brought to the fermenting houses to be trodden by the men in the huge wooden troughs you have seen. It's as much an annual fiesta as a time of very hard work, and of course it is that too.'

'You make me sorry I shall miss it,' she said with genuine regret at the imagery he evoked.

'You could still change your mind,' he retorted, his voice implying that he hardly cared whether she did or not.

'No, I could not. I need to go home.'

And please don't tell me that this is my home, she pleaded silently. It wasn't—not yet, and she wasn't sure that it ever could be, if Eduardo García continued to live and work here, and in time would presumably bring a wife to share his life at the Casa de Montalban. It was something Serena hadn't even considered until that moment, but it must surely happen in time. Eduardo was too vital a man to want to live for the rest of his life without a woman, especially now that Doña Adriana had lifted her restrictions...

'There are more people who wish to see you before you leave for England,' he was saying now, still in that expressionless voice.

'Really? I cannot think who else is in the least interested whether I go or stay, since I've met so few people apart from the family.'

Not even all the prospective Spanish husbands who were to make her ardent offers of marriage, she thought cynically, and whom Eduardo had apparently seen fit to keep well away from his English cousin.

'*Los gitanos,*' he answered, and she felt a stab of irritation.

'Would you mind speaking in English? I don't understand what you mean,' she said stiffly.

'Of course. You will be wanting to revert to your old ways,' he said, as if there were some demerit in it. She stared at him unflinchingly, wondering how she had ever found a tenderness in this unyielding man.

'Well, are you going to tell me? I warn you that I have no desire to meet any new people at this late stage,' she said in a low voice.

'You have already met them. *Los gitanos* are the gypsies——'

'Oh, no. I can't—not again——' She felt a new kind of panic at the very thought of it. To be alone with Eduardo again beneath a starry night sky on the way to the gypsy encampment, and then to feel enveloped in a wild and passionate culture as old as time...

'They will be very offended if you do not,' he said relentlessly.

'Does it really matter to you? I cannot see that it is of such great importance. They are gypsies——'

She felt her face colour, but he seemed not to notice any disrespect in the English dismissal of gypsies as vagabonds and rogues.

'They wish to put on a display for you, Serena. There will be the flamenco, naturally, and the old one wishes to look again in the crystal for you.'

To Serena it was all mumbo-jumbo, and she was incredulous that Eduardo seemed to take it so seriously. Or perhaps he did not. Perhaps he had schemed with these gypsies to entice her to stay by telling her of dire consequences if she took a sea voyage at this particular time. Immediately she thought it, she dismissed the idea, knowing that Eduardo would not stoop to such deviousness.

'Tomorrow night,' he said, his eyes seeming to burn into hers with their intensity. Black, mesmerising, gypsy eyes, she thought, or so similar as made no difference.

'All right, tomorrow night,' she said faintly.

And then they would see whose will was the stronger, hers or that of everyone else whose sole mission, it seemed, was to persuade her to stay. But she too was a Montalban, and was single-minded enough to do what had to be done.

She thought that some of the other younger members of the family might like to come to the gypsy encampment too, but her query came to nothing. She was told that Elena was too young to visit the gypsies late at night. Juana did not care for the wood-smoke which always made her eyes sore, and Ricardo simply said it was a special night for Serena and he would not intrude.

'But if I ask you to come, you would not be intruding,' she objected.

'My brother understands the ways of *los gitanos*, Serena, and I suggest that you respect his wishes,' Eduardo said calmly. 'It is your company that is requested, and for you that they wish to perform.'

'But they do not object to your company too.'

'They do not, but perhaps you would prefer to go alone? It can be arranged.'

His eyes challenged hers, and she knew they had reached an impasse, and gave up arguing. She accepted that the following night was to be a virtual repetition of that other night, when she had firstly been nervous and suspicious, and finally enchanted. And she lay sleepless in bed, wondering how she was going to deal with all the sensations that night had produced, knowing that this time she was about to turn her back on everything that Spain was offering her.

She turned her face into the pillow, dragging her English sensitivities to the fore. Was she mad, to have her head turned by the wildness and colour of gypsies? She must never forget the cruelty of the bullfight, and not be swayed into grudging admiration for the splendour and courage of the matadors. She must remember that she had been brought here for the sole purpose of being looked over and assessed, that her father had been denied his home and heritage and her mother never accepted.

Even more, she must forget all about a lover's arms holding her captive, crushing her to him in a passionate embrace that almost took her to the stars...and remember that both he and his brother had been instructed to woo her with the intention of marriage to either one of them, and for no other reason than to prevent fresh English blood being brought to the house of Montalban...

She stifled a sob and hardened her heart against all her softer feelings, feverishly assuring herself that the sooner she resumed a normal, ordered English life, the better. And refusing to let the slightest thought of how terribly dull it all sounded enter her mind for a single moment.

It was almost a repetition of all that had gone before, Serena thought, as she sat beside Eduardo in the little cart and allowed the plodding mule to wend his leisurely way towards the gypsy encampment. Almost...except that she felt as though she must try to savour every instant of it, as if it would never come again.

She had promised Juana she would return for the wedding in December, and she wished for the hundredth time that she had not. But it would be a brief visit, she vowed, just for the wedding celebrations and nothing more. This was not her home, and nor did she want it to be. Ramón de Montalban's house, that he had depicted so well in his painting, was best left as a dream after all.

'Why so silent tonight, *querida*?' Eduardo said, and she felt her heart leap. They had become so distant with one another lately, and it seemed so long since he had used any endearment to her.

'Since it's my last night here, I naturally feel a certain sadness at leaving, despite my longing to go home,' she said honestly.

'Do you want it so badly?'

'Don't you always feel the need to return here whenever you go to England?' she said.

'Of course. My heart is here.'

'Yet you expect me to forget so readily that my own heart is in England?' Unintentionally, he gave her the lead.

'How can we forget when you have made it so abundantly clear?'

They countered and countered back, until there seemed little else to say, and they rode on in silence. It was a relief to them both to see a group of the gypsy girls running to meet them in a swirl of brilliant skirts and with bright flowers pinned in their black flying hair. They carried garlands of leaves and flowers and they swathed them around the necks of the visitors, and escorted them towards the clearing where the dancing was to take place, just as frenzied and emotive as before.

When it was over, the old crone made her way towards Serena and sat down cross-legged. Even at her advanced age, the single movement was done with agility and grace, and she looked keenly into Serena's face before consulting the crystal cupped in her hands and held firm in her lap.

The gypsy's own face was shadowed since she sat with her back to the fire. The firelight played through the wispy grey strands of her hair and gave her a somewhat grotesque appearance, while everything there was to see in Serena's face was portrayed in the glow of the crackling flames.

This time the girl Rosanna sat beside Serena and translated the old crone's words.

'She reminds you that she told you your time here would end before the end of summer.'

Serena had forgotten, but it would have been a fairly obvious prediction. Except that until very recently she had more than half planned to stay until October... Rosanna went on.

'But you will return to discover what you really want. Now she says there will be much conflict to come, and a breaking of ties. There is a man who causes you pain, but it is not of the physical——'

'I don't really want to hear any more,' Serena said huskily. Any minute now and the old crone would be intoning that Eduardo García was her undoubted destiny, and she didn't want to hear that either. Not until he came to her with love and not the calculating need to better his own life through Serena's inheritance.

Rosanna spoke swiftly to the old one in their own tongue, and the woman nodded.

'She has a gift for you, which you must place beneath your pillow each night for twelve nights and on the next night you dream.'

Serena resisted the urge to laugh as she felt Eduardo's fingers digging into her arm. It did not do to scoff at the dukkeripen. She took the skin bag the old one held out to her in tentative fingers and made to open it, but the woman spoke sharply.

'No. You do not look inside or you will break the spell. Besides, you would not wish to know the contents.'

The girl smiled for the first time, and she was truly beautiful, Serena thought with sudden envy. Who could blame any man for being charmed by such a comely girl, even a gypsy...?

Rosanna went on translating. 'You may begin the twelve nights at any time, but when they are done the bag must be burnt, still without being opened.'

'What am I supposed to dream about after the twelve nights?' Serena asked, feeling slightly foolish.

Cook would say she had been bewitched by the devil to take heed of such things. Mr Price, her staid London solicitor, would think her head had been turned completely, and perhaps it had... It was Eduardo who answered her question.

'You dream of your husband, of course. What other spell does a young girl ask of the wise one? She says that the first man you see will be the one for you.'

She hadn't asked for any spell at all, Serena thought in annoyance. She wouldn't even do as she was instructed. It smacked too much of invoking dark spirits... but even as she thought it, however heathen it sounded to her English ears, she knew she wouldn't dare to disobey. If only because she was too incurably curious to know if there really was any substance in a gypsy spell... and she told herself fiercely that that was the one and only reason.

CHAPTER ELEVEN

IT WAS the twelfth night of placing the skin bag beneath her pillow. Serena had followed the gypsy's instructions with a growing sense of how ridiculous it all was. She was home in London now, among people who spoke the same language as she did, and most of them viewed gypsies with distaste and suspicion. And here was she, paying heed to the old one's words as if they were a religious ritual.

She shivered, remembering how intense it had all been, and how very different a Spanish gypsy encampment had been from the door-to-door pedlars or fairground fortune-tellers. Remembering how easy it was to be seduced by the firelight and the sweet herbs they burned, the heat and the music and the wild passion of the night. How easy to believe implicitly that when she dreamed tomorrow night, she would dream of the man who was to be her husband...

Her eyes pricked. Supposing that when she dreamed she saw a man whose face was totally unfamiliar to her? Anyone at all, other than Eduardo...? For a moment she was tempted to fling away the skin bag, to break the spell rather than risk such a disappointment. And then she told herself not to be so irrational. Was she a woman of spirit, able to choose for herself, or was she a mouse who would meekly follow wherever the dream led her? And was she beginning to believe so implicitly in gypsy spells that she could no longer think for herself?

Angrily, she tried to dismiss the notion, and remembered that Cook certainly hadn't thought her a mouse when she had arrived back at the house more than a month ago now, weary and travel-stained. The woman had gaped at her as if she were seeing an alien being.

'Oh, my good Gawd! Begging your pardon, Miss Serena, but it is you, ain't it? You look so different, so—so...'

'Oh, Cookie, it's only the effect of the sun,' she said in a choked voice only slightly tinged with impatience. 'Are you going to let me in and make me some tea, or do I have to stand out here attracting attention all day long?'

The woman's eyes spilled over with ready tears. 'It's my young lady all right, sharp tongue and all. Come inside, my duck, and tell me all that's been happening. I'm more than glad to see you back where you belong, despite that stuffed-up Mr Price telling me you'd probably end up staying away for good an' all.'

She gave a great sniff and then she and Serena were crying on one another's shoulders, until an older version of Cook came out from the parlour to see what the noise was all about, and ended up making the tea herself since the other two seemed quite incapable of managing it.

Serena gathered that this was Cook's sister, and, since they never referred to each other as anything else but Sissie, Serena did the same as far as the other woman was concerned, which simplified things all round.

She had no intention of being a recluse now that she was back in England. Although she had few real friends, she joined the crowds still visiting the Exhibition in Hyde Park, and felt herself part of the still-curious and excited throng. She watched the riders in Rotten Row and on several occasions she glimpsed the Queen and Prince

Albert taking exercise with the royal children. She did her needlework and wrote dutiful letters to Doña Adriana, not knowing when or if she would get a reply.

It was well over a month after her return home, long after the lengthy explanations to Cook were over, with many gaps on Serena's part as to what had really been happening in Spain these last months, that she finally decided to experiment with the gypsy's spell. She was as edgy about keeping it as doing nothing with it.

But finally, she decided to follow the gypsy's instructions, being careful to remove the skin bag from beneath her pillow every morning, and lock it safely away in a drawer. Sissie had insisted on acting as lady's maid now that Miss Serena was back, and it wouldn't do for the woman to find the heathen-looking object and report to Cook that the young lady's mind had been turned by black magic.

In any case, now that the twelfth night was over, it was time to burn the skin bag. Once Cook and Sissie had left the house for their daily visit to the vegetable market, Serena dropped the bag quickly into the fire with shaking hands and prodded it into the glowing coals with the poker.

It caught and flared almost at once, burning with an acrid stench that made her cough and pinch her nostrils together. Whatever had been inside the bag, she agreed fervently with Rosanna that it was better not to know of it.

And the next night she would dream of—whom? Now it was done she began to wish she'd been brave enough to throw the bag overboard on the voyage home, and she was becoming more uneasy by the minute.

When the sisters returned she said that she was going to take a stroll around the park. It was a fine late

September day, the air crisp and bracing, the earth green with autumn grass, completely unlike the sun-scorched countryside of Spain. She pushed the memory out of her head before she started getting nostalgic. She wondered just what was wrong with her. She hadn't settled there and now she couldn't settle here...

She deliberately never thought of Eduardo, and she certainly hadn't dreamed about him yet. In fact, although normally she often dreamed, it struck her that while the skin bag had been beneath her pillow she hadn't dreamed at all. There was probably nothing significant in the fact, but it was odd all the same, and she wondered if tonight's dream would be of spectacular proportions.

'Oh, that reminds me, Miss Serena,' Cook said, and she paused on the stairs on the way to fetch her cape and bonnet. 'We met an acquaintance at the market, and she said her ladyship had been asking after you.'

'Who was it, Cookie?'

'One of Lady Darbyshire's maids. Apparently she was talking about you with some guests in the house recently and was wondering if you were back in London.'

'The maid should learn not to repeat what she hears in her ladyship's house,' Serena commented, knowing it was a futile wish since servants gossiped incessantly.

Her words covered the fact that her heart was thudding, reminding her as it did of the time Eduardo had taken her to Lady Darbyshire's house. She didn't want to go there again, and hoped the maid wouldn't pass on the information and cause her ladyship to issue an invitation.

Serena's fears were well-founded, because by the time she returned invigorated from the park a little card had arrived, inviting Serena to a musical soirée that very night. She read the scrawled words the Lady had written.

'I know it's terribly short notice, my dear, but I had no idea you had returned from Spain, and I would so love to have news of Eduardo. I will send my carriage for you at eight o'clock and do hope you will come.'

There was no way she could ignore the invitation, and she wouldn't demean herself by pretending an illness she didn't have. Besides, it would put off the moment of retiring to bed and awaiting the dream...

'You are quite mad,' she told her reflection in her mirror when she had dressed suitably for the evening at Lady Darbyshire's home. 'I refuse to look at you a minute longer.'

She turned away from her reflection, but she hadn't been able to suppress a fleeting moment of pleasure at her appearance. She was woman enough to know that she looked in the best of health, her complexion glowing with an inner well-being as well as the radiance of the Spanish sun. It was odd, she thought, that on the outside she looked so well, when inside she was all turmoil...

'My dear!' Lady Darbyshire exclaimed when she greeted Serena, holding her at arm's distance with both hands. 'How splendid you look. Quite the continental, I declare, and such a contrast to us pale things.'

Serena wasn't sure if it was meant to be a compliment or not, but decided she might as well take the words at face-value. Besides, the gentlemen in the company seemed to be glancing her way approvingly enough.

'And how is dear Eduardo? Such a darling man. Is he well? We do look forward to seeing him next month, and you must come along with him too. I shall give a small supper party for you both.'

Artlessly, she linked them together, prattling like the social butterfly she was, but to Serena's surprise she began to find her oddly endearing, and surmised it was due more to Serena's own newly acquired poise and ability to handle the situation than to any change in the Lady herself.

'Serena, you must sit here beside Lord Edwin Brownley, who has been dying to speak with our lovely Spanish-looking gel. I've told him all about you, and he's mightily intrigued, my dear.'

Serena couldn't think beyond the fact that Lord Edwin Brownley was young and eager and personable, and that his name was far too much like Eduardo's for comfort. She pushed it out of her mind and turned to give him a dazzling smile as they settled themselves to listen to the songs and pianoforte duets. The young man spoke in her ear.

'I'm so delighted to know you, but please call me Teddy, Miss de Montalban. Everybody does.'

'Then I shall too, Teddy.'

It was such a relief she nearly laughed out loud. He was so definitely a Teddy, nicely mannered, cuddly as a child's soft toy, and quite ineffectual. And Teddy was not a name that anyone could ever ascribe to Eduardo García, lean and intense and so much a man...

Serena concentrated on the music, but she was seeing Eduardo's face everywhere she looked. His hands turned the sheets of music. His eyes smiled into hers. His hand touched her fingers...

'A glass of wine, Miss de Montalban?' Teddy Brownley asked hesitantly. 'Lady Darbyshire provides a splendid table, does she not?'

Serena started. The evening's entertainment had come and gone and she couldn't have told anyone what she

had heard or what was played or sung. She was aghast
at her inattention, but it seemed to have gone unnoticed,
and she accepted the glass of wine gratefully. How different a reaction from a few short months ago, she
thought, when her head would have spun alarmingly
from the thought of it, let alone the taste.

'May I call on you, Miss de Montalban?' Teddy
Brownley was saying now. 'I am in London for only a
short while and perhaps I may escort you to the theatre
one evening?'

'You are very kind, Teddy, but I rarely go out. I am
still in mourning for my aunts, and even this evening is
quite an ordeal for me,' she said honestly. 'Besides that,
I have only recently returned from Spain and feel the
need to get my bearings again.'

She heard herself, and thought she sounded more like
a matron than a young woman on the brink of life. But
Lord Brownley was the kind of young man who never
persisted in his attentions, and backed down gracefully.

'I quite understand, dear young lady. Some other time
then, perhaps.'

'Perhaps.'

Her attention was caught by someone who had travelled in Spain and wished to speak with her about the
country. And Serena wondered just what kind of fool
she was, to rebuff a young man with obvious connec-
tions and breeding. Many a young girl would leap at the
chance to be escorted by such a man, for who knew where
it would lead...?

But that was something Serena didn't want. No
attachments, no broken hearts, no inevitably painful en-
tanglements with a man she couldn't love. How could
she, when she already loved, unwisely and far too well?

She was so thankful when the evening was over. She wanted to be home, to be alone in her room and to will sleep to come. She knew she was being naïve and foolish, pinning so much hope on a dream. Her aunts would have said she was selling her soul to the devil, giving credence to spells and witchcraft, but she couldn't seem to help herself.

She tossed and turned in her bed, until the dark, starless night lightened into a pearly dawn, and still she hadn't slept. Sleep was the very thing that eluded her, just when she needed it most. Her distress wasn't helped by the fact that she could hear the loud, rhythmic snores of Cook and Sissie through the walls, and it was impossible not to listen to them.

She almost wept with frustration, and finally wrapped herself in a dressing-gown and crept downstairs to the kitchen to heat some milk in the hope that a drink would settle her nerves.

She was still waiting for the fire's embers to heat the saucepan when she heard a noise outside the front door that made her heart leap in fright. She thought immediately of thieves and made to rush upstairs to waken Cook, who would see anyone off in a hurry.

And then she paused, taking deep breaths, angry with herself at such weakness. It might be no more than a stray cat, looking for a saucer of milk, as restless as she was. Besides, it was almost daylight, and thieves usually lurked about under cover of darkness. Everyone knew that.

She peered through a chink in the curtains beside the front door, reminding herself also that thieves wouldn't come announcing their presence so obviously. She saw a tall, dark shape standing on the step, peering just as intently at the upper windows, as if debating whether it was too early to waken a sleeping household of women.

The morning light revealed his face quite clearly. It was angular and taut, and it was one she had hoped so desperately to see in her dream, but never thought to see in the flesh. The crazy, unbidden thoughts whirled in her head.

'...the first man you see will be the one for you...'

And so he was. She discounted Teddy Brownley. The spell was intended to produce results on the night after she had slept with the skin bag and its contents beneath her pillow for twelve nights. Was that the reason why she hadn't been able to sleep, to keep the dream at bay? Because Eduardo had already been on his way to her...? He wasn't due for nearly three weeks yet, when Prince Albert's Exhibition ended, but obviously he hadn't been able to wait that long to see her...and she hadn't needed a dream after all, because he was here, only a door's width away...

She couldn't think sensibly at all. She forgot all about decorum and that she was hardly dressed for receiving visitors. Her heart was pounding so joyously because he had come for her that she flung open the front door and breathed his name, her eyes glowing.

'Oh, Eduardo, I'm so happy to see you!'

She threw herself into his arms, and didn't notice that his reaction was a mechanical one. If any young woman had thrown herself at him, his arms would have moved of their own will to steady her. But after a blissful few seconds she realised that he didn't move to kiss her, nor to sweep her off her feet in the way of a lover. He stood quite still, and hers was the only heart that was hammering so wildly. His might have been made of stone.

She looked up into his face, and, although few folk were about in the streets yet, she drew him inside quickly, knowing they must look a questionable pair to be standing on a doorstep at such an early hour.

Her heart leapt with something more than pleasure now. Almost as if some sixth sense told her, before he said the words, what they were going to be. And even now, she thought, hating herself for it, she could feel a small selfish pain that he hadn't come totally on her account.

'Can't you guess why I'm here? Doña Adriana is dead,' he said brutally. 'It happened quite soon after you left. Once you decided to return here, she had nothing else to live for——'

'Stop it!' Serena gasped harshly, after a brief, painful silence. She backed away from him. 'I'm not responsible for her death, and you have no right to make me feel guilty——'

'Is that all you have to say? No remorse, no grief?'

'Of course I'm sad! But you've hardly given me time to gather my senses, have you?'

And what was grief, if it wasn't this rush of tears blinding her eyes, and regret as sharp as a knife at all the years she and her grandmother had missed that could never be recaptured, however hard Serena had tried? She knew all about grief, and he had no right to censure her like this.

'I should have broken it to you more gently. I'm sorry,' he said stiffly. 'It will have been a shock to you.'

Especially as this night had been intended for frivolous things. For depending on gypsy spells and dreaming of a future husband... The innocent shame of it seemed to change Serena's thoughts from those of a silly girl to a grieving woman.

'Tell me what happened,' she said quietly.

'*Abuela* was old and tired. She went to sleep one night and never woke up. There was nothing dramatic about it, and it is the way she would have preferred to die. I believe she had some premonition, though. She made certain statements that led us to think so.'

His simple dignity choked her. Her head throbbed with the enormity of what he was telling her, and she couldn't think properly at all.

'And—the arrangements? You will want me to go back to Spain with you, I presume.' And she would want to be there to make her last goodbyes to Doña Adriana. It was the correct order of things.

He caught her hands in his, and his grip was firm and strong. It gave her a sliver of comfort, as did the slight softening of his voice.

'Serena, there was no time to reach you. I could have written, but a letter would not have got here in time for you to do anything. In any case, I preferred to tell you myself. But the funeral took place some weeks ago, arranged with the usual expediency.'

His unspoken words reminded her of the hot climate, and she gave an involuntary shudder.

'The family thought it best to do nothing until it was all over, and then I would come to tell you personally. It has been a strange time for us all. We were busy with the harvest, because of course the grapes did not stop ripening because of one old lady's death, but there was no fiesta this year. The whole time was a mixture of sadness and joyfulness. We celebrated a good harvest and we rejoiced for Doña Adriana's life even while we mourned her death.'

He spoke in a monotone that somehow conveyed more emotion than if he had wept. It touched Serena in a way she couldn't explain, but he didn't seem to expect any answer and went on talking in the same flat manner.

'Now I have come here straight from the ship and am desperately in need of a few hours' sleep, but no matter. I have to carry out some business in London, but I shall not be here now for the end of the Exhibition. Tomorrow I shall instruct our agents as to procedure with our wines, and you and I will go back to Spain at the earliest possible time.'

The words flowed over her. The Exhibition...the Montalban wines...she must return to Spain with him at the earliest possible time... She stared at him, loosening her hands from his grasp.

'I must go to Spain with you? There's surely no need for that...' she stuttered.

'There can be no reading of Doña Adriana's will unless you are present. Other members may make genuine excuses, which will be accepted if not approved, but you are the heir, and it is expected that you attend.'

'And what if I refuse?' For some reason she felt the need to object, to voice her own opinion and show that she still had a mind of her own and was not still dominated by Doña Adriana de Montalban, even from the grave.

'Is it so much to ask?' Eduardo said tiredly. 'She loved you, Serena, even though she found it difficult to express, and you are the last link with her son.'

'The son she discarded,' she said bitterly.

Eduardo stood silent for a moment.

'You have it in your power to continue her empire in the way she always wished it. But you are quite right. You may refuse to attend the hearing, even though it will not be a welcome decision. I will try to pacify the outrage the others will feel, but no doubt they will understand that you consider it an eye for an eye. The house of Montalban rejected your father, so now you reject it in return.'

Her voice was sharply defensive. 'You are quite wrong, but I never sought wealth and property. I never had it before, so why would I ever miss it?'

'As you say. Then your decision is to stay here?' he challenged her.

She wilted then, just as she had known she would.

'Naturally I will return to Spain with you. I owe that much to her. I loved her too——'

Without warning she was crying in his arms and he was comforting her like a parent with a child. But even in her grief she knew that her feelings towards him were anything but filial. She loved him so much, and he was being so formal and correct... She knew that he too suffered grief at Doña Adriana's death. He had known and loved her for so much longer than Serena had.

'I'm sorry I'm such a trial to you,' she mumbled against the cloth of his outdoor coat. 'This has been a great shock.'

'I know.' She could feel the rumble of his voice from deep in his chest where she leaned her head. 'You hardly expected to see me, especially at such an ungodly hour.'

Something inside her froze for a second as she remembered the crazy thoughts that had tumbled through her mind on seeing him when she had only expected to see him in a dream. She had desperately wanted him to be the one whose face would appear to her in that dream, but instead she had come downstairs and peered through the window, and there he was... Again, Rosanna's words swept into her head...

'...the first man you see will be the one for you...'

'Are you all right? You're so still. Do you have some brandy?'

'I don't want it. I'll be all right in a moment,' she whispered, ashamed that she should even think of such frivolous things when her grandmother was already dead and buried and she had known nothing of it until now.

They heard footsteps coming downstairs. Cook's apprehensive face preceded that of her sister, both women fully dressed despite the early hour, and clearly having no intention of being seen by robbers or beggars in their night attire.

'Bless my soul, it's the foreign gentleman!' Cook exclaimed, her voice filled with dark suspicion.

Serena could read her thoughts with almost comical clarity. Gentleman callers did not appear at this hour of the day, and nor did well-brought-up young ladies greet them half dressed.

'Cookie, my cousin has come to tell me that my grandmother has died,' Serena said quickly. 'I shall have to return to Spain with him very soon.'

Cook was briefly shocked into silence at this news.

'I'm sorry to hear it,' she said then, her voice betraying no sign of sorrow whatsoever, since she had always considered the unknown Doña Adriana a harridan. 'But you're not thinking of going away forever, I hope?'

'That has not even been discussed,' Serena said, hardly realising how she skirted round a direct answer. 'But since we're all awake now, Don Eduardo is in need of some breakfast, so will you please prepare it for us both?'

She looked at Eduardo and saw how weary he looked. She spoke impulsively, longing to trace the lines of tiredness from his face, but not having the right. 'Why don't you have a short sleep after you've eaten something before you go about your business? I'm sure a few more hours will make little difference. I too had little sleep last night, and may well do the same.'

She had had no sleep at all, and the restless hours were suddenly catching up with her. That, and the news about her grandmother, which was beginning to have more and more of an effect on her. And she wouldn't want to be seen weeping for all the lost years except in the privacy of her own room.

'I will do just that, if I may,' he said gratefully. 'There is a limit to how long you can survive without sleep, and I feel as if I have had very little these past weeks.'

Serena guessed that much of the business of the harvest and the demise of her grandmother had fallen on his shoulders. One particular family member nearly always seemed to bear the brunt of any crisis, and she guessed instinctively that in this case it would be Eduardo. His were the broadest shoulders in the Montalban hierarchy.

'How are the rest of them faring?' she said, when they were sitting at the dining table with thick buttered toast and Cook's plum preserve and a welcome pot of tea.

'Well enough,' Eduardo said. 'Paco seems not to know what has happened, and it's probably better so. We have engaged a permanent nurse to care for him now.'

Serena guiltily remembered her grandmother's poor brother, whose twilight days must surely be numbered too. As Eduardo said, it was far better that he didn't realise his sister was dead. She resolved that when she returned she would read to him sometimes, and then realised the futility of such a thing, since he spoke poor English. But she could read to him in Spanish. Even if she didn't understand all the words herself, Paco would.

'The men take it well enough, but my sisters are devastated. One of the strange things *Abuela* said shortly before she died was that on no account must Juana's marriage be postponed for any reason. It was as if she knew.'

Without him saying so, Serena knew that he meant her to stay at the Casa de Montalban until after the wedding, and that Doña Adriana would expect it. From now until December. And then what? She hadn't had time to consider it yet, and the present situation was still too new to her to think about plans for the future. But all that Eduardo's news entailed was making her head throb.

'I would like to take advantage of your bed now,' he broke into her thoughts, and she felt the colour flood into her face until she realised what he meant.

'Of course.' She stood up at once, all fingers and thumbs. 'Cook will show you to the guest room and I'll see that you're awakened in about three hours. Will that do?'

'No longer than that,' he agreed. 'I will conduct my business with all speed, and I have booked our passage on a ship leaving for Cadiz at noon the day after tomorrow. That should give you enough time to pack your clothes.'

Serena drew in a breath angrily. 'Are you saying you've already booked my passage? Before you even knew what my answer would be?'

'I knew there was only one answer you could give, *querida*.'

He knew her too well. She might rage inside, but he was perfectly right. How could she refuse to go back? Hearing the will was the last thing she could do for her grandmother, and it didn't matter a jot to Serena that what she would hear would be unquestionably to her advantage. It was the fact of being there that mattered.

Cook appeared in the room and announced that the guest room was ready. She led Eduardo upstairs and held open the door for him as if to ensure that the foreign gentleman didn't dare to invade her young lady's territory.

Serena thought that Cook hardly need have worried. Eduardo looked exhausted, and she felt the same. In her room she removed her dressing-gown with fingers that shook uncontrollably, and crawled beneath the cold bedcovers. She curled up like a wounded animal, feeling her loss keenly, and within seconds all the pent-up emotion was flooding out.

She cried until she could cry no more, and finally slept from sheer physical exhaustion. There were no dreams to haunt her sleep, and even if there had been she would have dismissed them totally. They had no place in her thoughts now. Bound up in her grief for her grand-mother was the thought of the next few months in Spain, and then deciding what to do with her life.

The last thing she had expected was such an early return to the Casa de Montalban, but it seemed as if fate was dictating things for her. She shivered, won-dering if there was something in the hand of destiny after all.

When she awoke it was late in the morning, and she dressed quickly, hardly able to credit that Eduardo was here in London. She was half disappointed, half relieved to discover that he was no longer in the house.

'He had a short sleep and then went off out. He don't give himself time to breathe, that one,' Cook said with a sniff, but Serena could sense a grudging admiration in her voice. Cook always said she liked a body who got on with things . . .

'I'm going out too,' Serena announced. 'I'm not sure when I'll be back, so you and Sissie have something to eat and don't bother about Eduardo and me until this evening.'

'You'll do yourself no good by rushing about——'
Cookie began, with one rule for Eduardo and another
for Serena, but she was talking to herself by then.

Serena took a hansom cab to the chambers of Messrs
Phillips and Price. She had called here on her return
home to inform Mr Price that all was well. She remembered that the time before that she had been there to
check up on Eduardo García, and previously for the
reading of another will, when she had learned the truth
about herself and her family...

'My dear young lady.' Mr Price shook her hand and
ushered her into the brown-panelled room. 'It's good to
see you looking so well, and I trust that you're enjoying
your homecoming?'

The dignified words she meant to say stuck in her
throat, and then everything came out in a rush, and the
elderly Mr Price silently gave her a freshly laundered
handkerchief and waited for her to compose herself.

'What exactly do you want me to advise you, dear
young lady?'

'Tell me what you think I should do! Should I stay
at the Casa de Montalban or give up my claim to it?'

'You should certainly not do that! Many people would
give their souls to come into such a fortune, and you'll
please take no exception to my taking a rather mer-
cenary view of it, Miss de Montalban. In my business I
see too many poor unfortunates to waste pity on young
women who do not appreciate what they have inherited!'

'I do appreciate it,' she said in a small voice. 'I just
don't know if I want it.'

And the solicitor didn't know of the added complications caused by her tormented feelings regarding
Eduardo García.

'Only you can decide on that,' he said more kindly.
'Whatever you wish to do I will see to everything for

you here, rest assured of that. The previous arrangements regarding your cook will continue as before, I take it?'

Serena seemed not to be listening for a moment, and he repeated the question. She answered quickly.

'Of course. And if ever I wanted to make a gift of the house to Cook, would you be able to arrange that too?'

He was shocked. Young women simply didn't bequeath London town houses to servants on an apparent whim of the moment. 'My dear young lady, don't act too hastily——'

'Can you draw up a document for me to sign, to the effect that if I wish it in the future I can write to you from Spain and it can all be done legally without my having to return to England?'

She hardly knew why she was saying it. It was as if the words were entering her head and expressing themselves, whether she meant them or not. It might never happen, but if she wanted it to, she intended to get the legalities organised now.

'Such a document could be drawn up, but such things take time,' Mr Price blustered.

'I don't have time. I leave for Spain the day after tomorrow. I will call back tomorrow afternoon and expect you to have the document ready for signing at that time. Or I can go to another solicitor who can arrange it——'

'That will not be necessary,' he said at once. 'I will see you at three o'clock tomorrow afternoon, Miss de Montalban.'

'At three o'clock,' she said, giving him her hand.

She left the chambers with her head held high, still wondering what on earth she was thinking about, yet feeling a sense of calm inside, again as if something was directing her to take the correct course.

Her aunts would approve, she thought suddenly. It was right and proper that Cook should have the house after her years of faithful service to them, if it was what Serena so decided. And she knew all the time that this was only a formality, after all. There were no ifs or buts about it, and in her heart the momentous decision had already been made.

The London house would be her gift to Cook, and she might or might not make her permanent home at the Casa de Montalban. But whatever happened there was no need to let Eduardo know of it yet.

CHAPTER TWELVE

'DON EDUARDO will be staying with us for two nights, Cook, and we will leave the day after tomorrow,' Serena told her as soon as she returned to the house. The woman burst into noisy tears, holding her apron to her face.

'Oh, please don't cry, Cookie, or you'll just start me off——' Serena began in distress.

'You mustn't go, lovey! I know I'll never see you again if you go away with that man. I reckon he's bewitched you, and no good will come of it, no good at all.'

'Now you're being silly,' Serena said, ignoring the small shiver at the words. 'He's my cousin and I'll not hear anything against him, so please be respectful when he comes back. And naturally I feel that I should be with the family now that my grandmother has——'

Somehow she couldn't say the word. She was more affected by Doña Adriana's death than she had ever expected to be. Instead she gave Cook an embarrassed hug, seeing nothing odd in wheedling her way around a servant she had known since she was a babe in arms. She spoke huskily.

'Will you be an old love and make us one of your special meat pies for this evening? I'm sure Eduardo would appreciate that.'

And despite her intention of leaving this house in Cook's safe keeping, whether legally or not, Serena still wouldn't accept that she was going away for good. It wasn't final, and she could always change her mind and come home, if not to this house, then to another.

She was perfectly aware that she was blowing hot and cold, but presumably she would now be financially secure with her legacy. She was as free as a bird, and Doña Adriana had given her that means of independence. But she certainly intended to live at the Casa de Montalban for the present, to see whether she and it suited each other now that they belonged to each other.

To occupy her mind she began to think about packing her clothes and possessions. Half the time she felt numbed by all that had happened, mourning Doña Adriana with a quite primitive feeling of loss. The rest of the time she tingled with guilty anticipation, knowing she was as drawn to the Spanish house as ever. To the house and the man...

Eduardo returned late in the afternoon, having completed much of his business, but with a few more details to finish the next day. Serena awaited him with all the anxiousness of a young bride, and told herself it was madness to think that way, just because the gypsy's foretelling had come true. In her saner moments, she decided that it hadn't at all. She hadn't dreamed of Eduardo or anyone else, and perhaps that indicated that she was never meant to marry. She was alternately plunged from elation to gloom.

'I hope you've quite recovered from the shock of hearing my news, Serena,' he said quietly, after they had enjoyed Cook's savoury meat pie and potatoes that evening and were sitting companionably together in the parlour.

She gave a small smile, evading a true answer. 'I'm still trying to imagine the Casa de Montalban without Doña Adriana's presence in it,' she said. 'She was so tiny, but there was no mistaking her character.'

'The Montalban women have always had that streak of independence in them.'

'Do you think I have it?' she asked.

Neither of them thought she was angling for compliments, and he was thoughtful before he answered.

'I think you would be a true friend, but a bad enemy. I think you have the strength in you to turn your back on anything you thought less than perfect, however much you desired it.'

'What an odd thing to say,' she said crossly. 'I don't like riddles and I didn't ask for a character analysis.'

'Yes, you did,' he said maddeningly.

'Why should you think I would make a bad enemy?' she demanded, unable to leave it alone. 'I'm not aware that I have an enemy in the world.'

'I think perhaps your English sense of fair play is your personal enemy. You still can't rid yourself of the wrong that was done to your father, and refuse to accept people for what they are, with all their weaknesses and faults. You expect a perfect world, Serena, and you will never find it. We're all vulnerable in some ways.'

'And you're so wise, being ten years older than I!' she said, stung at being dissected so thoroughly, and knowing to her chagrin that there was so much truth in what he said.

'That's right. Ten years is a big difference, and, no matter how hard you try to grow up quickly, you will never catch up.' He spoke in a teasing way now, but to Serena he seemed to be saying that she was far too young and immature for a man of the world like himself.

There was also something she hadn't considered before. Now that she had inherited her grandmother's property and land, perhaps Serena de Montalban was too far removed in the social scale for him to aspire to.

Which was complete nonsense, as far as she was concerned, but was quite a possibility in that autocratic family.

'I don't care to talk about myself any more. You mentioned Juana's wedding. It's not to be postponed because of *Abuela*'s death, then?'

'Most definitely not. Life continues, and Doña Adriana was the first person to say so. The wedding will take place at the beginning of December in Cadiz.'

Serena intended to ask more about the wedding arrangements, to keep the discussion less personal than before, but they were interrupted by Cook.

'A young gentleman has called to see you, Miss Serena,' she said. 'Should I tell him you're not at home?'

Serena took the card she handed and saw the name of Lord Edwin Brownley flamboyantly embellished in gilt. It was such a contrast to the stark announcement of Eduardo García's name on his own calling-card, she remembered in a flash. Even as she thought it, she sensed the atmosphere in the room, and knew that Eduardo was not altogether pleased that a young gentleman should be calling on her uninvited. She inclined her head at once.

'Please show the gentleman in,' she said with more warmth in her voice than she had first intended, and she saw Eduardo's eyes narrow as she smoothed down her skirt and rose to her feet to greet the newcomer with an outstretched hand. It wouldn't do any harm, she reflected, for Eduardo to realise that she still had a life of her own and wasn't bound hand and foot to the Montalbans...

'How very nice to see you again, Teddy. May I introduce my cousin, Don Eduardo García? This is Lord Brownley, Eduardo, whom I first met at Lady Darbyshire's home. You remember her, of course?'

Quite neatly, she shifted all their roles. Eduardo was the foreign visitor who had some time met the Lady in question. She implied that she herself was a regular visitor to Lady Darbyshire's home, and that this young titled Englishman was a welcome acquaintance, if not already more than that.

'I'm sorry to intrude, Miss de Montalban,' Teddy said hastily after the introductions were made. 'It was wrong of me to call unexpectedly, and I had no idea you were entertaining, of course...'

For a lord, he was incredibly flustered, Serena thought fleetingly, and she smiled dazzlingly.

'I'm hardly *entertaining* my cousin, Teddy!' she said brightly, knowing how Eduardo was hating all this. 'I'm always happy to see you, so please stay and take some refreshment with us. We have some splendid Montalban wine which I think you will enjoy.'

She was amazed at her own self-confidence, but beginning to enjoy the situation all the same.

'Well, then, I'd be happy to stay a while,' Teddy said, with all the eagerness of a young puppy. 'As a matter of fact I came to ask if you would care to join a picnic party in Hyde Park at the weekend.'

'Oh, it sounds delightful, but I'm afraid I shan't be able to——' she began with genuine regret, when to her surprise Eduardo broke in.

'I also would have mentioned it to you, Serena, but I knew we would be unable to attend, so I didn't think it necessary.'

Serena and Lord Teddy both turned to look at Eduardo. He was calmly pouring a glass of wine and handing it to Teddy, completely unperturbed by the other's presence.

'What do you mean, Eduardo?' she exclaimed. 'Do you two know one another after all? Were you playing with me when I introduced you both?'

'I have never met this gentleman before,' Eduardo said gravely. 'But I believe the picnic he mentions is the same that Lady Darbyshire is organising, and that's the one to which I refer.'

Serena realised instantly that today had not been all business then. He had had enough time to pay at least one social call, and the fact that he hadn't mentioned it annoyed her intensely and irrationally.

'You're quite right, sir!' Teddy said with a smile. 'You're a friend of Lady Darbyshire, I take it?'

'We are old friends,' Eduardo acknowledged.

Serena remembered her ridiculous notion that those two were possibly more than friends, and was angry for even thinking it. The Lady was so much older than Eduardo, and had a husband . . . Even as she thought it, she knew very well that that was considered little hindrance in certain quarters! Her life had been so closeted in the past she knew nothing about intrigue, except that it existed.

'Anyway, I'm afraid neither of us will be available to attend the picnic,' Eduardo was saying easily now. 'We return to Spain the day after tomorrow.'

The way he said it immediately spoke of an intimacy that didn't exist. They were cousins, for pity's sake . . . and yet the blood relationship between them was so distant, and anyway, even if they had been closer, the empathy between them was too strong to be denied. Serena admitted it freely. She couldn't deny that she loved Eduardo García, whatever his darker reasons for paying court to her.

Not that he had paid her the slightest compliment of late, she realised. Not since arriving, and not for a while before she left Spain. There was a constraint between them now that hadn't been there before, and it was emphasised by the fact of Doña Adriana's death. In the small silence following Eduardo's words, Serena felt obliged to speak quickly, and said the first thing that came into her head.

'Unfortunately, my cousin has brought me sad news. My grandmother has died, and I must go to Spain to pay my respects to the family.'

Teddy leapt to his feet, his face ruddy with embarrassment.

'Then you must forgive me for intruding. I had no idea—but you surely could not have known of this when we met at Lady Darbyshire's, Miss de Montalban?'

'Naturally I didn't know of it then. But now you see why I am all of a rush——'

'My dear young lady, don't trouble to explain yourself on my account. I offer my sympathies to you both, and will take my leave now. But perhaps when you return to England I may call on you again in happier circumstances?'

'Of course you may, Teddy,' Serena said, deciding it was far better to leave things as they were than to go into garbled explanations of whether or not she would ever return to England...

When he had gone she moved restlessly about the room, while Eduardo lounged easily in an armchair, perfectly at home.

'Is his lordship the kind of man you would choose to marry, *querida*?' he finally asked.

'I think that's my affair,' she said quite calmly. 'It has nothing to do with you——'

'On the contrary. It has everything to do with me.'

'I think not!' she answered with some spark in her voice. 'You are under no obligation to *Abuela* now, remember, and neither am I, for that matter.'

'Did you ever think you were?'

She looked at him blankly. 'I don't know why I even said it. I never felt that I owed her anything.'

'Yet it weighed on her very heavily that she owed you something. However much she hated what your father did, she could never hate him. She could never hate you either, nor deny that you existed.'

'No? She managed to do so for a good many years.' She spoke in a brittle voice now, caught up in the memory of that painful moment when she had learned the truth.

'Serena, can't you be as forgiving as she was?'

At his censure, she felt her spirit droop a little. 'I really don't know what we're arguing about. She's gone now, and there's nothing left to forgive. It's over.'

She didn't know how the conversation had developed in this fashion, when it had begun by his asking if Lord Teddy Brownley was the kind of man she wanted to marry.

As if he remembered it too, he got to his feet and came to the window, where she gazed out at the dark night. She hadn't yet pulled the curtains and their reflections merged into one as he came to stand close by her.

'Can't you guess why I asked if you cared for your English Lord?' he said roughly. 'Hasn't it become clear to you yet?'

If only he would tell her he loved her, she knew she could forget everything else but her own desires. Even if it was a small white lie, she would bear it ... She felt his arms close around her, trapping her inside his embrace. She leaned her head against him for a moment and closed her eyes. It would be all so simple to turn around and be held to his heart. His lips were on the nape of her neck and she felt the weak trembling in her limbs. The impropriety of it all didn't escape her either, but it hardly seemed to matter now. The music of the flamenco was inside her head, the mingled scent of flowers and wine and sunlight was heavy and strong in her senses...

'You belong to me, *querida*. You were always meant to belong to me.'

Slowly her eyes opened, and the illusion vanished. For a second the temptation to agree with him had been overwhelming, but her head still contained enough English common sense to tell her to beware of his seductive voice and her own vulnerable state. She still couldn't be sure whether he wanted her for herself, or for who she was. Confused as she felt, she knew there was a great difference. She twisted out of his arms.

'I belong to myself, Eduardo,' she said huskily. 'And I've no intention of rushing into marriage with the first man who asks me.'

Not even with the right man...

He spoke distantly. 'I regret that you find my attentions so unpleasant, and I'll remember in future that the Señorita de Montalban chooses her own husband. You may be interested to know that in gypsy folklore the women have no hesitation in asking a man to marry them if they so wish. Perhaps there's more of the gypsy in you than you realise, though I confess I find it hard to believe. You constantly show me your English side.'

'Good. Then perhaps you'll remember that I *am* English, as I keep reminding you.'

She turned to the fireplace where a low fire was still burning, and heard his terse goodnight as he left the room and went upstairs. She looked unseeingly into the flames, and saw instead the flamboyant swirling skirts of the gypsy dancers. There was a slightly musty smell from a fall of soot from the chimney, and she fancied instead that she inhaled the fragrant wood-smoke of the gypsy encampment.

Her eyes were drawn to her father's painting above the mantel. The Spanish house was so beautiful and welcoming in its inanimate state, so filled with turmoil in reality.

'Just who am I, Ramón de Montalban?' Serena whispered, as unwilling tears salted her eyes.

The next day passed in a whirl of activity as Cook and Sissie insisted on washing and ironing everything that showed the slightest sign of soiling or creasing. Serena had already begun her packing, and by nightfall everything was waiting and ready, and she knew she was probably spending her last night in this house. At least for some months... but in her heart she knew she would never return as its mistress.

She was tempted to tell Cook what she had arranged with Mr Price, but she couldn't bear the tears and gratitude, and so she left it that Cook would be expecting her back at some date in the future, and certainly not before the beginning of next year.

She felt a little shock at the thought, but it was simply impractical to be forever plying back and forth between here and Spain, and there would need to be a breathing-space after Juana's wedding. Besides, the weather at the end of one year and the beginning of the next might not be conducive to sea-travel. With every objection, she

knew she was digging herself more deeply into the idea
of remaining at the Casa de Montalban.

She left the painting in its position above the mantel.
When she wrote to Mr Price with her final decision about
this house, she would say that it was her special gift to
Cook, knowing that she would understand. She didn't
need the painting now that she had the reality. Nor did
she need this one gift from her father when she had all
those other paintings in the sad little room at her grandmother's house that now belonged to her.

Two months after she left it, Serena returned to the Casa
de Montalban. It was clearly a house still in mourning,
but gradually coming to terms with the new order of
things. Elena was more subdued than when Serena had
left, but greeted her with an embarrassed show of
warmth.

'I'm glad you're here. It's been so dull, and I've had
nobody to practise my English on properly,' she said.

'I'm glad I'm useful for something, then,' Serena said
mildly. Everyone else seemed pleased to see her too, and
she thought fervently that she was thankful she had come
earlier, while Doña Adriana was still alive, and not
waited until now to descend on this family. How different her reception might have been, seeing her as the
covetous Englishwoman.

'How has Uncle Paco been?' she asked at dinner that
evening, and Leandro García shrugged his shoulders.

'No different from before. We've tried to explain that
his sister is dead, but he can't grasp it, so it's kinder to
let him be. His nurse is with him constantly, and he seems
to think that she's his family.'

'I shall sit and read to him,' Serena said.

Leandro grunted. 'He won't understand, but you do credit to your grandmother, Serena. You do not discard your old ones.'

He was giving her the Spanish approval, she thought wryly. She saw Eduardo raise his glass to her and knew his thoughts were similar to her own.

The day after their arrival he took her to the family graveyard to show her where Doña Adriana was buried. She placed a sheaf of flowers on the mound of earth and turned away. Death was too matter-of-fact among these dignified people, who could cry their tears away and come to terms with their grief so readily.

Even the García sisters, pale beneath the amber hue of their skins, told her that Doña Adriana wanted no tears shed for her, and that they were to get on with the business of living. She had always thought that hot-blooded people displayed a more noisy grief, but perhaps these did their crying in private, and were more controlled than most.

Perhaps on the day of the will-reading they might show more emotion, Serena thought. Ricardo had returned for this day from his new position in training for his new career, and hugged her wordlessly for a moment. He had already grown in stature, Serena thought in surprise, and then gasped with horror as the nurse and two helpers pushed in the prostrate form of Paco de Montalban on a narrow wheeled bed.

'Must he be here?' Serena said quickly to Eduardo. 'He hardly knows what's happening.'

'He has the right, and the solicitor insisted on it since he's naturally mentioned in the will.'

At her look he added icily that no, he wasn't aware what it contained. She realised that she was very nervous. She was about to hear that this beautiful house, the vast estate and vineyards, and the entire *vitícola* production, now belonged to her alone. In a sudden panic, Serena thought it was too great a responsibility, and she didn't know if she really wanted it after all. All these people around her had earned it, while she had not...

'If we are all here, I will begin,' Señor Rodriguez, the family solicitor, began. 'For the benefit of Señorita de Montalban I shall repeat all the bequests in English once I have read them in Spanish. I shall do this individually, so that you are all completely aware of the contents as they were dictated to myself and my witnesses.'

Serena inclined her head to the man and the two stalwarts who had arrived with him. She felt a small surprise at hearing the date of the will, which they were told superseded all others, and had been drawn up shortly after Serena's return to England.

It was a lengthy document, and she knew at once that this reading was going to be very different from that day in Mr Price's stuffy London chambers when she had read her aunts' and her grandmother's letters. That day seemed so far away now... She realised she was blocking out the reality of these proceedings, and that Señor Rodriguez was clearing his throat very deliberately as he broke the seal on the will of Doña Adriana de Montalban.

By the time much of the lengthy reading and translations had been conducted, she realised that Doña Adriana had been very astute in her intentions. There were the expected personal bequests to Leandro García and the three younger members of the García family which would see them all handsomely through their lives, together with personal mementoes.

There was the provision for the infirm Paco de Montalban to remain under the protection of the Casa de Montalban for the remainder of his natural life. There were minor gifts to maids and servants and estate workers.

'And now we come to the main section of the will,' Señor Rodriguez said patiently. People shifted in their seats, and Serena saw Elena glance outside longingly, where a small breeze moved the leaves of the brilliant bougainvillaea bushes and wafted a fragrant scent of blossom into the room.

Señor Rodriguez was speaking in rapid Spanish now, and she heard everyone in the room gasp. She hadn't caught much of it, except that it concerned Eduardo, and that everyone else was looking at him to see his reaction. Serena looked at him too, and saw that his neck was a dull fiery red. It was the first time she had ever seen him discomfited, and he leapt out of his chair to confront the solicitor.

'There must be some mistake! *No es possible!*' he said angrily.

'I assure you, Don Eduardo, there is no mistake, and Doña Adriana was of sound mind when she dictated this will. Will you please return to your seat while I inform Señorita de Montalban of this content, before I go on to the final bequest?'

Eduardo refused to sit down. He stood with arms folded, his gaze never leaving Serena's face. She had no idea what was happening, except that it was totally unexpected and something of vital importance. She could see it in Elena's round, disbelieving eyes, and Juana's embarrassed face.

Señor Rodriguez began intoning the contents of the will in English again, and it was as though Serena could hear Doña Adriana's thin voice dictating her wishes in a final triumph.

'"I bequeath to Eduardo García the entire parcel of property known as the Casa de Montalban, in the wish that he will reside within its walls for as long as he so desires, and that he will house as many of his family and mine that choose to share it with him for the foreseeable future. I cherish the thought that in due time its passage will echo to the sounds of his children's voices. The one proviso I make is that the room known as Ramón de Montalban's studio shall be left in its present state and that this one room shall belong irrefutably to my granddaughter, Serena de Montalban."'

Serena felt as if all the colour drained from her face. She couldn't gather her thoughts together. She had never wanted anything here, and had come to Spain under sufferance at the whim of this old woman. But she had been led to believe that she was the rightful heir to this house, and instead she was to have possession of one single room...

It was nothing short of evil. How could Doña Adriana do this to her? And then she realised that it was total revenge. Doña Adriana threw back any thought of inheritance into Serena's English face. Doña Adriana could do as she wished with her property, and the fact that Serena was its heiress-presumptive had been no more than a farce.

She could have wept, never realising until this moment how fiercely she had wanted all that she believed was rightfully hers.

Someone was thrusting a glass of brandy into her shaking hands, and she looked up through blurred eyes at Eduardo's set face.

'Congratulations,' she mumbled. 'I presume you got what you really wanted after all.'

She drank the bitter liquid too quickly, and felt his iron grip on her arm as she rose to leave the room.

'Señor Rodriguez hasn't finished yet. You must hear him out, please. And, believe me, this has been as much a shock to me as it has to you.'

She couldn't deny him that. His reaction had been too involuntary to have been otherwise. So what was her bequest to be? Just the roomful of her father's paintings? Her thoughts still spinning, she suddenly realised there had been no mention yet of the land...

'For Señorita de Montalban's benefit I will read the last section in English first of all, since most of it concerns her,' the solicitor said. He cleared his throat.

'"To my beloved granddaughter, Serena de Montalban, the daughter of my much-loved son Ramón, I leave all of his paintings as already stated above, and the room which houses them. I also leave to Serena de Montalban the remainder of my entire estate, which includes the land, the vineyards, cellars and the wine-production. Because of my affection for the last two persons named as beneficiaries in my will, I instruct that all proceeds from the wine-production will in future be shared equally between Serena de Montalban and Eduardo García in perpetuity.

'"I further instruct my solicitor, Señor Fernando Rodriguez, to calculate the value of the Casa de Montalban and the value of my bequest to my granddaughter, and to divide the remainder of the monetary assets equally between Serena de Montalban and Eduardo García, in the hope that this will put them on equal terms, since they will both be sharing all that was mine. As my granddaughter, she will, of course, inhabit that part of the house that was mine, and Eduardo will continue to live in the García wing. That is to be clearly understood.

'"I want no animosity among my family as a result of my instructions, and, in an attempt to right any past wrongs, I declare the two people mentioned above as equal partners in all future dealings of the Montalban property and enterprises. I wish to declare again my verbal wish that the former requirements for the young men of the family to perform in the bullring before they marry are to be ignored forthwith, and request that Serena de Montalban will never bring back such an ultimatum. I entrust her with the proud legacy of the Montalbans."'

Serena sat as if stunned while the solicitor quickly repeated Doña Adriana's instructions in Spanish. She was the heir, but the house had been taken away from her. She was entrusted with the Montalban legacy, whatever that high-sounding phrase meant, but the house belonged to Eduardo, not to her...

'Señorita, I would like to explain things more clearly to you, so perhaps we may have a few words in private?'

She realised the solicitor was speaking to her now, and she nodded. She needed to be somewhere private, if only to get away from everyone chattering excitedly around her in high-pitched voices, speaking so quickly that she couldn't catch any of it.

'I would like Eduardo to accompany us,' Señor Rodriguez went on, 'since it was Doña Adriana's wish that both of you should be absolutely clear as to her wishes.'

Why had she done it? Serena raged. To bind her to Eduardo more tightly than if they had been married...?

Was that it, after all? Giving her no chance to break away from this close-knit family, as it became more ob-

vious to her that she and Eduardo were now two halves
of a whole. To unite the estate fully, there was only one
answer. Even from the grave, Doña Adriana was
scheming to get her own way and marry them... She
had turned everything upside-down in her will in a way
that no one had anticipated.

She glared at the solicitor now as she sat opposite him
in the library where she had so often enjoyed the books
and maps collected over the years by past Montalbans.
Eduardo sat as rigid as stone, not looking at her, and
Serena wished herself anywhere but here. She longed
fervently to be back in England, where she belonged,
where she should never have left...

'Why did she do this?' she burst out, unable to wait
for any formal beginning to this meeting. 'She must have
known how upset we would be. Besides, it's so unfair
to Eduardo. If anyone should have the land it's
him——'

She stopped. It wasn't what she had intended to say
at all. She wasn't sure just why she was so upset on
Eduardo's behalf! She should be angry for herself, and
so she was... In the normal order of things, she had
presumed that the land would have come to her along
with the house, yet now she saw only too well that the
land was in Eduardo's blood. It should have been his.
The bequests should obviously have been reversed. The
more she considered it, the more enraged she became.

'I never wanted this house. I never expected it, nor
did anything to persuade Doña Adriana into thinking
so. You must believe that.' Eduardo spoke only to her
now, and it was as if the solicitor was an interloper in
a very private meeting. Perhaps he chose to see it that
way too, because he made no attempt to intervene in
those first moments.

'I do believe it. It's all *her* doing,' Serena said bitterly. 'She thinks she can undo past wrongs by throwing us into an impossible situation.'

'Is it so impossible, Señorita de Montalban?' Señor Rodriguez finally made his presence felt. 'Doña Adriana thought very carefully before making this new will. She was greatly influenced by what she sensed to be your love for the land here, and she was humbly gratified by it.'

'I hardly think my grandmother was a woman to be humbled by anything,' Serena muttered irreverently.

'But why leave the house to me?' Eduardo said angrily. 'It should belong to Serena. It's the natural order of things.'

Señor Rodriguez smiled faintly. 'My dear Don Eduardo, you know as well as I that the revered lady chose her own way of doing things. She revoked the scandalous need for Montalban men to face *el toro*, for one thing——'

'For her own reasons, I think,' Serena put in.

The solicitor spoke decisively now, as if he mentally gathered up his papers and prepared to go. He hadn't moved, but the sensation that he was finished with this ungrateful pair was the same.

'Whatever the reasons for that and the document I have delivered today, I am certain of one thing. Doña Adriana knew human nature. She wished very much that the house of Montalban shouldn't continue to be divided, and the solution is in both your hands. I will say no more, since it is your personal affair, but I think you are both intelligent enough to know what I mean.'

CHAPTER THIRTEEN

'I HAVE no intention of marrying you for the sake of a house and a parcel of land,' Serena stated flatly once they were alone.

'I'm not aware that I had asked you to marry me,' Eduardo retorted just as keenly.

'You've made it clear in the past that you had some kind of amorous intention towards me——'

'That was then and this is now.'

She stared at him, finding nothing in his voice to tell her anything. There was a growing lump in her throat at the way they were sparring so bitterly, and it was all so adverse to what her grandmother had obviously intended when she made the unexpected bequests in her will. Doña Adriana did not know human nature so well after all.

'You find something funny in this situation?' Eduardo snapped, seeing her wry smile.

'On the contrary. I find it sad that one frail old woman thought she could twist the future of two strong-minded people.' She took a deep breath and went on. 'Anyway, I see no reason why anything should change. The solicitors and accountants will see that we are not cheated out of the proceeds from the wine-production, I presume. I have no knowledge of the *viñas* and hope that you will continue to manage them exactly as before. And I assume that you have no objection to my taking up residence in my grandmother's part of the house as she decreed?'

She tried not to sound sarcastic and to stay as unaffected by him as possible in the circumstances.

'Naturally I have not. I would be offended if you thought otherwise.'

Oh, why didn't he take her in his arms and tell her he loved her, and that if this was Doña Adriana's way of giving them her blessing in uniting the two halves of the Montalban estate they should accept it unquestionably? Why didn't he say that, with or without the inheritance that was now divided between them, he would always love her...? And if he did, would she believe him?

The small hope dwindled away. What had Doña Adriana really done? In dividing the estate, she had divided them still further, and Serena felt drained of all emotion.

'I think I've had enough talk for one day,' she said now. 'I'd like to be alone for a while.'

'Of course.' He rose at once, always the gentleman. 'We shall meet again at dinner this evening, Serena, when I imagine we shall all feel much calmer. But there's just one thing more I want to say. If I am to continue to manage the *viñas* for you, then I ask that you run the house for me. It's a woman's task, and you walk very adequately in Doña Adriana's shoes.'

It was the strangest kind of compliment and she was more moved by it than she wanted to be. She murmured her agreement to his request and went quickly out of the room with her head high. She wondered ruefully what there was to run in this house, after all. It organised itself, with the small army of servants taking care of everything, and only the daily menus to be approved... Her eyes gleamed.

That was the one small way in which she could make her presence felt here. She was an able enough cook, having been allowed in the kitchen to watch Cook many times as a child, and frequently to participate. She could pass on many suggestions to the Spanish cook here, and she decided that from now on there would be plenty of English dishes on the menus as well as Spanish.

They would be truly integrated, and she could wave a small flag for England in the process. It would certainly be no hardship to instruct the kitchen staff here on how to bake meat pies that weren't smothered in olive oil, and to make the clean-tasting English syllabubs for puddings. She felt her mouth water at the thought, and at the fact that she needn't be entirely useless.

There was an odd piquancy too, in the knowledge that regardless of Doña Adriana's bequest Eduardo was best suited to managing the vineyards and the wine-production, while she was far more suited to domestic dealings. They each recognised the fact and would find their own roles, whatever the matriarchal wishes.

In the next few weeks she managed to infiltrate her traditional English ways into the household, and found surprisingly little objection after the cook's initial outrage at the invasion into her domain. But she found a strong adversary in the Señorita de Montalban and finally gave in quite gracefully.

The family seemed to enjoy the novelty of English food. It was almost more frustrating than if they had all protested violently, preferring the less strong-tasting and oily flavours of some of the Spanish dishes. But one person who definitely benefited was the elderly Paco de Montalban.

Serena discovered a strange kind of peace in sitting with the old man in his room and reading from some of the Spanish books as eloquently as possible. She no longer feared the smell of senility in the room and all that it implied.

It was astonishing that he had outlived his sister, but Serena was beginning to adopt the Spanish philosophy that death was the natural progression of life, and she gave the old man her company, knowing he listened as if following every word, whether he did or not. He rarely spoke, but just occasionally he did so lucidly and clearly, and often quite out of context.

'Meat pie and brown gravy,' he said in his quavering voice on one gloriously warm morning.

'What?' She laughed. ''You're not thinking of your dinner already, are you, Uncle Paco?'

'And the sloppy stuff.'

'Do you mean milk jelly?' she suggested.

'Milk jelly,' he said, with a broad smile on his lips. 'Does your England have more cows to milk than bulls to fight?'

'I think it probably does,' she answered, feeling her eyes blur. It was simple logic from a simple man, and after it he lapsed into silence again. It was the last thing he ever said.

They buried him with dignity as befitted an elder statesman of the house of Montalban. There was no formal will to be read, as he owned nothing. Serena was bereft and wept over him in the privacy of her room in a way she had not even wept over her grandmother.

In so short a time, a closeness had built up between herself and Paco de Montalban that she could hardly explain, even to herself. Perhaps it was to do with the fact that in Don Paco's declining days there had been a gentleness in him that she hadn't seen in her grandmother, and certainly couldn't see in any other male member of the family.

Her father probably had the same trait, she thought. His artistic talent would have given him a sensitivity that was lacking in the rest. Not even Eduardo, despite his resistance to fight in the *corrida*, had the same perception of a woman's needs. She put the thought away from her, feeling that she was the insensitive one to allow its intrusion when she mourned yet another family member. She had never known she had so many, and already they were dwindling. But just as before, life went on...

If she and Eduardo had been shaken at the knowledge of Doña Adriana's will, everyone else accepted it without question. They accepted that she belonged here far more than she did herself, but after all that had happened in the past six months Serena began to feel a great need to be settled. It was ridiculous now to reject this family who welcomed her, and she dismissed any idea that if she ever thought of selling the land they would all be homeless.

They certainly would not, because Eduardo García owned the Casa de Montalban, and Serena acknowledged that, in doing that, Doña Adriana had been more canny than any of them might realise.

But she wrote to Mr Price in London informing him to sign the London house over immediately to Cook, and to tell her that she had decided to reside in Spain for the foreseeable future. After a lot of heart-searching she came to the conclusion that it was what she most wanted to do, and that all other considerations were just a waste of energy.

At the beginning of November Juana sought her out and spoke to her cousin quite freely in the easy friendship that had sprung up between them.

'I'm so happy that you've decided to stay here now, Serena. It was what Jorge and I hoped for.'

'Did you?' She couldn't think why Jorge should have been so interested, and saw Juana blush.

'I think it's true that all lovers wish for everyone else to be as happy as themselves. And both Jorge and I could see the attachment between you and Eduardo and still hope that it will become more.'

'Please don't build up your hopes,' Serena retorted. 'The attachment between Eduardo and myself is not of our making, but that of Doña Adriana!'

Juana shook her head. 'No, you are wrong, *querida*. I see the way he has always looked at you, and I know my brother. No other woman has reached his heart.'

Serena's laugh was forced. 'You just said yourself that lovers wish for others to be as happy as themselves, and I think you see the world through rose-coloured spectacles right now, Juana. Be happy for yourself and let the rest of us take care of ourselves.'

'Just as long as you don't mistake pride for duty, then. Eduardo would never marry out of duty. But we'll talk of it no more. The dressmaker is coming today for a fitting of my wedding dress, and wishes to consult with you and Elena about your dresses. I hope you don't think it tasteless to be thinking of such things so soon after Uncle Paco's death, but it cannot wait much longer. Jorge will bring his sister along too.'

The awkward moments passed when Juana obviously thought Serena took her brother's desires too lightly. She assured the girl that the wedding should go ahead. It was always her grandmother's express wish that nothing should stand in the way of Juana's wedding, and later that day Serena tried to take an interest in the bolts of shimmering fabrics the dressmaker brought for their consideration.

The smell of the new material was sharp and fresh, recalling instantly the time that Eduardo had taken her to the Crystal Palace in London and she had gazed in wonderment at the exhibits in Prince Albert's lavish spectacle. How young and gauche she had been then, and how long ago it all seemed...

'I am to wear the mantilla and lace veil that all the Montalban women have worn for generations,' she heard Juana saying, her voice a little awed. 'I don't believe you have seen it, Serena. María can fetch it and we will have a proper dress rehearsal.'

Serena paid attention to what was happening around her, instead of letting her thoughts stray to that faraway dreamworld where she had suspected none of Eduardo García's intentions, and had found herself the object of a young man's desire for the first time in her life. She remembered with a pleasure that was almost pain the heady, wonderful moments that would never come again...

'You seem to be favouring the rose-pink silk, *señorita*,' she heard the dressmaker say, and realised she had been fixing her gaze on the material without seeing anything but the dreams in her head. She gave a start, barely glancing at the lovely watermarked silk, and nodded quickly.

'It's beautiful. It will do very well,' she said.

'And I will have the yellow,' Elena announced, barely hiding the challenging look she gave to Jorge's young sister, Veronica, as if daring her to choose the same.

Veronica capitulated at once. 'I think pale blue for me,' she said. 'It will be more flattering.'

The small exchange between the two girls was quickly forgotten as María returned with a box containing the beautiful heirloom mantilla and lace veil. The dressmaker helped Juana into the heavy cream satin wedding dress that still needed a few alterations, and then arranged the head-coverings lovingly over Juana's dark head. Immediately it seemed as if the girl had changed into a princess.

'You look breathtaking, Juana,' Serena said softly. 'Jorge will fall in love with you all over again the moment he catches sight of you.'

Juana preened in front of the long mirror for a few more moments and then laughed self-consciously as the others made similar comments.

'I think I had better remove my finery before my head is turned by my own importance!' she said. She touched the precious mantilla lovingly. 'These will be for you to wear next, Serena. It's a tradition in our family.'

Serena didn't want to try to picture herself in the elegant head-dress and was glad that Juana didn't suggest she try it on. It was considered bad luck, the other girl informed her, so she was spared the moment of imagining herself in a bridal gown and repeating the vows that would join her to a man until death parted them.

She spoke abruptly to the dressmaker, with sufficient knowledge of Spanish now to converse fairly fluently.

'You will have the dresses finished in good time?'

'Of course, *señorita*. My women will work on them day and night.'

She hardly need have asked. It was obviously to be the wedding of the year, and any member of the house of Montalban deserved every consideration by workers and minions eager to please.

She saw little of Eduardo these days. He threw himself totally into his work. As well as overseeing the processes in the *bodega* with the great oak vats of fermenting wine that had to be carefully monitored until it was exactly right for bottling, there were last year's vines to be pruned and a new crop for next year to be planted.

The seasons didn't stop for a wedding, and the men had their own concerns, but the excitement among the women accelerated until the December day when they left for Cadiz the day before the wedding. They were all to stay in a lavish hotel overnight so that they would appear fresh and uncreased the next morning.

Serena had never stayed in a hotel before, and she found it difficult to sleep in the unfamiliar surroundings. She knew that Eduardo was in a room along the corridor, and she wondered what he was thinking now as the family wedding came ever closer.

She was haunted by memories. She remembered the twelve nights of placing the gypsy charm beneath her pillow. She remembered the sleepless night when she was supposed to dream of her future husband and how she had gone downstairs for a drink, and seen Eduardo García's face outside the front door. It was all nonsense to believe in such charms, and yet...

She moved restlessly in the bed, wondering if she had been so foolish after all to throw away the chance of happiness. In the dark of the night it was so easy to remember only the good things, and to forget the calculating ways of ambitious men.

There was much that was good in Eduardo, and any woman should consider herself fortunate in having his love. And there the musing ended, because she didn't have his love and never had. Weak tears rolled down her cheeks, and she blinked them angrily away, knowing she mustn't let Juana down by looking a sketch tomorrow.

The day was as beautiful as any bride could wish for her wedding day. The sky was a brilliant cloudless blue, and even in December the sun blazed down quite fiercely. A little guiltily, one of the bridal attendants could have wished for a faint hint of English mist to lessen the impact of heat on the bustling crowds eager to watch the spectacle of Juana García's marriage.

But such a thought was soon banished from Serena's mind as they entered the hushed cool interior of the church where soft music was playing and people filed reverently into the pews for the ritual to begin. Serena had never witnessed a wedding ceremony before. She couldn't follow every bit of the address, but the vows were simple and emotive and easy to understand, and her throat had thickened long before Jorge finally slid the ring gently on to Juana's finger.

Afterwards, out into the sunlight again, the carriages took them back to the hotel for a wedding breakfast. And in no time at all, it seemed, the couple had changed out of their rich finery and had become ordinary mortals again, ready to drive away for two weeks at some secret destination in the mountains. And yet they were still not quite ordinary, because they each wore that special glow that filled Serena with a pang of envy.

As head of the Montalban family now, she had been continually escorted by Eduardo, and she hoped he wouldn't see how vulnerable she was today. It was the perfect time to take advantage, but he was being very formal and correct, and she didn't know whether it pleased her or not.

She was hopelessly irrational where he was concerned, she thought, and would be thankful when they returned to the Casa de Montalban and this emotional day was over. For the time being she had to sit beside Eduardo at the bridal table and enjoy the last of the wine and titbits of the wedding feast while the bridal pair made their way around the guests to pay their respects.

'Juana will soon be throwing her flowers to the *señoritas*,' Eduardo said now as some of the guests began wandering towards the courtyard of the luxurious hotel. 'It's an old custom, and it's said that the *señorita* who catches the flowers will be married within the year.'

'It's an English custom too,' she said. 'You don't have priority on all the traditions in the world, Eduardo!'

'Then we are not so unalike, are we?'

Without warning he stretched out his arm across the table, caught her fingers in his and raised them to his lips. She couldn't analyse the thoughts behind his enigmatic eyes at that moment, but the sudden caress was enough to make her heart beat too quickly for comfort.

'Please don't,' she said in a low voice.

'Why should I not? Cousins have certain privileges.'

'We are not close cousins, Eduardo, and you do not treat me that way nor look at me that way——'

She stopped abruptly, seeing the small, sad smile curve his wide, sensual mouth.

'Nor do I think of you in that way, as you so quaintly put it, *querida mía*, but I shall never expect you to understand it.'

She was still trying to make sense of that smile and the sudden depth in his voice, when she heard Elena's excited voice.

'Serena, you must come! Juana is about to throw the flowers!'

'Oh, no, I think not——'

'Do you think it such a demeaning tradition, then? You would offend Juana greatly if you did not join in,' Eduardo said, and she knew she had no choice.

Nor did she think it in the least surprising when the posy was tossed high in the air, and, despite all the eager, laughing young girls who tried to catch it, the fragrant blossoms seemed to fall unerringly into her own un-seeking hands. The next second she felt Juana's exu-berant kiss on her cheek.

'I'm so glad! Now do as your heart tells you, Serena!' Juana said, so that only she could hear.

Then she turned quickly to join her new husband, and the carriage was taking them away to a heaven of their own. Serena buried her nose in the posy for a moment, and knew at once that the sweet, seductive herbs of the gypsy dancers had been included in this bridal token.

She saw Eduardo advancing towards her, and for a wild moment she wanted to fling the flowers away, feeling that she was being inexorably drawn towards something against her will. However much she wanted it, she was still feverishly denying it, pitting her will against Eduardo's, and even more so her grandmother's, and her head ached with the stress of it all.

'So you were the lucky one,' he commented, and she gave a short laugh.

'I don't believe in luck. And the more that people try to persuade me by such foolishness, the more I refuse to be swayed by it.'

'Well said,' he said calmly. 'It's wiser to use your head to see what's under your nose instead of looking for hidden meanings in everything.'

'I suppose you know you constantly surprise me,' she said. 'I fully expected you to take advantage of this situation and make some significant remark. Instead of which you tell me to use my head, and it was Juana who told me to follow my heart.'

'Perhaps your head and your heart are in agreement for once. It's not impossible, Serena.'

He moved away before she could think of a reply. She couldn't fathom whether he was proposing to her or not. He spoke in riddles that were both frustrating and irritating.

She wandered among the guests, receiving their compliments on her appearance, and frequent congratulations on her new status as the Señorita de Montalban, the slight emphasis on the name telling her in no uncertain way what an honour it was.

'I knew your father,' one old gentleman told her in English. 'Such a fine man, and so brave to risk the wrath of your grandmother in the way he did. I hope you will forgive an old man for saying as much.'

'Of course,' she said with a smile. 'And it's so nice to talk with someone outside the family who knew my father. I don't suppose——' She hesitated. 'I don't suppose you knew my mother as well?'

To her surprise he nodded. 'Only slightly, and I confess that I had a sneaking admiration for her myself. But she and Ramón only had eyes for each other. From the first moment it was obvious that they were destined to be together.' He sighed, remembering, and Serena hardly dared to interrupt. Besides, it was intriguing and poignant to hear the story from outside the family circle.

'Ramón de Montalban had two loves in his life, my dear. One was his painting and the other was your mother. Nothing else existed for him, and I see the same passion in Eduardo now.'

Serena felt her face flood with colour, but the man was rambling on and seemed not to notice.

'Eduardo possessed the same courage in defying your grandmother, and his life is dedicated to the land that he loves. He is almost as fulfilled as a man can be.'

She decided the time had come to leave the elegant old gentleman, before she had to hear any more about Eduardo, and she certainly wasn't going to ask why he wasn't quite as fulfilled as a man should be...

'It was so good to talk with you,' she said. 'Perhaps we shall meet again one day.'

'I hope so.' He smiled, his old eyes twinkling. 'It's always a privilege to be invited to a Montalban wedding.'

She escaped quickly, but somehow he had opened up her eyes to something other than Eduardo. When she returned home she intended to go to her father's room and examine his paintings again. She was the one lacking in courage since returning to Spain, because she hadn't been able to face that room and its memories since learning of her legacy. But suddenly she wanted to be among her father's belongings, to absorb all that was his, and to be a real part of all that was now hers.

'We should think about leaving soon, Serena. It will be dark before we get back to the house as it is,' Eduardo said at her elbow. 'Ricardo is leaving for Toledo, but my father and Elena have decided to stay at the hotel for another night to make a small holiday of it. Do you want to come back with me, or stay on here with them?'

She looked at him, and for the first time she thought she detected some flicker of doubt in his face. He was always so strong and decisive, master of all he surveyed, but she sensed that at last he thought he had met his match in Serena de Montalban. She made her own choices.

'I'll come back with you,' she said. 'It will be rather special to be in the house without the others there—for myself, I mean.'

It would hardly be any different, she thought in confusion. She would be in her own part of the house, and he would be in his, and she hadn't meant her words to apply to the two of them at all. To her relief he didn't make any mocking answer to the ambiguity of her remark.

She said goodbye to the others and they finally made their way out of the hotel and into the courtyard where the rows of carriages stood waiting, tended by the hotel grooms.

'We'll take the smaller one and Father and Elena will bring back the baggage tomorrow,' Eduardo said.

She climbed into the small enclosed carriage beside him. It was stuffy and hot, and she wished briefly that they were in the ornate little open cart drawn by a mule instead of the elegantly trotting horse, frisky at being released from the hours of inactivity and constantly needing to be held back on the reins Eduardo held so competently through the grille at the front.

But the sun was already lower in the sky by now, and the oppressive heat of the day had lessened. December in the south of Spain was nothing like an English winter day, Serena thought fleetingly, though she knew it was foolish to expect constant summer. They needed the rain to feed the vines as much as they needed the sun.

'A peseta for your thoughts,' Eduardo said when they had travelled some way in silence. Serena laughed.

'How odd that sounds to me!' she said.

'It should not by now. You are becoming used to our way of life, surely? Sometimes I even forget that you

are half English, in spite of the number of English meals
you organise for our table without any prior warning.'

'You noticed, then! But I thought you liked English
food. You appeared to when you were in England.'

'So I do. I like everything about the country, especially its women.' He spoke arrogantly, and she glanced
at his profile, darkly handsome in the gradual dusk of
evening.

'And you have known so many, of course,' she said.

'I have not lived as a monk,' he acknowledged.

'Have there been many women in your life, Eduardo?'
She persisted without really knowing why. It was only
twisting the knife—or perhaps it would prove to her that
he could toy with a woman's affections when it suited
him, and forget her just as quickly.

'Are you trying to pick a quarrel with me?' he asked,
turning to glance at her.

'I'm just asking a civil question——'

'No, you are not, *querida*. You are trying to provoke
me. Yes, I have known many women and enjoyed their
company. But I have loved only one.'

Her heart jolted. She hadn't expected that. His tone
was flat, as if daring her to question him further. She
wondered instantly if the love of which he spoke had
happened a long time ago. Her thoughts raced on. Had
it been doomed because of Doña Adriana's rigid rule
that the Montalban men had to face *el toro* before they
married? Perhaps the lady in question hadn't been prepared to wait . . . even without his own set face, she knew
it was something she couldn't ask him.

Then she gasped in sudden fright at the crack of gun-
shots followed by the sounds of horses hoofs thundering
through the night. The noise came from somewhere to
their right, where the foothills of the mountains rose in

stark outline against the blue-black sky. Eduardo spoke quickly.

'Don't be afraid, we're not about to be robbed. It will be the gypsies on the move. They go to their *cuevas* for the winter months about now, and they see their removal as an excuse for the young men to race their horses. The shots are no more than a signal for the races to begin. The winners choose the best quarters.'

It was one thing to tell Serena not to be afraid. It was another to still the sudden excited fear in the horse pulling their small carriage. It reared up suddenly and then galloped off in a frenzy, pulling the reins out of Eduardo's hands and throwing them both against the back of the carriage.

Serena screamed as she clung to the side, knowing enough Spanish to recognise Eduardo's stream of oaths as he grappled to reach the loose reins through the small grille. It was useless, and the carriage careered on with the horse lathering ahead of it, away from the track and over the rough, uneven scrubland that stretched for miles alongside.

'Hold on tightly. I'll try and stop him,' Eduardo shouted, and she reached desperately for the leather strap fixed to the roof of the carriage.

She saw his intention at once as he threw open the door of the carriage and began to inch forward along the wooden shaft of the lurching vehicle.

'No, Eduardo, you can't. It's too dangerous!'

She screamed again as he seemed to fall backwards for a second, and she fully expected him to drop beneath the hurtling wheels of the carriage. But somehow he managed to hold on and haul himself forward again while she hardly dared to breathe.

If Eduardo were killed... She felt the sob in her throat and knew that she couldn't face life without him.

The carriage threw her from side to side and she thought every bone in her body must be broken. Eduardo's dark shape moved forward painfully slowly, and it seemed like an eternity until Seréna saw him grasp the animal's back and work his way forward to lie low over its neck. She heard him talking and soothing the frightened animal, until at last the snorting stopped, the horse slowed to a trot and finally stood still.

Only then did Serena realise how badly she was shaking, and when Eduardo slid off the animal's back and came slowly back to her she almost fell out of the carriage and into his arms.

'I thought you were going to be killed,' she sobbed incoherently. 'I thought I was losing you, *mi amor*, and I couldn't bear it——'

She realised what she had said, and so did he. She had called him her darling so naturally, and it was too late to bite it back... but she realised he had cradled her close to him and that he was telling her over and over again that she only had to say the right words and they would never lose one another for the rest of their lives...

'What words?' Serena said thickly, feeling helplessly that all her resistance was sliding away as she was held so blissfully close to his chest. How incongruous they must look, she thought for a moment, sitting as close as any lovers in the wilderness scrub in all their wedding finery, while she ached in every limb, and so must he...

'The words that tell me you love me as much as I love you,' he said roughly. '*Te adoro, mi querida.* Surely you must have always known it?'

She looked up into his face, shadowed against the silver moonlight, but infinitely dear to her, and melted against him, knowing she had no more strength to fight against her own feelings.

'How can you expect me to ever believe it when I always thought it was not me you loved but the land and all that went with it?' she whispered.

He tipped up her face to his, and there was anger mingled with passion in his voice.

'Serena, if I asked a woman to marry me, it would only be because I loved her, not because I coveted her property, or because I was instructed to do so. *Por Dios*, if you think me capable of such weakness, then you do not know me at all.'

Juana had known him, Serena remembered. Juana had said much the same thing in defence of her brother...and how could she ever think him weak when he had risked his life with a runaway horse? Facing *el toro* in the *corrida* was no more courageous than this.

'Are you asking me to marry you, then?' she said, before she stopped to think.

Somewhere in the distance now she could hear the faint sounds of gypsy music. It seemed to merge with the sweet, pungent fragrance of herbs from Juana's bridal flowers that was still on her fingers and forever entwined in her senses.

She held her breath for Eduardo's answer, knowing that this night was turning into one of the most bizarre in her life, but caring nothing about that. Caring only for him, and for these moments that were so intense and all-important to them both.

'I'm not sure,' he said, his voice suddenly light and teasing. 'I seem to remember Señorita de Montalban telling me she would choose the man she would marry.'

She felt a wild exhilaration flowing through her veins, knowing instantly that they were only fencing, and that now the fencing could have only one ending.

'Perhaps I should ask you, then, the way the gypsy women do,' she said daringly. 'Is that what you want of me?'

He held her so close she could hardly breathe. His mouth was in her hair, on her lips, her throat, and her spirit soared to meet his.

'I want *you*, my darling, for all time,' he said. 'I love you more than anything in the world, Serena.'

She answered him tremulously. 'No more than I love you,' she said.

'Then together we will begin a new life,' Eduardo told her. 'We will be married just as soon as it can be arranged, for we've wasted far too much time already. Do you approve?'

'I approve,' she said, her heart too full to say anything more.

And so would all those others, she thought, for now was the time to set free their gentle ghosts... her father Ramón and her English mother, and her stoical little grandmother and their turbulent past. The house of Montalban had a bright new future ahead of it, beginning for Serena right here in Eduardo's arms.

The other exciting

MASQUERADE
Historical

available this month is:

KNIGHT'S PAWN

Polly Forrester

Treason and intrigue were rife! In this year of 1100, King William Rufus was a hated man, and his brother, Duke Robert of Normandy, wanted England's throne.

Eloise Emeron – a refugee from the havoc in Normandy, she counted herself lucky to be employed as a minstrel by an English lord, though this was far below her station.

Richard de Sable of Brittany – whom did he support, in his travels around England? And why had he embroiled Eloise, when she made it no secret that she disliked Duke Robert.

Look out for the two intriguing

Romances coming next month

MADEIRAN LEGACY

Marion Carr

Brought up in an orphanage in Cornwall, life was stark for Coriander May, but her bright vivid personality refused to give in.

So when a mysterious stranger from Madeira came, claiming to know her background, Coriander was intrigued. Raul Beringer told of an inheritance awaiting her, and that he wanted to buy her out. But the lure of a family, at last, was impossible to resist, and Coriander insisted on travelling to Madeira with Raul – into danger, and deceit . . .

THE SPANISH PRIZE

Joanna Makepeace

Dona Maria Santiago y Talavera understood only too well what the corsair, Captain Giles Norwood, was threatening.

Despatched by her uncle to Cartagena to marry her betrothed, Maria had rebelled against a loveless match to cold autocratic Don Luis Ortego y Castuero. But Cartagena had fallen to Drake, the notorious English pirate, and now Maria was aboard Norwood's ship, her fate entirely in his hands.

Would Don Luis be prepared to furnish her ransom; did she wish him to? Yet how could she endure life as this Englishman's prize of war?

Available in September